I0555936

The Road Builders

Tales of The Aura Weavers, Book 2

LizAnn Carson

The Road Builders
(Tales of the Aura Weavers, Book 2)

© 2021 Elizabeth Carson

All rights reserved. No part of this book may be reproduced, stored, or used in any manner whatsoever without the express written permission of the publisher except for the use of brief quotations in a book review.

ISBN: 978-1-7770993-3-6

Cover photos used under license from
Deposit Photos

Thanks to MadJik for Paint.net's Page Curl plugin, which was used for the cover.

To my critique group: Ladies, once again you have helped me shepherd a book to its conclusion. I couldn't have done it without you. Thanks!

Prelude

Twelve-year-old Neve Farmer squirmed. The interview – did she really have to go through with it? Would she even survive it? Would she ever know another mild, autumn day like this one again?

Her mother, sensing her panic, put a solid hand on her back and rubbed. "It's fine."

Sure it is.

Usually, a trip to Orlan meant a day in the market selling apples or vegetables, with free time to explore the stalls, sample the food, and run a little wild with the other stall children. But today was different. While her mother sold their produce, she would be facing, on her own, an ogre.

Her father had laughed when she said this. It's an audition, he'd assured her. Nothing to fear. Gauvain, the mage in the Black Tower, was neither more nor less than they themselves. And if he could help her, so much the better for them all.

They'd dreamed this up, her parents had, to help everyone make sense of the unusual capabilities their daughter had manifested recently. Things like screening an apple tree from the predations of worms and birds. Predicting the sex of soon-to-be-born lambs, with one hundred percent accuracy. Keeping the hail off their farm when everyone else's crops were flattened.

Not that these weren't boons in themselves, but no child should be able to do such. Neve was losing sleep, growing thin when she should be filling out with the onset of puberty. All knew of the Black Tower, with its fearful occupant and his ability to command unseen forces. Was Neve another such?

Her mother halted the cart in the plaza fronting the Black Tower. "Now, you just knock on the door like you belong there," she said to a cowering Neve. "Hold your head high. Nothing bad's going to happen. He'll see what you're capable of, and with luck give you some training."

Like she believed that. She'd never forget her years-ago first glimpse of the Black Mage – grim visage, whip-thin under his flowing black cloak, hair like midnight. She'd not been the only child to run for the safety of their parents' stalls that day.

"Do I have to?" she asked now. There must be another way...

Her mother rewarded her with an exasperated sigh. "I'll wait here until you're inside. Come straight to the market when you're done. I've brought pasties for our lunch."

Along with a full cartload of produce to sell. Neve would give anything to be praising their tomatoes, weighing apples, accepting coin or goods in exchange. Anything but this.

Her mother dropped the reins over the back of their elderly donkey and hopped down, then reached up and hauled her daughter after her. On solid ground, Neve broke all the rules of being twelve years old, almost a teen, soon to be adult, and clung to her mother, burying her face in the familiar, well-padded shoulder. "Please..." she whimpered.

"It's for the best, my love. Come on. I'll see you to the door."

Their knock was answered much too soon. Neve clung to her mother's hand and studied the man standing there.

Elderly, long gray hair in a tail, beginnings of a stoop, and twinkling eyes... surely those happy eyes were a good omen? This wasn't Gauvain, no way, but if someone living in this fearful place could be happy, perhaps it wouldn't be so bad? Maybe?

"My daughter requires testing and training," her mother said, wasting no breath. The market called, and competition this time of year was fierce. "I've heard to come here."

"You've heard correctly. I am Leo. I run the household." He grasped her mother's hand in a gesture of welcome. "The Master will want to interview Neve alone, you understand?"

"You know her name already?" Suspicion flashed across her mother's face as she jerked her hand free. How was this possible?

He nodded. "We knew you were coming, yes. Nothing mysterious about it, really. I've an excellent network of people who pass on tidbits of information." He turned to Neve, who had moved ever closer to her mother's comforting bulk as they stood there at the door. "Young lass, please come in. I will announce you for your interview. There will be tea and cakes after. It's all perfectly normal, if a bit gloomy. But you can ignore that, I'm sure."

He reached out his hand. Almost as if she had lost all free will, Neve took it. She shot one last, hopeless look at her mother before finding herself escorted into the dark entryway. Behind her, the door closed of its own accord, making her jump and whirl around. But Leo's hand stayed attached to hers, warm and – in a funny way – comforting.

Leo led them down a short hall and rapped on a door to his left. "It'll be all right," he whispered, then the door opened by itself. "Miss Farmer," he said, and suddenly she was inside. The door closed silently behind her.

She froze.

The man at the desk – oh yes, she recognized him. His face, as much as she could see of it in the gloom, held no welcome and a fair bit of displeasure, as if her presence disrupted an otherwise pleasant morning. Not that he could possibly tell it was morning, given the dark walls, lack of windows, and minimal light.

"Your first name, girl." His voice was not overly deep, which surprised her. It was commanding, however. This was a man who expected to be obeyed, and instantly.

"Neve," she croaked. Her own voice seemed to have been left behind on the wagon, going to market with her mother.

"Stand here." The man barely moved but somehow gave her to understand she was to place herself in front of his desk. So much closer...

"Now," he snapped, like the crack of a whip.

Her limbs unfroze but threatened to melt instead. Somehow, she managed to wobble closer.

"What can you do, girl? I take it your powers have manifested?"

"Started to," she mumbled to her shoes.

"What? Light, sound, weather, mind reading? What are you capable of, that you considered it worthwhile to interrupt me? *Speak!*"

An energy not her own seized control of her voice. "Some weather. Some... I guess you'd call it nature. Like making seeds sprout and grow."

The door opened behind her and the old man appeared. "Yes, sir?"

"Leo, I've need of seeds. Can you procure some?"

"Certainly." The door closed behind him, this time with a solid *thunk*.

"An attempt to demonstrate weather magic from within these walls would be pointless, so tell me what you have managed."

Her voice sounded strange in her ears, as if it weren't herself speaking. "Changed some hail to rain once."

"Have you brought in clouds? Caused rain?"

"Don't think so." If she kept her eyes fixed on her boots, it wasn't so terrifying. Boots were familiar, ordinary, not like this place with its strange instruments and more books than she'd ever dreamed existed, never mind in one place. She thought of her own book, which had come down through her family from who knew when, full of receipts to make tomato paste, what to feed pigs to produce the most flavorful bacon. She'd bet the Black Mage's collection didn't deal in such mundane things.

"But you don't know?"

She shook her head. It had been only the once, but whether she had done it or the hail changed on its own... well, it was months ago, one of the first signs of these scary powers. Back when it was all still a game.

A game. She almost snorted at that. The man could eat her alive before anyone stopped him. The way he sat there, unmoving, staring right through her... she shivered.

The door opened, and Leo brought in a plate of sunflower seeds. "These should be viable," he said as he put the plate on the desk. Then he bowed himself out again.

After a pause, Gauvain said, "Well? Go on. Make them sprout."

"I... I'm not sure how."

"You said you'd done it before."

"Yes, but in the field. Maybe it wasn't even me. Maybe they were just ready to grow. Maybe the weather—"

"I suspect you did it. Now, do it again."

Neve looked up from her boots, her eyes darting from one object to another in the intimidating room. On the land it felt natural, but the energy here was all wrong. "I can't," she said.

The Black Mage closed his eyes and his lips narrowed, as if he was holding in a ferocious temper, but for how long? Neve's gaze dropped back to his boots.

"Would you care to tell me why?"

"It's... it's like... maybe it's the sun or the soil or something? It's all wrong in here."

"Ah." He spoke as if her words had revealed some great truth, and gestured. "Sit in that chair, girl."

She sat. It was easier than keeping her knees locked so she wouldn't fall over.

Gauvain stood and circled the desk. As he passed behind her, he said, "You are not yet a woman."

Heat flooded her face. How did he know that? She'd had cramps once, but no monthly flows. It was early days, her mother assured her. She was in no hurry; womanhood held too many mysteries, and too many restrictions.

"I don't train children. But as you're here, let's see what we can discover."

The moment he put his hands on her head, her control broke. She jerked to her feet and scrambled for the door. Leo was there, as if he had been waiting for her. He put a comforting hand on her shoulder. "It's all right, Neve. Calm yourself, child."

She gasped and nodded but couldn't stop the tears coursing over her cheeks, or the profound shudder that wracked her body.

"Take her away," Gauvain said.

And with that, the interview was over. The old man wrapped his arm around her as they left, turning not toward the front door as she might have expected, had she been able to think of anything at all in that moment of horror, but to the left and into what proved to be a large, comfortable kitchen.

"We'll nourish your body while your spirit sorts itself out," he said as he steered her into a chair pulled up to an old, marred table. A plate of cakes had been set out, and once she had been seated the old man poured a tisane into a stoneware mug. "I think you'll find the pastries tasty, but the tisane is of first importance. It will calm your nerves and call you energies back into your body. You've had a fright."

And nor are you the first one, she thought she heard him mutter as he placed himself in a chair across from her.

It took some time for her to control her breathing and stifle her sobs, but once she did, she discovered that the cakes were indeed the best she'd ever eaten, and the tisane somehow removed the ache that clutched at her heart. Eventually she almost relaxed.

"As I told you before, my name is Leo," the old guy told her. "Remember that. You aren't ready for training yet, as I'm sure you realize. But I do believe we will meet again. When you return, I'll be here. And when you're older, this whole thing won't be so frightening. It's merely his way, you know. He'd never harm you."

"Tell that to the pigs," she muttered. Pigs were good listeners and generally recognized when people lied.

He laughed. "It's true, though. Come back, Neve. In a couple of years, when you've got your maturity. You'll do fine."

Later, Leo personally escorted her to the market and had a few quiet words with her mother. Some agreement was struck, and for the next few days Neve experienced was a great deal of kindness from her parents and a slight reduction in her workload. Other than that, life went on as usual.

But when, on her sixteenth birthday, her parents proposed another visit to the Black Tower, she had flatly refused. By then she had discovered the notes hidden in her book and had learned through experiment to do the things that brought prosperity to the farm. That was enough, and the Black Mage would not be allowed into her life again.

Chapter 1: The Summons

The day should have been nicer. High spring, two nine-days past spring equinox, crops growing nicely, apple trees showing every sign of a good yield. Neve should be pleased; so much of this came down to her, her work and also some subtle tweaking she had done along the way, drawing on the Aura to give extra vigor to the crops.

And even better, John, her younger brother, was home. His training kept him confined to Orlan most of the time. Gauvain, the dreaded Black Mage, was a harsh master.

Should have been perfect. But after supper, John hit her with the message from the Black Tower. As they strode long the path, she slightly in front, he persisted, "Come on, Neve. It's not like you have a choice."

She glared, something she got the chance to do all too seldom lately. "Because the old man decrees?"

John nodded. "Scoff all you want, but when Gauvain says to come, you come. Even the Orlan council kowtows to him."

"You know what, kid? Ever since that man got his claws into you, you've been insufferable. Telling me what to do? I don't think so."

"I am not a kid." John had turned seventeen recently, but despite a significant height advantage, at eight years younger he didn't even try to look domineering. Instead, he hoisted himself onto the fence rail, adolescent legs every which way.

He knocked his hair, dark like hers although hers bore reddish highlights from the sun, from his forehead. In front of him, apple trees marched in orderly rows toward the hill on the horizon; behind him lay a market garden, tomatoes, beans, and leafy vegetables. "I'm nearly a man grown, as you seem determined to forget. Anyway," he added, "if I ever got above myself, Gauvain would shoot me down. He doesn't have any tolerance for cockiness."

Neve snorted.

"But something's going on," he continued. "You're not the only one he's called." He paused, staring out over the orderly rows of trees. "I've been wondering for a long time how many others like you are roaming around, untrained because the mages decided not to train you. You could have been great, Sis."

"I'm as great as I need to be. I see no reason to jump to your mage's demands."

She leaned against the fence, so they were both staring out across the apple orchard instead of looking at each other. They'd always been a close family, Neve and John and their parents. Since John had left almost five years before to undertake mage's training, a process she happened to know he hated, craved, and feared in equal measure – no one could say Gauvain made a sympathetic teacher – she had felt some of that closeness slip, but it was still there, strengthened by their shared bond through the Aura. John already was aware of exactly what she thought of Gauvain, and her bitterness at having been denied training herself.

"Gauvain won't like it."

She grinned. "All the better."

"We'll leave tomorrow after lunch, sell some turnips and overnight in Orlan, hit the market for breakfast..." He dangled the market with its famous food stalls like a carrot before a hungry donkey. But then, he knew his sister's weaknesses well.

"Would you come to the interview, too?"

"I doubt he'd let me."

"But at least—"

"Afraid?"

Neve thought it over. Afraid didn't quite describe whatever it was that clutched her abdomen, trickling upwards toward her heart. She knew that feeling, although it was one she hadn't experienced in years. It was...

Excitement. Something the farm was notably short of. She shut her eyes a moment, hoping this wouldn't prove to be a stupid decision.

"Okay, I'll go."

John must have caught an almost hectic flash in his sister's eyes, because he questioned the very position he'd argued for. "You're sure? Because I'm just the messenger, you know? If you really don't want to—"

"Oh, no. You don't get to change sides like that." She grabbed his hands and hauled, tipping him off the fence rail. "Let's see to the chores, then I'll pack. What should I take?" She was already striding along the path skirting the orchard, her loose linen pants whipping around her legs, pulling John by sheer force of enthusiasm along behind her. "Maybe I'll dress all fine, that should throw his nibs off his pace for half a second. You sure you don't know what this is all about?"

"I'm guessing, but perhaps something about that road they're building to the south." John easily caught up. "Donkey or pigs?"

They did rocks paper scissors to allot the tasks, then went about the evening's work.

Chapter 2: Return to the Tower

Wearing her best embroidered tunic, her stomach comfortably full of flatcakes topped with roasted vegetables, Neve arrived at the door of the Black Tower in good time. She remembered the elderly man who opened the door to her knock; he had been the only kind presence all those years ago, when Gauvain had casually dismissed her bid to become an apprentice as if she were mere dirt under his royal foot. "Please, step in," he said formally. "You've grown well." At her questioning look, he added, "I remember you, of course."

Neve crossed the threshold she'd thought never to pass again. The Black Tower represented her best chance at governing and maximizing her Auric abilities, which had grown over the years, leaving her itching to know what she might now be capable of. Whatever Gauvain wanted, whatever game he was playing, she was sufficiently intrigued to take this gamble.

With gracious formality and no further words, the elderly man – Leo was his name, she remembered now – ushered her into the lion's den.

The door clicked closed behind her. The flatcakes and vegetables weren't sitting quite so comfortably in her stomach now. But she'd never let *him* know. She stood for a moment, gathering herself and surveying the room. It was much as she remembered from that long-ago, fateful interview. She had been but a child, with parents concerned about the 'oddities' their daughter was manifesting.

The room was dark, with heavy wooden bookshelves and no windows. Odd instruments and books were strewn on tables and shelves. How Gauvain worked in this obscurity was beyond her. Neve had pestered the local archivist until he agreed to teach her to read – a useless skill for most – then spent her spare time poring over the ancient, faded writing in her book. Most of it was farm records, but there were a few pages in a different hand that let her know she wasn't the only person in her lineage with Auric powers. She always sought daylight to puzzle out a new learning, because the light helped in deciphering the old, crabbed writing. She had studied from that book, about the Aura and how it interacted with herself, imbuing her with abilities that had frightened her at first, refining her into an agent of prosperity for the farm.

You're not helpless, nor untrained. Remember that.

Prominent in the room was a large, black desk fronted by two chairs in dark wine upholstery, and behind it the man himself, gaunt, black hair and eyes, black attire, a black expression on his face.

Well, he'd invited her here, hadn't he? She wasn't that twelve-year-old anymore. Neve sat uninvited on one of the chairs and waited.

Having extracted, she supposed, all he could from her appearance, Gauvain placed a paper from a drawer in front of him and made a mark on it. "Neve Farmer, correct?"

"Yes." She refused to say 'sir', although it was on the tip of her tongue.

"Excellent. Prepare to leave within the nine-day. Leo will provide a supply list."

Leave? John had hinted at travel, but... "I don't think so."

At the simple defiance in her words, the man rested his elbows on the desk to form a tent of his fingers, then studied her over them, very much as if he had just added a bug to his collection. "I beg your pardon?" His voice could have sliced through the stone wall.

With some effort, Neve neither stammered nor hesitated. "I require to know what this is about, and if I *choose* to go anywhere, I'll need to return home first to make arrangements for the farm. A minimum of a nine-day, I should think, as well as whatever is needed for whatever you're planning." She felt she could be excused for the emphasis on the word *choose*, given Gauvain's irritating assumptions.

"I see. That feckless brother of yours failed to provide you with this information?"

She resisted smirking. "Actually, it seems you failed to give the information to him."

Gauvain's face grew even tighter. "That is impossible. However. We are opening a trade route across the hills in the south, where, they say, the effect of the spells is less. You will be part of an expedition to the far south of Borgonne, a land of plains and sparse settlement, I'm told. We require the road to be improved as you go. For this we require your technical skills in earth-based Auric energy. Landscape assessment, for instance. Once there, you will establish a base of operations. And management once the depot is operational."

Neve let the silence stretch while she thought that over. Centuries of spells on the hills prevented any commerce between Borgonne and the Midland, other than by those connected to the Aura. She had learned, through John, about the trek two of his classmates had made across the hills. She'd never heard that those mysterious spells might be lessened in the southern part of Borgonne, which was almost as unknown as the Midland. That Gauvain intended to pack her off to a place she knew nothing about, merely for the sake of commerce, when what was needed was more support for local agriculture... well.

"It doesn't sound appealing," she said. "I'm sure you can find someone else."

His head jerked back. "What did you just say?"

"I have no experience in road building or administration. It sounds like you need engineers and businessmen, not untrained mages."

His voice was chilling. "I suggest you refrain from using that word, even with its appallingly accurate modifier, in the context of yourself." There was a threat in there somewhere.

She shrugged, faking a nonchalance she didn't feel. "I don't see why I should. My powers have come in strong since I last saw you. I use my abilities to benefit my community." She was on a roll now and almost forgot to fear him. "If you check, I think you'll find that my little part of Borgonne has survived the drought better than almost anywhere else. We're superior at trade as well. Why would I abandon my people for some wild scheme of yours?"

He smiled. The bastard actually smiled. "Naturally I've noticed. I'm perfectly able to track the source of permutations in the Aura. You've done surprisingly well. You are aware that the College of Mages frowns on manipulation of the weather?"

She was on her mettle now. "Why should I be, since you denied me the opportunity to join the College?"

"One thing you should remember, Neve Farmer. I am far more powerful than you will ever be. Your prosperity is fragile until we've fully recovered from the drought. Continued success is not guaranteed."

"You threaten me."

"Yes."

Well, that was bald. But Neve doubted the Black Mage would deign to waste his time and energies on something as insignificant – to him – as her family's farm. Time to at least get more facts, find out if agreeing to this odd pilgrimage might be better for her community than her refusal would be.

"Tell me why you need me, specifically."

"Simple." He sighed, as if reconciling himself to the tedium of explanation, and leaned back. "Trade with the Midland is essential. You are probably aware of the food shortage in Orlan, despite your farm's meager contributions."

Neve took offence at 'meager' but said nothing.

Gauvain continued, "But trade means crossing the hills. The Midland mages – they call them Weavers for some reason – will in fact control the trail, as their spells have held more strongly than ours. In short, they can come in our direction, but we cannot go in theirs. We need strength in the south to monitor them and be sure they honor the terms of the agreement. I should add that there is no possibility of removing the spells."

Control. Just as he was controlling her now. It was subtle, but she felt him in her mind, tipping her toward a favorable outcome – for him. The man was truly a master.

Still...

"Why don't we just use the northern route? At least we know we can get across."

Gauvain sat very still for a moment, as if gathering his patience. "Two very obvious reasons. First, even for mages the northern route is fraught with peril. Second, we will be trading for horses."

Neve felt a pulse of excitement. "We'll be getting horses?"

"No, foolish woman. We will be sending horses to them. There's a large herd on the southern plain. And surely it's evident even to you that a horse could never navigate the steep entrance to the northern trail. It's hard enough for humans on hands and knees."

"Still, if we could bring some of them up here—"

He cut her off with a gesture. "Good for farm work, faster communication, I'm aware of the arguments. Later, perhaps. Getting grain and vegetables from the Midland is the priority."

Neve shelved this information for further consideration. "But why me in particular?"

He nodded, for once appearing pensive rather than belligerent. "Your connection to the Aura is strong, which I admit surprises me. At the moment, we find ourselves with an unfortunate shortage of trained mages. Although one crop of apprentices is soon to graduate in my lineage, they are boys yet. You combine both Earth power and maturity, and what you lack can be trained into you on the journey."

Training. What she'd dreamed of over long years. "You are going also?"

The disdain was back. "Hardly."

Neve thought it preferable to leave aside the question of who would conduct the purported training and move on to more practical matters. "How long will this trek be?"

He waved a hand, dismissing the question. "A season. It hardly matters. As long as it takes to improve the road."

"An estimate. Weather might play a role, you know."

"I'm sure you will arrive before the weather turns. In the south, you'll find it more moderate."

"In time to build your warehouses?"

"That will be your problem to solve. Yours and the others. You won't be traveling alone."

"Those aforementioned engineers and businessmen?"

"No doubt there will be some of those, for whom you will provide support as needed. Initially your companions will be construction workers. I'm told the road is little more than a track. However, my primary concern is with security, preventing the Midland mages from taking advantage of our weaker position."

"Oh, honestly." She stood. "You're presenting me with a half-baked plan that benefits me little, snatches me away from my life, and without even the essential facts to let me know what the challenges will be. I can feel you in my head, you know." His eyebrows rose slightly. "But it's not enough. I need a much better plan than you've provided to convince me to take this on."

"I've told all you need to know. I concede your point about finishing up your life here, but I will expect you in the plaza in front of the Tower in a nine-day. Now, kindly leave."

"One more thing."

He started to rise, as if to herd her through the door, but froze momentarily at her question. That more than anything else suggested she had flustered him behind his carefully constructed frost. "Now what?"

"What's the pay?"

His eyes blazed as if the very question was an affront. "Pay?"

"You propose to remove me from my usual occupations. I'm entitled to compensation."

Gauvain's face suggested he was swallowing down some deep disgust. "I don't sully myself with such trivialities. Speak to Leo." He stood and stepped toward her. The vegetables, which she had nearly forgotten during their sparring, produced a tentative gurgle. With a hand on her arm, he hustled her from the room. The door closed none too gently behind her.

Leo appeared from nowhere, a smile on his face. "I see you've rattled the Master. Well done. It doesn't hurt him every once in a while to realize there are people his equal. Will you join me in the kitchen? I've made a tisane and a cake."

Leo's smile went a long way toward restoring her nerves. With half an idea this might work out after all, she followed him through a door at the end of the hall and into his remarkably pleasant kitchen.

Chapter 3: Tisane and Cake

The cake lived up to her memories. She wondered what ingredients Leo used to create the drink, which was... well, tasty enough, she supposed. She sensed a powerful herb, romarin perhaps, disguising something much less pleasant. Or maybe it was the honey, which she rarely included in her tisanes. She had just opened her mouth to inquire when he shook his head.

"There are mysteries in my kitchen which I choose not to share – yet. You must know that more goes into the tisanes than kitchen herbs."

Neve met him head-on, as she had his boss. "You magic the plants? Or the Tower does?"

Leo sat at the table and took a deep draught from his mug. "There's nothing magic about the Tower. It's just a tall, black building. As for myself, I daresay you are sensing a hint of something extra. No one who touches the Aura could possibly work with herbs and not add a bit of themselves to the mix, don't you think?"

Her second sip went down more smoothly. She absorbed this new fact – Leo could apply magic to herbs. He might well be a man of hidden competencies, not a mere underling. Was he still doing it, changing the brew to make it more palatable? The question tickled at her mind, but she shoved it aside. Besides the drink, which seemed to be mending the frazzled endings of her nerves, this man had been consistently kind, and in no way intimidating. Anyway, she needed information, all the details the Black Mage had felt it beneath him to divulge.

Or, she thought with half a smile, perhaps Gauvain didn't have the answers. Why should a man of such powers demean himself with petty details?

But Neve was a farmer, a woman whose life centered on the earth, its cycles and bounty. She knew full well the imperative for attention to detail. The health of the soil, the abundance of crops, depended on a hundred things, not all of which could be left to nature. If the land was to be tilled, it must also be husbanded, and that was her skill, one she'd nurtured as assiduously as she cultivated beet and broccoli seedlings.

And she did it well, so she knew better than to press Leo. The mystery of the tisane lay in the Aura and in her own powers to tap it; she would memorize the flavor and deal with it later. Instead, she applied herself to the dried berry and nut cake he had served her, mumbling her gratitude between bites.

Leo calmly waited until she had fortified herself with sugar – clever man – before gently prodding. "Tell me what you need to know. I'll assure you up front that the offer is sound. If your farm can spare you, your presence would be invaluable."

Remembering her manners, Neve sat up a little straighter and made a polite blot of her mouth with the small scrap of linen provided. "Several broad questions, I suppose. Scope, timeframe, compensation, future prospects. Probably more I haven't thought of yet."

Leo grinned, cradling his mug before him in gnarled hands. "You have tidy mental habits. That's good. Part of the benefit to you will be further training, to formalize your powers and rid you of any bad habits you may have picked up over the years. You'll find the work goes more smoothly and with less effort when you handle power correctly."

Don't bristle. The idea that her techniques, the ones she had refined through years out in the fields, experimenting, coaxing the crops to her bidding, might not be adequate...

No. That isn't what he was saying.

"I think you should know," she said coolly, "I would refuse any tutelage under...," she jerked her head in the direction of the study, "... *him.*"

"I see." Leo's voice held a note of disapprobation, but his eyes laughed. "That won't be an issue. I assure you, Gauvain has no wish to participate in this venture, beyond administering it from afar."

"Controlling it, you mean."

"Only insofar as he handles recruitment and purse strings."

"So, if he isn't pleased with progress, he'll withhold compensation."

Leo stood and removed the empty plates from the table, piling them into the deep sink. Then he turned back to her. "I tell you what. Let's start this over, shall we? I think we're on a wrong footing."

Neve nodded. It was unlike her to show so much belligerence, but it seemed as if hostility had been her theme since John had brought the summons to the farm.

Leo sat, then poured more tisane into each of their mugs. "Here are the basics, as you have outlined them. The scope, initially, is to support the surveyor and laborers in improving the road to the south. Once at the destination, you'll establish a base as the Master outlined. The primary item of trade, at least at first, will be horses, so expect to construct some kind of barn or corral. You won't bear sole responsibility, of course."

How did he know what Gauvain had said? Did Leo listen in at keyholes?

"A major concern to everyone," he continued, "is defining procedures for dealing with our counterparts in the Midland. I'm sure the Master mentioned we need a person with strong Auric abilities to keep an eye on them. Nobody quite trusts anybody else yet."

Neve nodded, although she had no clear idea how her powers, so valuable on the farm, might translate to a venture such as this.

"Timeframe is uncertain. With the amount of roadwork needed, it will take the summer to get to the southern plains. Beyond that, much depends on how things progress and how soon trade can begin – which involves the people in the Midland as well, and we don't know their status. It's reasonable to expect a full year before the commitment is fulfilled. I'm assuming your parents can manage the farm this season, but if necessary, we can send John home to help. He's far enough along in his training that he doesn't require constant supervision.

"Compensation will be more than adequate." He named a figure that had her widening her eyes before she caught herself and resumed a neutral, blasé expression. "The amount will be disbursed every four nine-days, as you direct.

"And future prospects... that one is trickier. There is always the possibility you will elect to stay in the south. If you come back, you will bring new, stronger powers, which can only benefit your farm – if the farm is your choice. Other opportunities may open up. But no one will control what you decide."

When Leo stopped speaking, Neve couldn't seem to find words to reply. She found nothing to fault, certainly. And no reason to decline... and...

...and why would she? Hadn't she been ignoring a niggle under her skin for several years now, like an itch telling her the farm had become too small? Had she not longed for adventure beyond the market in Orlan? New people and sights? Hadn't the stories John told of his friends' venture beyond the hills created sharp shards of jealousy?

"Who does the training?" she asked. "I've told you, I won't have anything to do with your boss. And if all mages are like him, then forget it."

Leo shook his head. "No mages. As you surmised, I have some minor abilities myself, and a fair understanding of the ways of the Aura. I can tell you, for instance, that your strength is earth magic, something Gauvain isn't highly skilled in. Without contact with the land, you become disoriented, as if the Aura itself has deserted you. This can be corrected, or at least adapted, giving you greater scope. I'm a decent teacher, Neve. You won't lack training."

"I hadn't realized you'd be going." In her mind, Leo was a part of the Black Tower.

"I am, but keep it to yourself for the moment. I've yet to inform Gauvain of my intentions."

Was that even possible? "Why on earth not?"

Leo shrugged. "There are moments to share information, and moments to fade into the background. This expedition... while Gauvain accepts the necessity, it isn't exactly to his liking, the organization of it even less so. He feels the stress, I fear."

"And you lie low. I see." That he would dare manipulate the great Black Mage delighted her.

There were a few niggly points to clear up, sure. But the only major question remaining was one for herself alone. Did she have the courage? To leave her family, the farm, everything familiar...

But she was well into her twenties. There wouldn't be another opportunity, that was certain.

He read her mind. "You can do this, Neve."

She licked her lips and took a breath. "I need a day or two."

"Which you may have, but no more. We depart in a nine-day, and there is much to do beforehand."

Neve nodded. "I understand. I'll let you know tomorrow by messenger. It's just... it's such a big decision."

"Take this." Leo retrieved a paper from a drawer in the table and passed it to her. "A packing list, primarily for your personal needs. We will be able to acquire necessities along the way, at least at first."

Of one accord, they both stood. Leo opened a door leading to a back alley. "This exit isn't scenic, but I see no reason you should brave the Tower's formal spaces again today. Goodbye for now. I look forward to our travels together."

She made her farewell and left, replaying the morning in her head. Leo believed she would go. And really, he wasn't wrong. Was he?

Chapter 4: Leaving Home

Neve stared out over the field. Only a few hot-season varieties remained to be sown, mainly specialty crops like basilic, which they grew in small quantity but would command a high price during its short season. All about her, plants poked up through the soil in tidy rows which curved around the central hub of the farmhouse. Beyond them, the apple trees had finished their bloom and leafed out, promising a healthy trade in cider, come autumn.

The work was never-ending, but it suited her. Being out here in the sun, encouraging the growth of the fledgling crops... was she really about to leave it behind to go off adventuring?

Tomorrow, she would be gone.

In the next row, her father clearly had the same thought. "Reckon we could send you off with a load of apples from last year, if that would be a help." His way of reminding her of her roots.

"There won't be room. We're starting out with only a couple of carts. We'll pick up more as people join the caravan down the road, I guess."

"And he's gonna magic the food into your stomach, is he?" He rubbed at his grizzly beard, matching her stare over the new-sown field. Far away on the western horizon, the hills quivered, eerie in that you never felt you were seeing them clearly.

She wouldn't be in the hills, she reminded herself firmly. Only skirting them. People lived there, worked there. An ordinary survey and construction job. Surely it would be safe.

"You'd like Leo," she retorted. "He's older and knows more than he lets on. I'll be safe enough with him. I am a woman grown, remember." Funny how it was sometimes hard to grasp that simple fact when she was around her parents, as if she reverted to being a girl again. Annoying.

Her father nodded and switched his gaze from the far hills to survey her as if she were a new apple sapling. "It won't hurt you to get it out of your system, Neve. You've been – you *are* – a fine daughter to your mother and me, and a first-rate farmer." She wondered if he meant the occupation or their family's last name, although when you came right down to it, they were the same, her family no longer separable from the land they tended. "But who knows what wonders there might be out there, waiting for discovery?" he went on. "We know you're not like us, with the things you can do, and John, too. We'll get by for a season, lass. You're not to fret."

"I know, Dad." She stepped across the furrow to give her father a hug. Better parents couldn't be found, which only made leaving them harder.

Back at the house, her mother displayed the products of her morning's toil – a pair of neatly laundered and mended tunics with trousers and a new woolen wrap. She'd traveled to the market for the wool and had been knitting every free moment since Neve told them of her plan. "Because you'll be near the hills, it could be chilly."

"You're a queen, Mom." Neve didn't hug her mother, knowing that she preferred to keep the farm's dirt on her husband and child, not on herself, but she did smile her biggest smile before taking herself off to the wash tank.

Freshly cleaned and suitable for her mother's table, she dug into her stew and spoke around a mouthful of potato. "I'll need to go to town this afternoon to make arrangements for my salary and pick up last-minute stuff from the market. Is there anything you need?"

Her dad shook his head. "Nothing at all, lass. And set up your own account at the banque. The farm brings in enough income, and food toward the winter. Your wages will be for you."

"No." On this point she was firm. "I can claim them later, should I choose. If I put them in the farm account, you'll have an emergency fund." Because who could say what might befall the farm without her powers protecting it. Hail, pestilence, another drought season... she shuddered and forcibly kicked the thoughts of calamity from her mind.

She had another reason for the trip. The expedition left on the morrow, and she intended, if at all possible, to bring John home with her this evening. His presence would ease the sting of her departure. She well remembered when he had left to begin his training with the Black Mage, the wrench it had caused her parents to break up their tight family. Her going would be no less traumatic, for all that her parents were both supportive and stoical. Perhaps they had always assumed she, at least, would go, because that's what daughters did – find themselves a partner and wed, and thereafter devote themselves to another family's prosperity. That she had never felt whatever it took to commit to another had been a boon, as far as she was concerned. This was where she belonged.

Belonged. Past tense. Now, she was going to try her wings, and in a most unexpected way. The unsettled feeling around her heart and stomach, which had been fluttering on and off since she had received the summons to the Black Tower, tickled at her again. Nerves, she told herself firmly. Nothing but nerves.

She ordered the afternoon in her mind. Take the cart to Orlan, first to the Black Tower to drop off her small pile of supplies. Speak to Leo about where to deposit her wages. Invade the apprentices' lodge to find John. Run her errands in the marketplace. Then back to the farm for one last meal, one last evening with her family, in the security of her home.

And so it had unfolded. Typical of mid-spring, departure day promised clear skies and moderate temperatures. John and Neve arrived in Orlan with the dawn, guiding their donkey – for the last time, but she was determined not to dwell on that – and bringing not only a shipment of early greens for one of the up-market restaurants in town, but also a breakfast of fresh barley bread and jam. Comfortable in her usual attire of linen pants and tunic, she sat on a stone wall by the market – no point enduring proximity to the Tower until it was necessary. With John next to her, they shared their mother's lovingly prepared meal. Words were unnecessary; John of all people would be able to sense her trepidation.

Nerves had never hampered her appetite, or her brother's either, come to think of it. When the barley bread was gone, she dusted off the crumbs and turned to him. "Time to go."

John bounded to his feet and gave her a full hug rather than his usual brotherly shoulder bump, then grasped her arms to fix her with a look. He had almost a handspan on her now. Sometime in the last couple of years, he had shot up. How much would he change before she got home again?

"You be careful out there."

"Wish you were going?"

"Yeah. Life in the Tower without Leo's gonna be the pits."

"Get your training, Bro. Your magic's not like mine. He's awful, but you're learning a lot."

John shrugged. For all practical purposes, the Tower and its apprentice wing were his home. "One thing I do know, you don't want to be late."

They steered their cart along the street leading north to the Black Tower and the chaos caused by the imminent departure of a small wagon train. Neve spotted Leo on the front step with a paper, probably a checklist, speaking to a couple of workmen. Two donkey carts had queued, the drivers awaiting instructions. Behind them, an oxcart loomed. The pack holding her small pile of belongings lay in the back of the first cart, along with camping gear. The second held provisions. The oxcart carried machinery of some sort; Neve concluded it had to do with road construction. The carts were of a style she had never seen, with tall poles at each corner. A small crowd milled about the square. Seeing relatives off, she speculated, or just curious. Whichever, they certainly contributed to the atmosphere, a mix of festive and pandemonium.

All three animals waited with a patience that, in a human, might be called boredom. Their own donkey gave her a gentle head butt, demanding a treat. She retrieved a carrot from the bed of the cart – she never came unprepared – and fed the beast while fighting off a sudden twinge of nostalgia for the farm, for the simple life of walking the furrows, brushing the plants and ground with her fingers, harvesting... and all with nary another human voice other than one of her parents calling her in to lunch.

Well, no time for sentimentality, they'd be on their way soon enough. Leo would have them mustered and rolling out soon, despite the perceived chaos.

"Neve, over here." Leo's voice rose above the ruckus. After a final hug from John, she reluctantly left the sanctuary of the known and crossed the small square. Her brother gave her a final wave and led their donkey away toward town, where he would deliver the greens before heading home. Neve watched him go, all gangly body and mussed hair. Winning his freedom from the apprentices' lodge for a day had required Leo's intervention, one reason for her to feel gratitude toward the old man.

Neve was working her way around the carts when Gauvain stepped through the door. The Black Mage scanned the gathering with an expression that suggested a bad smell, then spoke to Leo. Whatever he said didn't go down well at all. Leo's mouth tightened as he listened.

From her position behind one of the carts, Neve strained to hear. This was too good to miss. The Master, as Leo called him, was ticked. And Leo was, too.

"...a mistake. As I've told you before." Leo started to turn away.

Gauvain put a hand on his shoulder. "That's nonsense. He's virtually a mage, fully trained. Whereas she—"

"Will surprise you. You're mixing what should be kept separate. This is nothing but trouble."

Did Leo not want her on this trip? Was that what they were talking about?"

Gauvain shrugged. "A couple of kids. You can manage them."

"Yes." Leo's eyes flashed. The two men were almost nose to nose, the argument flaring between them. "But manage their powers? I doubt it."

Gauvain shrugged, but Neve sensed a lack of his usual insouciance. "You're the one who insisted on going along on this journey."

"I'm the only hope we have that they won't kill each other or release..."

Kill each other? Metaphorical, surely? Neve felt a chill in her bones. Something was going on here that she hadn't allowed for.

Gauvain stepped back and put his hand on Leo's arm. "This is my realm, and I'm telling you there's nothing to worry about. Let it go, my friend."

Leo's lips twitched. "It will be an adventure, that's certain."

"Stay in touch." Gauvain hesitated. "And don't fail me."

"We've been over everything imaginable. Should this mission fail, it'll be none of my doing." Leo squeezed the other man's arm, murmured something Neve couldn't hear, then turned away, making for the oxcart. Gauvain remained on the step briefly, then re-entered the Tower.

After a brief word with the oxcart driver, Leo approached her. "That was interesting," he said, acknowledging that she had been witness to the scene. "Don't let it worry you. Now, I'd recommend riding on one of the carts until we've cleared Orlan, but you'll be welcome to stretch your legs thereafter. No one says travel by donkey cart is speedy."

"Who am I likely to kill?"

"His name's Santon. We'll meet him late tomorrow. Hop up."

She nodded her acquiescence. Asking about this mysterious other person could wait. Leo offered her a hand up to the seat of the first cart. Higher than their own, it would afford a fine view of new vistas. Leo walked down the line to speak to the drivers of the carts, then returned and swung up behind her with surprising ease, given his probable age. The driver twitched the reins, and the cart lurched forward.

Neve looked back, counting. She, Leo, and the driver on the first cart, only the driver on the second, driver and two other men on the oxcart. Not as many as she expected.

Leo anticipated her. "Besides Santon, we'll be picking up construction workers along the way for the next few days. The administration types will join us later, taking the new road south... once we've built it." His eyes twinkled, as if laughing at the softness of city-based administrators.

The carts headed east toward the road circling the city. Neve twisted on the seat, but John had already vanished. Then everything familiar ended. The adventure had begun.

Chapter 5: Tension in the Tower

Turning from the door and the departing caravan, Gauvain strode to his study, glowering. He and Leo went way back, to his young days when the soldier took him adventuring, teaching him about the land, responsibility, and self-defense. Leo was majordomo, friend, moral touchstone, cook, and the one person in the world Gauvain trusted unconditionally. Glumly, he wondered how the Black Tower would function without him.

Well, it wouldn't be forever. Leo would return home once they reached their destination. And the potential benefits far outweighed whatever discomfort he might endure over the course of the summer.

Gauvain was grimly aware that 'destination' had only a nebulous definition, and there was no guarantee what they would find once there, or even if the planned crossing point would be recognizable if no one from the Midland was present. The southern part of Borgonne was a mystery, sparsely populated and having virtually no trade or other contact with the more prosperous and urban north. Gauvain allowed himself a tiny shudder, then he chided himself. What had happened to the young man he had been, open to all possibilities, eager for new experiences?

Frankly, he admitted to himself, the last venture across the hills had destroyed his curiosity about the unknown, possibly for all time. That monster, the slaughter...

But the south wasn't like that. Leo and his little entourage would be fine.

Irritated with the situation and more with himself, he turned to business and the small stack of paper awaiting him.

A memo from Esther Sauvage, one of six town councillors who collectively were the bane of his existence, lay on top of the pile. It suggested – no, stated – that the time had come to release more grain from the storage warehouses. The previous year's drought had devastated the food supply, and rationing was triggering unrest. Her note was well reasoned; thank the Aura there was someone with sense on the Orlan council.

The council. His pen hit the table, spattering ink. Wearily, he used a ready rag to wipe up the mess. This was far from the first time he had smacked a pen to the nearest available surface.

He scribbled a note to himself on the sheet and set it aside. There was yet another council meeting later, wasting yet another afternoon. Losing Cedric Prudhomme, the late mayor – his position remained vacant – had resulted in a return to partial rationality, but the remaining councillors consistently failed to acknowledge the wisdom of his guidance. Fools every one, always excepting Esther.

Gauvain opened his mouth, about to shout for Leo, but closed it in time. Leo was gone.

Where the council was concerned, Gauvain had his ways, and generally, when it mattered, his position won the day. Still, watching the caravan prepare to depart had shaken him in a way he couldn't readily define. At times like this he felt intensely, vulnerably human, a feeling he tried to avoid at all costs.

The next two items in his pile were applications from parents eager to see their offspring attend his classes. Apprenticing in his school led to prestige and reward later, so demand was constant and he could afford to be choosy. He quickly perused the two letters. One of the children, it seemed, was a girl. He was on the verge of tossing the letter into the waste basket when he hesitated. That other girl, Neve... he had not foreseen that she would become such a force, in both personality and Auric ability. There had been one or two other girls over the years, although none had completed his program. Perhaps he should at least grant this new girl an interview.

He read through the application letters, finding nothing he hadn't seen dozens of times before. Boys – almost always boys – manifesting powers no one could explain, parents concerned for their offspring but also with a thought to improvement in the family's means. The children were universally presented as obedient, smart, likeable, self-starters, and undoubtedly ideal to receive his tutelage.

Gauvain roughly calculated the admission rate at one in ten, the success rate once admitted at fifty percent. The current crop, John, Reed, and Conor, bade fair to be the first class ever to graduate with no failures. Later, he might call the apprentices together for an impromptu lecture. Or maybe not. With John's absence, only two of them were in residence, and they could wait.

Gauvain rose and stalked to the currently empty kitchen, thinking that a mug of Leo's special tea might improve the day. As expected, he found everything in the cheerful room tidily labeled and stored. With his usual efficiency, Leo had arranged for a local woman to come in daily to prepare meals. Gauvain had agreed only on the condition that the woman stay in the kitchen and he never had to lay eyes on her. His privacy trumped any possible culinary advantage – or so he'd thought at the time. He supposed she would turn up later and wondered what future teatimes might be like, should she be present.

He had to admit, the thought of that tea without Leo's company to give it spice fell flat. He brewed a mug anyway – the blend had been divided into individual portions, so even he couldn't mess it up – and carried it back to his desk.

Well, there was always the council meeting to look forward to.

With a groan, Gauvain returned to the pile of papers demanding his attention.

Chapter 6: On the Road

Neve's father had said often enough, "Don't wish for excitement, girl. It usually means something's bad wrong. Slow, steady, and peaceful. That's the ticket."

Well, her dad would appreciate this journey. Slow, steady, and peaceful. Just the way Neve herself preferred it.

It took much of the morning to clear the environs of Orlan. She swayed with the cart, her head swiveling in an attempt to miss nothing. This was unfamiliar territory. She knew the market and the handful of individual customers, mainly restaurants and street vendors, who bought their vegetables and fruits. She knew the route home and the road to the Tower, a few city blocks from the market. But the extent the town sprawled to the east surprised her. Small dwellings lined side streets. The occasional market square might be home to a well, a butcher, a greengrocer, perhaps a healer with bunches of herbs hanging by the door. From her perch, she could see fields unfolding across the shallow hills, most of them showing early growth from first plantings.

The greening of the land was hopeful after last year's drought. Her own village hadn't fared too poorly, but even they were pinched now, in the lean time between the end of one harvest and the beginning of the next.

Eventually, they passed through the last small marketplace, pausing briefly to stretch and make use of public conveniences. Leo distributed pasties and fruit leather. "To keep us going," he explained. "It's some hours before we stop for a meal."

As the donkey began its jolting walk forward, Neve munched through her pasty in record time, then asked, "Do you know this route? I thought you hadn't been along this way before."

Leo made himself comfortable in the back of the cart, nibbling on his own snack. He gave every indication of being comfortable on the hard floor, despite his age. "I'm familiar with the roads as far south as Vienne, near the enclave of a late mage. In fact, that will be our second overnight stop. Santon is one of his former apprentices. His magic is unlike yours, being more cerebral, more in tune with Gauvain's. The two of you will work together to get this road surveyed and improved."

"But you're not optimistic we'll work well together."

"It's never a good idea to rely on what you overhear," Leo chided.

Neve twisted to study the land, then her soon-to-be tutor. "Is it my imagination, or is settlement primarily east of Orlan, not to the west?"

"Not imagination." Leo munched a bite of fruit leather and swallowed. "Even the ordinary folk shy away from too great a proximity to the hills. And for mages, well, I'm sure you've heard enough to know that none of them are willing to be any closer than necessary. The old spells... some say that with time, they have become unstable. No one with even an ounce of Auric ability is willing to take the risk of seeing their magical powers perverted, or worse, losing them completely, by too much proximity."

Neve experienced a lurch in her chest. "I believe you said we'd be following a track closely paralleling the hills?" Other than the probable conflict with Santon, this was the first indication she'd had that the trip might be other than a straightforward roadbuilding exercise.

"Unfortunate but true. A number of mages have traveled the northern section of the route over the years and have reported no adverse effects, so we believe it to be safe. Much of it crosses the foothills, but... well, we'll see. At least there is a track, and we know it presents no real difficulties for the first few nine-days. Once we pass the settlements, it's wilderness to the east, which would be much more challenging."

"Great," she mumbled.

Leo nodded to himself, his gaze off to the west. The hills were merely a feature on the western horizon, but they were never not visible. Neve had lived with them all her life. "How about this?" he said. "One of the best skills we could begin your training with is to detect the spells on the hills, some of them anyway. No one is able to sense them all."

"I'm reading the earth now. Where it's healthy, that kind of thing."

"Good." Leo gave her a complacent nod. "That will be our starting point. Hopefully, sensing the spells will give you some reassurance."

"Or just the opposite." Neve had never had any formal training beyond the recipes in her book, so formal training made her nervous and excited in equal measure. "Are you sure I can do this?"

"You can. Scramble down here next to me."

Swinging a leg over the back of the high seat, Neve hefted herself over and down to the bed of the donkey cart, grasping Leo's outstretched hand as she landed. "How?" she demanded.

"Close your eyes." Catching her skeptical look, he said, "Just do it. Some of this will be earth magic, but you'll be tapping mental magic as well." When her lids sank closed, he said, "Relax. Feel the earth around you, cosseting you, and release to it. Earth will give you safety and surety. All is well. You can feel the energy from your element, from the earth. Touch it, be reassured by it."

This was semi-familiar territory, the energies of the earth, although accessed in a way she had never experienced. Leo's voice droned on, combining with the sway of the cart to lull Neve into a near sleep. A trance? She'd never bothered with anything like trance, it hadn't been necessary. But Leo's voice led her inexorably on, into...

... a different sort of world

... energies

... colors, so many colors. In swirls.

His voice prompted her. She told him what she saw... or perhaps didn't see. Perhaps felt. Or... experienced some other way?

"Hold on to the earth energies, Neve. They will keep you grounded. You're safe."

She let the strangeness float around her, enjoying the new sensations, following Leo's lead.

... dancing, colors dancing, almost like music...

... black. *Black*!

Her body jolted. Leo's hand tightened on hers. As the trance slipped away, her eyes flew open. She became newly aware of the high, clear sky, the sway of the cart in time with the donkey's steps, Leo's calm presence.

"Breathe," he said, "and put your hand on the bed of the cart. Draw up the earth energy."

Too shaken by the hovering blackness she had sensed, wiping out all the other colors, she did as he instructed. After a minute her breath steadied.

"Tell me," Leo said.

Neve swallowed, seeking her voice, which emerged with an unfamiliar, tremulous croak. "Black. Eating the other colors. It was lovely and then... it all got destroyed. What was it?" she demanded, her voice stronger. "How could something like that be here, so close to Orlan? Is it going to end the growing season? Is it dangerous? Is it—?"

"Whoa. Slowly, my dear." Leo shifted to face her, his gaze intense. "You need to explore these questions yourself. Replay the experience, watch for details. Open to meaning. Normally, you'd do these things while in trance, but it's worth reflection afterwards. As for what the black is, I can't say for sure, but I suspect it's leaking from the hills. I haven't sensed it myself, but my powers are much weaker than yours."

He passed a piece of fruit leather to her, folding her hand over it. "All manner of energy swirls around, constantly. Being a novice, I'm surprised you were able to detect anything that wasn't earth-based, frankly. But it needn't worry you. Most likely it's simply dissociated energy that can't do anything."

She chewed and swallowed. Abricoe and apple filled her senses. "Easy for you to say. I'm leaving home for who knows where, for a season or more, with people I don't know, and I'm attacked by that black *thing*."

Leo grinned. "Hyperbole, Neve. Not attacked. As I said, I'm guessing it's some kind of remnant, something that drifted down from the hills."

Neve sat straighter and looked around. The Orlan suburbs were well behind them, and the cart rolled through farmland on either side. The sun was past its zenith. Her stomach protested the paucity of lunch; she shoved the rest of the fruit leather into her mouth.

"Sorry about that," Leo said. "I wanted to be sure we got clear of Orlan on our first leg. But in retrospect, several pasties each would have been a better idea. I don't eat much myself, so give me a reminder when I underfeed you. They do say an army marches on its stomach."

"I can certainly do that."

Leo closed his eyes, seeming to abandon himself to the sway of the cart. Neve studied him. Elderly, to be sure, but still vital and clearly fit. In repose, his wrinkled face appeared benign, everyone's favorite grandfather, but she already knew enough to recognize that for the lie it was. How on earth had he partnered up with Gauvain? And for that matter, how did he stand life in the Black Tower?

Could she trust him? This was paramount. The sheer size of the vista drove home how alone she was. Going on this adventure suddenly felt like a child's whim, acted on without due care. She should be home now, working with the apple trees or helping her mother in the kitchen, not out in the middle of an unknown land.

In for a penny, she thought, and considered scrambling back up to the driver's seat, but decided to remain where she was for the time. The view was almost as good, and, Aura help her, there was something comforting about sitting next to the old man as they rolled along.

Chapter 7: Gauvain Bedeviled

Gauvain approached the council meeting as he always did – assuming he was facing a group of mindless cretins who had been put on the planet for the sole purpose of undermining his every move, no matter how well intentioned or rational his dictates might be. If there was a better method to tame the Orlan council, he hadn't found it.

The council chamber was on the second floor of the Orlan administration building, and Cedric Prudhomme, the previous mayor, had seen to it that the trappings reflected the perceived dignity of the office. The table rivaled Gauvain's dining table in size and quality, being of a dense, dark wood found only in the largely unpopulated forests to the far northeast. Chairs featured an ornately patterned upholstery, something rare in Borgonne where most chairs were plain wood. Heavy draperies guarded the windows, removing any hope of natural light or fresh air. The walls were painted deep green; Gauvain hadn't yet figured out how the dye had been created. All in all, the room was both impressive and depressing.

Today's meeting dealt with feeding the populace. Hunger, if not outright starvation, was rampant, and empty bellies led to unrest. But the stores sequestered in warehouses against just such an event as last year's drought were running low. So far, signs portended a good harvest, but that wouldn't occur for a season or more. While farmers had been encouraged to grow early season crops, in the meantime Orlan had to be fed.

As usual, Esther was the only council member with any grasp of the challenges facing the countryside. The others seemed to believe crops appeared as if by magic from the ground. And they expected he could provide that magic.

He chose not to admit he couldn't. A few, like that girl, Neve, had the knack for earth magic. He didn't. But council needn't know that. Better they believe him to be omnipotent.

Esther had no such illusions, however. As far as she was concerned, there would be an infusion of vegetables in five or six nine-days' time. Late season crops and grain for flour would appear much later. Until then, they had to ration what they had.

None of the councillors suffered from hunger, he noted.

Esther, who through sheer force of personality had assumed the role of interim mayor, cut through the bickering. "The question, in a nutshell, is this. Do we release the remaining stores over the next few nine-days, or do we hold some back in case this year's harvest is as disastrous as last year's?"

Lac, a sour man with nothing positive to say about anything, glared in Gauvain's direction without quite meeting his eyes. "There's no reason for the harvest to fail."

Lac had been part of the unfortunate party that had crossed the hills, so Gauvain couldn't completely blame him for whatever emotional hangover he still battled. Still, he had no right to put the weight, or the blame, on him. "I've told you numerous times. Not only is tinkering with the weather a bad idea, it is in fact forbidden by the College of Mages."

"The new road, then," Georges said. Georges was Gauvain's contemporary in age and ambition. He clearly resented Esther's assumption of control, and probably resented her presence altogether, given that she was both from a rural outlier and a woman. Georges had his uses, but keeping him under control was challenging.

"Next year, at the earliest," Gauvain stated, "as has been said several times already. It's possible some produce from south of here could be brought to Orlan, but frankly, I've never heard they grow more than they need."

Georges shrugged.

"You can't take food from their mouths," Esther snapped. "Just because they don't live in your fine city."

"Is your paltry little hamlet prepared to step up?" Georges shot back. "You go on about Orlan, but I don't see—"

"*Enough*," Gauvain roared through the main event and several side conversations. Silence fell abruptly, thick as fog. "Esther has summed up the situation accurately. Do we distribute now or hold back?"

"A little of both?" Justin, a timid man in his sixties whose thick mop of gray hair drew attention from a totally undistinguished face, asked.

"We've been over this," Esther said, making no effort to disguise her weariness with the subject. "A little won't pacify the population."

"Neither will none," Georges stated.

"We're being asked to gamble on the weather," Lac complained.

"Exactly. Can we vote now?" Esther folded her arms across her meager chest.

Gauvain sat back and watched. For him, the question came down to pragmatism. There had already been protests in the streets that only just missed being riots. They couldn't afford to worry about the future. The populace had to be pacified now.

"I demand a secret ballot," Georges said.

"As is your right," Esther said. She rose and crossed the room to a buffet against the wall, from which she retrieved a box with a hole in the top and a bag of wooden beads, tinted both white and black. "White ball is for distributing the stores now. Black ball is for holding back against a poor harvest."

"He get a vote?" Georges asked, nodding at Gauvain.

Esther paused to think it over. "Tie breaker," she announced. "Any objections?"

"A lot," Lac said. "But the hell with it. Let's get on with the vote."

The box and bag of balls made the circuit of the table. Each council member in turn dipped a hand in the bag, chose the appropriate color ball, and dropped it in the box, screening his hand from other eyes. They were all good at hiding, Gauvain thought as he watched the process. Not a one of them, other than Esther, was willing to be held accountable.

In the end, his input wasn't needed. The food would be distributed. And the Aura help them all if the harvest failed again.

On his way back to the Tower, Gauvain considered his apprentices. They were by far the best group he had ever instructed, but showing signs of posturing typical of young men. Such unruliness couldn't be tolerated, but even he recognized the boys needed to release pent-up pressures. Perhaps he would send them all to John's farm for a nine-day. John had a little of the earth magic that showed up so strongly in his elder sister. Perhaps exposure to another type of magic, as well as helping with ordinary, physical farm tasks, would give them more focus.

He snorted. Perhaps he should simply import three clean doxies. Even he remembered being seventeen.

Frivolous thought. The farm, though... that was an idea. When John got back, he'd talk to him about it.

His step lightened as he drew near the Tower, then returned to his normal, determined pace as he remembered Leo wasn't there to be a sounding board, and more to the point, to feed him. At least his home provided a bastion against the humdrum problems of the city. And Leo had laid in a supply of that superb wine from vineyards close to Duncan's enclave. Whatever slop the hired help catered, he'd enjoy a glass of the ruby elixir.

Chapter 8: Santon Is Fed Up

Shouts and singing from the tavern filled the streets of Vienne, no escaping it. The stable where Santon kept his tools was on the eastern fringe, all the way across town, but something had set the crowd off this evening – probably a futbol game.

Well, nothing new there. It just meant no quiet beer after work. He ran a hand through his dusty black hair – the scrap of linen he used to keep it out of his face had vanished somewhere during the day – and laid the survey equipment in place, locking the cabinet door securely. However dissatisfied he might be about his current circumstance, he respected the instruments.

The stable itself was quiet, only a couple of donkeys in residence. One of them glared at him with a baleful eye, as if it shared his frustration and was ready to kick out in disgust.

"You and me both, brother." He gave the beast a scratch between the ears on his way out.

The day hadn't been impossible. His assistant had been able to hold the survey pole upright and steady under an intense sun, a fresh breeze off the hills barely keeping the heat at bay. His head was sweaty, but he'd needed his wide-brimmed leather hat and the long-sleeved tunic he wore as a matter of course, to fend off glare and sunburn.

This evening, he was to meet the team from Orlan. He'd been promised a lot; he didn't believe it. But he was willing to give the representative from the Black Tower a hearing.

Black Tower. Gauvain. He had cause to hate the man. But sometimes you had to seize opportunities where they presented themselves. Duncan's death had left Santon neither here nor there, not quite a fully trained mage, but far too accomplished to be considered a mere town magician.

To relieve frustration, he sent shafts of energy into a few small stones lying along the street, shattering them. Nothing too dramatic, he wasn't out to hurt anyone. Just enough to create a minor explosion in the dirt. Grim-faced, shifting his shoulders to ease the ache of a day's labor and keep his tunic away from his sweaty back, he made it to the tavern yard.

Nothing grim about his reception. "San! Get yourself in there, grab a beer."

And he'd hoped to arrive unnoticed. Fat chance.

"Hey, Big Bobby. What's going on?"

"Ya didn't hear? Little Bobby's buying. Won the lottery."

The lottery was a scheme to keep the locals happy, dreamed up by the council. It seemed the town's burghers realized how much Duncan had exerted his Auric powers in their favor. Without his influence, the realities of their hardscrabble existence sank in. Grumbling was ubiquitous, as was gambling, so the lottery provided a pacifier to a restless populace. The prize was miniscule, but the weekly fascination gripped the residents – and kept them placid, Santon thought with a trace of bemusement. He couldn't care less about the lottery, although a couple of times since his exile from Duncan's sphere he had predicted the winning number – a fact he prudently kept to himself.

"Those winnings won't last long if he's treating the whole town."

Big Bobby shrugged. "What's it matter?"

Point.

A jovial punch to his shoulder. "How ya doin', man?"

A small group had formed, including both Bobbys and the other men who once had been the boys he'd grown up with. Farm workers, smithies, one who worked in the tiny village shop. Santon had become something vaguely exotic to them when he left for Duncan's enclave, but since he'd come back to Vienne, they'd simply absorbed him into their narrow culture. Or tried to.

He shrugged. "Long day. New houses going up out the north road."

"Got yourself filthy for a change. Must have been doin' some real work." Someone elbowed him in the ribs.

"It's dusty out there," he retorted. "Hot, too."

"Get your beer. No point to standin' there parched."

And free beer was free beer. Santon endured a few shoulder and back slaps as he elbowed his way into the dark tavern. The place was jammed, twenty or so men – almost all men – crammed into the space, the air murky with pipe smoke. Every step released a fresh puff of dust from the ancient wood floor. He claimed his reward and fled, huffing a large breath when he made it into the clean air.

One small taste proved the liquid in his mug was the stuff the tavern owner saved for just such an occasion, when the town was too drunk to know what they were drinking. He dodged a group of celebrating rowdies and tucked himself around the side of the building, away from both the sun and the hubbub.

Two choices, nurse the beer or gulp it down. Gulping had the advantage of getting rid of the horrid stuff faster while possibly giving him a buzz. Nursing limited the flavor hitting his tongue at one time but prolonged the disgust factor. Neither appealed, although Santon figured he was due for a good drunk. Since Duncan's death, his life and prospects had basically gone to hell.

Whatever the hell 'hell' was. One of the old words with no definition, but plenty of meaning.

Objectively, his life wasn't bad. It just wasn't what he'd expected, hoped for, been promised. What he was good enough for. As a mage, he would have had limitless opportunity. But being a mage meant training, and that meant Duncan. And damn *blast* it all. How *dare* he be dead?

Killed in Gauvain's Black Tower. He'd never forgive Gauvain for that. Never.

You're too old for this. Grow up. He'd started his training late, about the time he suddenly matured from a skinny kid the others picked on into a good-looking guy, or so the local girls said, packing height and muscle – and unexpected Auric powers. Duncan had found him soon after. Since then, mage training had been his life. Until it all ended.

Gauvain's people should be here soon. It wouldn't be wise to present himself to them without his wits firmly in place. He allowed the hand holding the mug to sag down along his side and tip. The beer streamed into the dirt. Santon placed the mug on the ground – it would be found eventually – and left, following the tavern's wall around to the back and cutting across a field through lengthening shadows to the shack he now called home.

Once, he'd lived in Duncan's enclave. A damn sight better than his single room with one tiny window. The enclave stood empty now. There were days he was tempted to simply walk in and take it over. He was close enough to his formal credential as a mage. But the potential repercussions from the College of Mages didn't bear thinking about. Assuming it even existed; the College was a mystery he'd yet to be initiated into.

Could he become Gauvain's student, complete his training that way? The thought had crossed his mind before. Rumor had it that Gauvain hadn't been responsible for Duncan's death, that it had been some lowlife with a knife who broke into the Tower. But Gauvain was his only hope.

And now this expedition. Surveying a new road didn't qualify as thrilling work, but at least it was a change. He would accept the job, travel to the far south, and see what possibilities opened up. From the door of the shack, he took in the drabness of it all. Vienne wasn't going to be his life forever, that much he could guarantee.

He grabbed a bucket, pulled water from the nearest well, washed the day's dust from his hands and face, and sniffed at his pits – clean sweat, nothing off-putting – before donning a fresh tunic and heading for the inn where he was to meet Gauvain's man.

Chapter 9: Meeting the Team

Neve slouched at a table in the inn's common room, grateful for the meal soon to come, and even more grateful for the soft pallet upstairs. They had camped at a waysite the night before. It hadn't been uncomfortable, exactly, but her body had ached with the tension of new travel – and maybe a little from the Auric exploration Leo had led her in that first day on the road.

The inn had proved a pleasant surprise. Her view of Vienne as they drove through had not engendered high expectations. But the room assigned to her was clean, if tiny, and the aromas emanating from the kitchen promised an edible meal. Leo had arranged hot water, allowing her a much needed wash before joining him over a mug of tolerable lager.

Neve felt the sizzle of energy – clashing energies, she thought, although she had no experience of such a thing – the moment the man entered the common room.

Of the stranger himself, he appeared to be one with the local culture. Black hair flowed to his shoulders; she could see the crimp where it had been tied back. A sleeveless tunic revealed muscled arms, while contemptuous eyes, closer to black than brown, poised to take offence. Even from across the room she sensed the tension in his body.

That the man in the door was the one they were here to meet, there could be no doubt. Although Leo had told her he had never met Santon Fernandez, recognition flowed between the two of them... and not a pleasant one. Instinctively, she sought a way to smooth the surges in the energy, so intense that several others in the common room looked up, frowning, as if sensing an obscure danger.

The man crossed the room to their table. "Who's she?" he demanded, glaring at Leo.

"This is Neve," Leo replied, his voice level. Neve watched, her gut clenching as it always did when she was faced with hostility. *Calm.* She repeated it to herself. If she let her cool demeanor slip, she might flee outright, and then what would this sardonic man think of her?

Santon stood above them, arms folded and no hint of pleasantness on his face. "I thought I was the mage on this project."

"I don't believe anyone claimed there would be only one person with Auric powers. Neve has her own skill set, which I believe to be quite different from your own."

The man's attitude was calculated to irritate. Tense she might be, but Neve stood, placing her eyes at a level with his. "You've no call to criticize before you've even met me."

Santon made a dismissive noise from the back of his throat. "Hedge witch, are you? Watch you don't get above yourself, girlie. I was promised—"

"Work, as a mage," Leo interrupted. "Shall we decelerate here, please?"

Santon wheeled on him. "And we'll all work together, and cooperate, and love each other? Give me a break. If you want my help, you'll do something about this *amateur*. If she gets in my way—"

"I get in *your* way? Mind what you're saying, *boy*." Neve trembled with frustration and insult. She hated confrontation but.... Without her conscious volition, the energy at the tips of her fingers flared, causing the table and mugs of ale to flash briefly in gold.

Santon elbowed her out of the way. "You want a competition?" His own fingers twitched. The mugs of ale sailed from the table over to the serving bar.

"Sloshed the ale, didn't you?" she taunted. "Poor control."

"*Children!*" Leo roared. They both froze. "Stop this. You're attracting attention we don't need. Santon, get the drinks back over here – by hand, if you please."

Neve looked around. The few other occupants of the common room were staring. Not in alarm – they probably all knew Santon and his abilities – but as if hoping for a show.

The energy faded as the man carried the mugs back. He hooked a chair from another table with his foot, dragging it into place. "Tell me more about this job," he said flatly as he sat.

The serving girl appeared with a third mug of ale. Setting it in front of the new man, she managed to brush against him, then placed a hand on his shoulder as she straightened. "Hey, San," she said, more breathily than the voice she'd used when serving Leo and Neve.

"Hey, Bethie. Good to see you." Santon spared a tight smile for the girl and squeezed her hand before it left his shoulder. That was all, though. If there was a story there, it wasn't a current one. Bethie disappeared into the kitchen and Santon, after a deep pull at the contents of the mug, focused on Leo. "Tell me," he said.

"Survey and construction work." Leo laid it out succinctly. "Which will undoubtedly rely on your Auric abilities as well. Improving the road to the south, in anticipation of establishing a trade route."

"Not that. I know that." Santon's mouth became hard. "What I want to hear is, how you can justify coming to me for any kind of help when you killed my master."

"Ah." Leo fell silent, considering, before he continued. "Duncan inserted himself into... a necessary action. His death was unfortunate, but not predictable. Or, I suppose, avoidable. Gauvain was not present."

"Were you?"

"Not in the room, no. Soon after, though. There were other casualties, although Duncan was the sole fatality."

"Somehow, that fails to make me feel better." Santon's focus shifted from Leo to the depths of his ale.

Leo offered a miniscule nod. "You might have come forward, you know. To continue your training with Gauvain, or one of the other mages."

"Others?" Santon's head came up.

"There are a few scattered around Borgonne. None to rival Duncan or Gauvain." Some subtle shift in posture signaled to Neve that as far as Leo was concerned, the topic was exhausted. "Now, unless you have more pressing questions, shall we discuss the matter at hand? Neve is tired, I've no doubt, as am I. It has been a hot, slow trip from Orlan."

A basket of coarse bread and three bowls of stew arrived from the kitchen just as Santon gave a curt nod. Neve smiled to herself. Leo had been sure enough of his man that he'd ordered the third bowl.

All three spooned up the stew. Neve sighed with pleasure; the flavor fulfilled every bit of the aroma's promise. For a few minutes she ignored the silent interaction going on between the two men. She was a daughter of the land. The stew connected her to the local agriculture, as well as sustaining her for the night and morning to come.

When she finally looked up, she realized that some form of deal had been reached. Santon wore an expression somewhere between contemptuous and resigned, while Leo's countenance was carefully neutral. Neve had spent two days with him, however, and was beginning to recognize his nuances. She saw hints of humility and gratitude. Leo hadn't been as certain of the outcome of this meeting as he'd let on.

"Tools?" Leo asked.

"I own my own survey equipment. Bought it when I left the enclave."

"How soon can you be ready? You can catch up if you can't get away immediately. I doubt there will be much work for you for some days to come."

"Not until you run out of well-traveled road," Santon confirmed. "I can leave tomorrow. I'm owed nothing here."

"Speaking of which..." Leo named an amount, the same Neve would earn. "Tell me what sort of disposition you prefer. A bank perhaps?"

"In Orlan? Sure, why not? I'm assuming expenses are covered."

"Of course. Have you transport?"

"Are you kidding? I walk where I need to go."

Leo extracted a leaf of paper from the leather bag he wore attached to the soft rope tied around his waist, cinching in his tunic. "Supplies. See how much of this you can round up. And anything you want for your own comfort or amusement. Or practice." The last was added with emphasis.

But Santon dismissed the suggestion. "My Auric tools got left behind. They were technically Duncan's anyway."

Leo smiled, the first genuine smile Neve had seen since Santon joined them. "Duncan always did rely too much on his devices. On this trip, you'll learn other techniques, if you're open to them."

There was that flare again. Santon, Neve speculated, was easily insulted. No doubt he met with scorn the idea this elderly man with questionable powers could teach him anything.

Leo ignored the reaction as he stood. Neve watched. From the day she had met him, years ago, she had thought of Leo as a hunched old man, well past his best years. A kindly elder who baked pastries and doled out soothing tisanes. But the man repositioning his chair now and reaching a hand to clasp Santon's was... virile, she decided. Strong, not someone to be dismissed lightly. Had the trip revived him? Or was it all illusion? One way or another, Santon clearly recognized the shift, and the spiky energy smoothed out. He rose and met the hand clasp with something approaching respect, although a thread of tension remained.

Round one to Leo. Neve also stood, bidding her companions a good night. Then she dismissed all thought of either man as she contemplated the nearness of a solid night's sleep.

Chapter 10: Confrontation

Sleep didn't come, however. Days were getting longer, so Neve slipped from her room, seizing the last of the fading twilight, and made her way outdoors. Riding or walking at a donkey cart's pace, followed by a heavy meal, left her longing for air and exercise. Farming was a physical activity, and her body ached for movement.

She walked toward the center of Vienne, looking about her. Some things were different from home, house styles and building materials and the way buildings sprawled along the main road rather than clustering around a square. Other things were familiar. Few windows were lit; the people here worked hard, just as her people did, and relished their sleep.

As she neared the center of town, she sensed she was being followed. Turning, she spotted a ginger cat stalking in the shadows. She squatted at the side of the road in front of a store and made a series of clicking sounds with her fingers. The cat approached cautiously. After thoroughly sniffing her hand, it relaxed and allowed her to stroke... *him*, she concluded, now that she was in direct contact with the cat's energy.

"You're hurt," she informed the animal. He let loose a low yowl. "Let's see to it, shall we?" Using both hands, she encouraged him to lie on his side. The cat struggled briefly, then relaxed into her touch. She channeled healing, seeking the knotted muscles guarding the old injury. It took a while before the muscles relaxed and she was able to target energy to the wound.

She sensed Santon before she saw him, emerging from what probably was a tavern. The dying light caught a reflection from the golden liquid in his mug... something else different, glass mugs were rare around her village, although she occasionally saw them in Orlan. The cat awoke from a stupor of relaxed purring and looked around, then twisted free and sprang to his feet. Neve stood, watching the animal bolt across the street and into an alley, his movements freer than before.

Santon left the mug behind on an outdoor table and strolled over to her. Behind him the lights in the tavern went out. "Abusing small animals?" he said with no welcome at all.

"Healing a small animal. Helping anyway. He was in pain."

"Lovely. A wildling and a hedge healer, all in one. You might even be useful if any of the laborers get hurt on the job."

Despite herself, her ire rose, but she kept her voice neutral. "I might be useful anyway. You know nothing about my skill set."

Santon folded his arms across his chest. Neve was thankful for her height; he couldn't glare down at her.

"Oh, I know all about your so-called skill set. I've seen my share of women like you. Some healing, and perhaps the ability to create a simple light ball or some other trick to impress the gullible. You're nothing but an untrained, unsophisticated charlatan, and you give real mages a bad name."

His words were calculated to insult, and he succeeded. "Just what's your problem? Challenged by working with a woman? Grow up, why don't you?"

He changed the focus of his attack. "I suppose where you come from, messy hair and a dirty face add to your mystique.

Why don't you find a mirror? Features like yours, you can't afford to let yourself look so slovenly."

"It's a mark of a slovenly mind to mix messages. My appearance has nothing whatsoever to do with whether I can heal a cat, or modify a landscape, or encourage growth in plants." She told herself to shut up, for all the good it did. "You're unbelievable. You go to a meeting looking like a bum, you're rude to me and to Leo. I think you need us more than we need you, buddy." As an afterthought, she added, "Maybe you should lay off the ale. You're hardly sober."

"I think it's time you learned a lesson or two from a real mage, *babe*." His voice turned wheedling. "Don't you want to go back to your inn, dear? Of course you do."

Neve felt it, a change in the air. He was doing something with the Aura, wrapping it around her, forcing her to turn.

Or trying to. Neve dug into the earth, found the energy she wanted, and sent it toward him. The ground heaved under him, breaking his concentration and causing him to stagger back. The energy dissipated, freeing her.

"You bitch."

"Don't you *ever* try something like that again."

He stepped toward her, fury on his face, a hand raised. Enraged, she felt power fill her hands, burst from her fingertips.

The air between them changed texture, becoming a thick, murky yellow-green that extended far up into the sky, emitting an eerie light. A rent appeared in the fog, as if the atmosphere itself had been torn apart, revealing... emptiness. Lightning flashed within the fog. A blinding burst of energy seared the road. Santon jumped back and Neve dove, her hands scraping across the hard-packed dirt. It wasn't until her breath was knocked out of her as she hit the ground that she realized she had screamed. Frantic, she rolled, gasping for breath. Santon cried out and twisted away as a deep rumbling emerged from the gap in the air.

Then it was gone. With a final crackle, the fog faded. Still unable to breathe properly, Neve struggled to sit. Her hands stung and her hip ached from the impact. She had never in her life been so terrified. Unexpectedly, Santon offered her a hand up. With him steadying her, she hauled herself to her feet, caught between grudging and grateful.

Her legs wanted to give way, dropping her back onto the ground. They held hands like children, both of them shaking, staring at the place on the road where the lightning had struck. The dirt was fused into a dirty glass circle a meter across. She studied Santon's free arm, where a livid burn ran from above his elbow to his wrist.

"What was that?" he said, not at her but at the night, or the Aura, or himself... she wasn't sure.

"I don't know." Her voice sounded faint in her ears.

Santon studied the glazed patch of road. "What the hell did you do?" he asked, puzzlement combined with a trace of his earlier superiority.

"Nothing. I don't know. I could ask you the same question." Neve swallowed hard. "I've never seen anything like it. Never knew it was possible."

He released her hand, crossed to the tavern, and slouched down on a bench against the wall. "We need to talk."

"We need to deal with your arm. That burn could be nasty."

She wouldn't ask if it hurt. He would probably deny it or take it as condescending on her part.

"It isn't all that bad." His voice had grown tight; the pain must be worse than he chose to let on.

Neve rolled her eyes. "We don't even know the nature of the burn. At least we can keep it from getting infected overnight. You don't think we'd travel without a pharmacy, do you?"

He snapped right back, "Given the ramshackle organization I've seen so far, it's possible."

"You haven't seen anything. Come on."

Neve knew full well she was only able to take charge because he had been the one hurt, not her. But he followed as she led the way to the inn. Even a stubborn male was capable of recognizing the need to doctor a burn this extensive.

In the quiet common room, Neve lined up a basin of water from the kitchen, clean rags and a pot of greenish salve from her medical kit. With a flick of her hand, she launched a small light ball to supplement the lantern light. "We can't assume it's clean, so best to at least flush it," she stated as she grasped Santon's wrist and positioned his arm over the basin. Without touching his arm, she used the rag to sluice the angry, blistered wound. Then a second rag gently blotted it dry – Santon winced but said nothing – and she smoothed on the salve. "This has analgesic as well as healing properties, so the sting should lessen somewhat. I can give you a dose of willow tincture if you need it."

"A case of the cure worse than the injury," he muttered, a sentiment Neve privately agreed with.

She placed a loosely woven linen rag over his arm, allowing it to adhere to the salve. "This will keep it clean, but the more air it gets, the better."

"Thanks."

Santon seemed disinclined to speak above a mutter, so she couldn't get a sense of his thoughts regarding the... what should she call it? No words were adequate when the heavens tore apart.

She packed away her medicines and extinguished the light ball, then sat across from him. His face looked ghostly in the light of the tallow lantern. "You want to talk?" she asked.

He turned those hostile eyes on her. "I want to know what you did. By all the demons of hell, you could have killed us. I've never seen—"

"Neither have I," she interrupted. "I didn't do it. I assumed you did. Leo did say your magic is different from mine. For all I know—"

"Stop. Wait." He glanced around. "Do you suppose there's any ale behind the counter? I could use some."

Neve located a small cask and pulled them each a mugful. With difficulty – now that the crisis was over, her internal tremors had eased, but she still had no control over the trembling in her hands.

"It wasn't me," Santon said before taking a long pull of the ale. "And you claim it wasn't you. So, what was it? When it tore open, it was like looking into infinity."

"Into things you don't want to see. And that color was sick. Tell me about your magic."

She thought at first he wouldn't answer, but at last he said, "Repatterning the air. To shift things, even time sometimes. Plans, music, communications. Lots of things."

"Can you clear the dust from air after an earthquake?"

"Not really. I can get a good wind going, but..." He shrugged.

"I can settle the dust, but I can't do the wind part."

"What else?"

It was Neve's turn to focus on her ale while she thought it over. "Growth, mainly. Crops, ripening, repairing, like after a hailstorm. I was able to call rain a couple of times last year, so my area didn't suffer from the drought as much as some."

"That's hard to believe. Growth is a natural process. It makes no sense that you can make a plant grow, much less yield fruit."

She shrugged. "How much of the Aura makes sense, really? We get used to the powers we have, but when you think it over, it's just so unlikely. Take healers, for instance. When I made that salve, I *knew* extra energy was going into it. I can't explain it, though. Does it still sting?" she asked in an abrupt segue.

He looked up, blankly. "No. Almost not at all. Amazing." After peering at the rag covering the wound for a moment, he added, "So we have different abilities, and not necessarily compatible ones. Do you suppose they clashed? And ripped the Aura somehow?"

"Yes," Neve said. "But it had to be more than that. Your energy's more like my brother's, and we've never triggered that kind of reaction. You and I were both flaming mad. The energy was so negative, I was feeling a little sick to my stomach."

Santon grunted agreement.

"But why didn't it happen earlier, here in the common room?"

Their eyes met. "Leo?" Santon suggested.

"Other people around buffering the energy?"

"Maybe both."

They finished the ale in silence. As he stood, Santon said, "One thing's for sure. We'd better not fight. That fog... It was like it could eat me alive."

Neve shuddered. "I know what you mean."

She stood in the inn's doorway and waited until he turned a corner and was out of sight before going upstairs. But it was a long time before she even attempted sleep. Instead, she sat in her window, watching the stars. Her grazed hands had been washed and salved as she tended to Santon, but her body throbbed where she had hit the ground; there would be bruises tomorrow.

The Aura had long been her friend, an energy she could rely on to enhance the life of the farm. There had been nothing life enhancing about what happened tonight. Not from the Aura or, she reflected, from her initial interaction with Santon. The conflict in their powers was beyond anything she had experienced. Now she wondered what the Aura was capable of, and if she could ever trust it again.

Chapter 11: Just the Facts

The next morning, Neve found Leo in the common room, made dim by a heavy overcast that had rolled in overnight. No bilious green – she had checked. She could willingly go through a lifetime without seeing that hideous tinge in the air again. After taking her time constructing a bowl of grains, fruit, and yogurt, she joined him at his table.

"Would you care to tell me what happened last night?" His voice held no hint of his previous supportive attitude. If anything, the kindly old man was intimidating.

Santon wasn't around. Good. She needed to tell Leo in her own way, without his prejudice. Still, she found it surprisingly difficult to explain the breach. Would he even understand? He had never made any pretense of having a strong connection to the Aura. Just the memory of the previous night's events triggered her nerves again; her spoon shook against her breakfast bowl.

Leo touched her hand. "Just get it out, my dear. Done is done, but we must understand what happened, to guard against it if for no other reason."

Neve swallowed hard. "We were talking, Santon and me." She shied away from the memory of the antagonism between them. Because it shouldn't be so intense. It shouldn't be at all.

It happened. All you have to do is explain.

"Then it... it was like the air split," she said, piecing her way through the explanation. "Like there was a jagged hole in the sky. And on the other side there wasn't anything. Just emptiness. The lightning... I'm not sure, but I think it came from the hole, not from the cloud."

"Just talking?" Leo sounded skeptical.

Feeling like she was revealing her deepest, most embarrassing secret, Neve mumbled, "Not exactly. He was...well, he made me mad. I didn't handle it well." She frowned. Why should she protect Santon by not speaking of his insults, how hurtful he had been?

"And between you, you nearly blew up the known world," Leo said flatly.

"You felt it?"

"My dear, Gauvain felt it. Go on."

"I have some bruises from diving to the ground, but Santon got burned. Red, some blistering. I cleaned and salved it."

"Good, good."

Santon entered the room and, like her, stocked up on breakfast before joining them at the table. He appeared pale but composed, and had donned a clean, sleeveless tunic, allowing him to favor the burn.

Leo's gaze took in the greasy linen on Santon's arm. "Your turn. What happened, from your perspective?" he asked.

"I wish I knew. It was different, not like what I learned from Duncan."

"It was the Aura," Leo stated. "Out of control, but the Aura just the same."

She and Santon spoke at the same time.

"The Aura heals, it's not—"

"Duncan never—"

"Hush, both of you." Despite his age, Leo's stern voice commanded the room. Even the couple sitting near the window, the only other people present, fell silent. Leo dropped his voice. "It was the Aura. The question is, what process brought it forth in this form? Think about it before you speak, please."

Neve took advantage of the enforced silence to eat. If nothing else, the events of the night had used up her resources. She was hungry. She glanced up and noted that Santon was assiduously avoiding meeting her eyes while attacking his own food bowl. Just as well.

"You were talking." Leo repeated back her words. "Neve, Santon angered you, yes? Describe the energy? Fury, passion, vindictiveness?"

With another glance at Santon – he didn't look up – Neve said quietly, "I don't think we like each other very much. I'm sorry for that. But I don't know what to do about it."

"More than that," Santon added. He tapped his spoon on the edge of his bowl as he organized his thoughts. The sound dug into Neve's nerves; she clenched her fists. "She got under my skin. It's my fault, I suppose. I tried to compel her to go back to the inn. But she did something..."

"I called on the earth. Just a little tremor. But... I think he was about to hit me."

"I never would have," Santon interrupted.

"And then—"

"That's when it happened."

Neve nodded.

Leo sighed. "I warned Gauvain about this." He stood and frowned at them; there was no warmth in his voice. "Do me a favor. Stay away from each other for a while. I want to see this place in the road, and my guess is that burn will require more healing, so we'll stay another day. Santon, use the time to gather the rest of your supplies. Neve, I'm going to give you an exercise involving lightning. It's time you knew more of the Aura's depth. We leave tomorrow, early. Good day."

Leo took his bowl to the serving counter and left them.

"I'm out of here." Santon also stood.

Neve looked up at him. "Do you want me to see to your burn, or will you go to the local healer? Either way's fine with me."

"Local healer, I think. We're supposed to avoid each other, remember? Just as well," she heard him mutter as he left the room.

In Orlan, Gauvain fumed.

Those idiot children.

After a disrupted night's sleep and a paltry, uninspiring breakfast, he was in no mood to deal with this new challenge. But the fact remained that he was the most powerful mage in Borgonne, probably on the planet, so it inevitably fell to him to investigate and, if possible, control the new manifestation.

He had direct knowledge of the Aura's less than positive capabilities, from his journeys across the hills and from his own experiments – but he at least had the experience to keep his trials controlled, unlike those two neophytes. It was better that the populace not know how terrifying the Aura could be, but after last night.... With any luck, most would conclude it had been a tremor, common enough throughout Borgonne. But some, no doubt, had been awake and abroad in the night to see the rent in the heavens. The danger Neve and Santon combined presented... well, he couldn't say Leo hadn't warned him. At least his old confidant had ordered them to stay away from each other, so there should be no immediate risk.

Thank the powers that be, Auric or not, that we developed our communication system. Were he not able to contact Leo, he'd be going mad, stuck here in Orlan.

Leo lacked a sufficiently strong auric connection to send him a message, so the protocol relied entirely on his own abilities. Leo could at least implant a message in the lower levels of the Aura. From there, Gauvain would retrieve it and send back his own. It was a convoluted technique based on a flimsy structure, but it had worked for them since the days, years ago now, when they had gone adventuring together, he a fledgling mage, Leo a soldier of fortune. Their friendship had been forged as they assessed and came to rely on their complementary abilities.

Leo shouldn't have to deal with this.

Well, done was done. He would spend the morning assessing the mood in Orlan, making sure no hint of the truth had leaked out. At the same time, he would lay to rest any reports or rumors before they could explode into a major crisis. The tear could be explained, possibly by blaming it on another ship of aliens such as had landed in the Midland a year or so ago. All handled very casually, as a matter of no moment. He would pretend a need to shop for fresh vegetables, as Leo did, to explain his unprecedented appearance.

Then, with the city calm, he could decide whether to take the route south. He fervently hoped it would not come to that. No matter how intriguing this new manifestation of the Aura might be, Leo's reports had made it clear conditions were dusty and primitive. And a donkey cart? Horror comes in many forms. Gauvain allowed himself a shudder of distaste as he flung his black cape over his shoulders.

If only there were a horse in Orlan; now that would be a way to travel.

He slung a lightweight black cloak over his shoulders and exited the Tower, headed for the marketplace.

Chapter 12: Building a Bridge

Santon had been pleased enough leave Vienne, although now, after five days on the road, he was still trying to figure out the dynamics of the wagon train's personnel, with special reference to Leo and Neve.

Neve gobbled up Leo's lessons, as Santon observed from his usual place, walking alongside the little caravan, now increased by a second oxcart and three more workers. The road had already deteriorated into deep wheel ruts running either side of a strip of rough vegetation. Not enough well-to-do or commercial traffic to justify investment, no doubt. He knew for a fact that Duncan, arguably the wealthiest resident in the vicinity, had never ventured further south than Vienne.

He tried not to listen as Leo put Neve through a series of exercises. What had he been fool enough to expect? An old man with limited Auric connection, a wildling with no training, and he thought he might gain by participating in this expedition? Beyond assessing Gauvain's setup, and incidentally getting out of Vienne, he doubted there would be any benefit to him at all.

The wound on his arm was almost healed, to his amazement. He'd been burned before; there should be tenderness if not outright pain, but instead the skin was already regenerating, smooth and healthy. Neve's salve? Nah. No village healer could pull off such speedy repair.

Of the incident that caused the burn, he preferred not to think. Somehow, Neve's energy had entangled with his, corrupting it – or so Leo had explained on behalf of Gauvain. Well, it wouldn't happen again. Keeping his distance from the woman wouldn't be a problem, at least until they hit their first major road construction project.

Keep your temper under control. Don't let her get to you.

To make the journey even more uncomfortable, despite his best efforts, the words of Leo's lessons occasionally got through his mental barriers, and he found himself practicing some technique along with Neve. His unspoken plan was to test and refine his abilities, but as often as not, whatever Leo was imparting proved beyond him. When that happened, he typically dropped behind and blew up a few pebbles while he worked through his frustrations. It made no sense. He was within a few months of qualifying as a mage. There shouldn't be anything he wasn't capable of.

Neve... against his better judgment, she intrigued him. Clearly, she was strong in Auric connection, for she had already exhibited a way of manipulating the Aura that was altogether new to him. Of no great interest, perhaps – not for him the nature-based techniques rooted in agriculture and healing, he preferred more esoteric practices – but still surprising in their power.

In the course of the walk, he'd realized how deeply he missed Duncan. The man had been brutal, not above inflicting bodily harm to drive his points home, but also capable of enormous generosity. Through him, a world of magic had opened to Santon, a world he had grasped greedily, for the sheer wonder of it as well as the promise of a prosperous future. Much of the wonder died with Duncan. Was it inching back, through Leo's unskilled hands?

Unlikely. Santon scuffed at the dust with his boot. The day had bloomed warm and dry, as had every day since they left Vienne, with only a few high clouds. Already the inhabitants of the occasional farms they passed were viewing the sky with worry, the fear palpable that last year's drought would be repeated.

His immediate surroundings broke into his consciousness. This low section of the road would become a quagmire as soon as it rained.

Leo called a halt, interrupting his musings. "Opinions, Santon? River valley, shallow ford. Scrub land, some forest. Can you make a recommendation?"

Santon climbed onto the back of the second oxcart, sidestepping the laborer snoozing in the bed, and surveyed the land around him. The road hugged the hills, but this particular valley was relatively wide and level. "The ford can't sustain heavy rain. The land's well vegetated, so erosion isn't an issue, but standing water may be. And backwash from that." He gestured at a large rock downstream that partially blocked the flow, then swung down from the cart.

"Neve, your opinion?"

"I disagree about erosion. The southern slope is overly dry. Rain won't penetrate easily, so there will be gully formation in a heavy rain. You can see remnants of earlier downpours."

Santon squinted to study the slope she indicated. Damn, he'd missed the evidence. Annoyed with himself, he walked forward to meet Leo and Neve, both now standing beside the lead donkey cart.

"What do you propose?" Before either of them could reply, Leo raised a hand. "We will stop here for a time. The two of you put your heads together. We'll meet later, over lunch."

Dismissed, Santon looked at Neve. "Ideas?"

"Some." She took off, heading for the north slope, her head movement suggesting she missed nothing as she walked. Santon followed but without hurry, forcing his mind to slow down, to assess. This would be construction, not merely surveying. Build something viable, capable of holding up against the probable spring floods, sustaining the weight of a laden oxcart.

He walked along the creek bed until it crooked around a bend. Out of sight of the wagons, he found a convenient rock and sat. He turned inwards, beginning the process of releasing the limits of his mind, step by step to a vision, which he then could superimpose on the physical landscape. The effort rendered him light-headed. But he kept at it, building a structure in the Aura, the drawing exact, an extended, raised roadbed stretching across the valley with arched supports spanning the river below.

After a time, he detected another awareness. Neve's voice impinged on his vision. "The south slope's gentler, so it needs to be longer on that side."

A suggestion trickled into his vision just before he lost his concentration, a use of local stone he hadn't considered to create the supports.

The vision evaporated. "What do you think you're doing?" he exploded – then looked around. Neve was nowhere near, only the sense of violation he'd felt when he was interrupted.

So, where had her voice come from?

He stood and followed the stream bed until the wagon train came into view. Neve was beside the cart, talking to Leo.

"You!" he shouted as he approached. "What do you think you were doing?"

"Helping?" she shot back. "Collaborating? Sharing ideas?"

Wildling. Beneath contempt to a mage. But most hedge witches had trivial powers, whereas Neve... no wildling should have the ability to access his plan.

His plan.

Leo's calm voice cut across his thoughts. "Enough. Tell me what you've come up with," he said, clearly referencing them both. He extracted dried fruit strips from one of the food crates in the bed of the cart and passed them each a piece.

Coldly, Santon outlined his vision. Neve interrupted him once, but at Leo's gesture said no more until he had finished. Then she explained her additions regarding the placement, roadbed, anchor points and construction material.

All based on the land. Santon's beautiful, abstract design hadn't connected to the land the way her additions did.

Leo wasted no time. "The men and I will make camp. You two get on with it." He left them, walking down the line to tell the drivers and workmen what to do.

Neve stared at Santon, bewilderment reflected on her face. "Just like that?"

He shrugged. "Looks that way."

"Where do we start? I've never built a road."

"Raw materials, I guess. Rubble, mainly."

The stream bed held a few smooth stones, and the dirt on either bank was undoubtedly rocky, but extracting it... "You can blow up stones," she appended. "I've seen you. So can I. We can use that." She gestured at the large outcrop on the bank a little way downstream. "Getting rid of it would improve the flow, too. Double win."

Feeling out of his depth, but unwilling to release his tenuous hold on superiority, he said, "We need a plan. We can't just start blowing things up. Someone will get hurt."

"True. What do we do?" Without consulting him, she began working her way down the valley to the rock she'd designated.

If he wanted a hand in this enterprise at all, he'd better keep up. Santon followed, ostensibly studying the land, wishing he understood what he was looking at. Surveying was a mechanical process, not an interpretive one. His strength lay in mental projections, not in dirt.

Nor, to be strictly honest, had he ever exploded anything bigger than a pebble. If Neve was capable of taking out the massive rock that partially dammed the stream... well. He might have to reassess his opinion of her power.

Grudgingly, he caught up, intent on learning all he could about this rock she proposed to explode to make the bed for his road.

Chapter 13: Another Inn, Another Stew

Neve scanned the common room as she entered, spotted a group from their caravan huddled around a table laden with mugs, and decided she'd prefer a table to herself where she could enjoy her stew in peace.

The inn, in the hamlet of Bergen, was a break from the slogging routine of their days. That first road repair, now almost two nine-days ago, had been exciting in a way, providing a chance to use her powers and to eavesdrop on Santon's. Between them they had produced a passable bridge, well able to withstand the weight of both oxcarts. Since then, though....

The track had deteriorated quickly. They now followed a rutted route scarcely able to accommodate the smaller donkey carts. Road construction wasn't an occasional break in their progress, it was constant. Nor had there been villages to relieve the monotony, until they had stumbled on this hamlet, with, miracle of miracles, a tiny inn. Leo booked one of the two rooms for her to share with the only other woman in the caravan, a member of the road construction crew. The second room he reserved for himself and Santon. The rest of the crew had tossed their bedrolls in the hay barn, which would likely prove every bit as comfortable. Still, the room meant a chance to bathe, standing in a shallow tin of tepid water, and wash some clothes.

The serving girl placed a mug in front of her. Neve took a cautious taste. The ale was tolerable; she offered the girl a nod and a tiny smile. Elin, her roommate, a woman in her thirties with brown hair cut almost to her scalp, waved a salute as she entered the common room and made straight for the men's table.

To each her own. Another day, Neve would have been happy to join the convivial group. Today, however, the unrelenting sun, work, and dirt of the trip piled up on her. Quiet – indoor quiet – clean sheets, and a meal not prepared over a fire struck her as bliss. She sipped at the ale, leaned back, and watched the scene.

The group at the table must be into their third or fourth ale, based on the volume of laughter and shouted, joking insults. Cards had appeared and a game of some sort was starting. One of the laborers gathered up the used mugs, trotting them over to the serving bar. He winked as he passed her table; she grinned back. The crew were okay, usually cheerful, up for a challenge. If she was in a bit of a funk, it was nothing to do with them.

She closed her eyes, just for a moment. It wasn't often she had time or energy to reflect on what weird chance had led her to this expedition. The farm, her family, felt years away, her old life something of dreams.

When she opened her eyes, Santon was pulling out a chair at her table. He dropped into it. "Hope you don't mind," he told her, although his look suggested that he wasn't really offering her an option. "I'm pretty worn out. I think you must be, too."

"Some, yeah."

The serving girl placed a mug in front of him. Neve noted that service for Santon was appreciably faster than for herself.

They eyed each other. She had seen the growing strain on his face as they designed, then built, yet another stretch of the road. She still eavesdropped on his mental constructs, but so far hadn't found a way to see them clearly, much less create one herself. But the creations cost him; his face showed less resilience, more fatigue, as the work progressed. She wondered if he saw the same thing in her.

"Doing okay?"

"Hmm?" Neve realized she had allowed herself to sink into a kind of reverie. In the warmth, fatigue crept over her, making her arms heavy, her mind muzzy.

"You zoned out there."

She blinked hard to remind her eyes to focus. "I'm grateful for the break. At home, accessing the Aura feels so natural, but here, it's as if every time I'm testing myself again."

"Yeah." Santon pulled hard at his ale. "Things I've never tried. Never thought to try. I had no idea there wasn't actually a road at all, just a dirt track."

Since the episode with the Aura, she and Santon had skirted around each other, rarely talking except when necessary to build yet another section of road. The last thing Neve wanted was a repeat of that near-cataclysmic disruption. But they were stuck with each other, so perhaps it was time to make tentative steps toward – what? Friendship? The colleague thing was working well, as long as Santon got over his self-importance and recognized the value of her contributions.

"You've never been here either?" she asked.

"Not this far south, no. I know the lands to the north fairly well. My family's from Vienne, but they moved to Orlan after Duncan took me. When I had time off – not that time off amounted to much – I'd go to Vienne or just hike around. Duncan was relentless. And mean, if he thought I was flagging."

Neve frowned. "Took you?"

"If Duncan decided he wanted you for a student, you didn't really have much choice." Santon shrugged. "He arrived one day, gave my parents some money and a promise of more, and away I went."

"But... that's appalling."

Santon appeared to be fascinated by the ale. "Not really. Practical, I guess you'd say. When my Auric connection manifested, it was scary. No one knew what to do with me. Duncan's interference was seen as a blessing, in a way. Questions answered, and prosperity for my family."

"And for you?" In her mind, Neve could see him in his early teens, much like her brother had been, probably a bit gawky, suddenly able to do things no one else could. An alarmed village probably was glad to see the back of him. But for the child, it must have been terrifying. She longed to put a hand on his arm, somehow support the boy he'd been, but sensed he would be offended should she dare. Instead, she fed him a few facts of her own, relating their stories. "My brother's a student with Gauvain, and he says the same – impatience, occasional cruelty. Nothing physical, though. Insults, humiliation in front of the class. Leo dropped that he's not so great at something called earth magic. I know my brother and I have different abilities, but I didn't know there were categories."

Bowls of stew and a basket of peasant bread appeared in front of them. Without further discussion, they both wielded their spoons.

Santon swallowed and picked up the conversation. "It makes sense, I guess, different kinds of magic. You can do things I can't. Demolishing those boulders."

It was the first time he'd acknowledged that the energy to create rubble from a boulder had been almost entirely hers. He'd given her something, though, so she made her own admission. "I keep trying to construct a mental diagram. It would help a lot. The most I can do is look in on yours, and then it's never clear."

"So, you're earth magic. I don't know what to call mine. Mental magic maybe? We do know we aren't compatible."

"I get the feeling," Neve said with a tinge of bitterness, "that Gauvain chooses to ignore powers he can't wield. He rejected me, and I lost my chance at training. I expect his magic's more like yours."

Santon wiped his bowl with a piece of bread. "If you learned on your own, that's impressive."

"Yeah. Maybe. But I wanted to be a mage. I wanted the training. Now it's too late."

"For me, too. With Duncan gone, there's nowhere to finish. I've heard Gauvain wasn't personally responsible for his death, but I don't think I could submit to him." He popped the bread into his mouth.

"Leo?" Neve asked.

Santon swallowed and said, "I hate to admit it, but those exercises are challenging. He has almost no power, but somehow he's able to bring his lessons to life."

Neve grinned. "Paying attention, were you? I thought you were above all that."

"Yeah, so did I," he said a trifle sheepishly. "I've stagnated lately. You have to find your teachers where you can. And a lot of his teaching is earth, wouldn't you say? It's not like anything I learned, anyway."

"He's geared it to me, or so he says. When he moves out of that realm, I'm hopeless. But it's pushing my mind, stretching me into different ways to manipulate the Aura. Not really earth, usually. Basics, the things I never had a chance to learn." Neve swirled her spoon through her remaining stew, staring at the pattern left in the thick gravy. "In a way, we've been lucky. We've both learned what we needed. You with formal training, and me on my own. Lots of kids get turned away like I was, I bet."

"Hedge wizards," Santon said with contempt. "Using tricks to earn a living, giving the rest of us a bad name."

"Think, though." Neve put the spoon down and leaned forward. "They can touch the Aura – who knows how many of them there are, but I bet a lot of village healers have some ability. They want it, and they don't know how to build their skills. The cabal called the College of Mages says no, and they're cast off. *We're* cut off," she added bitterly.

Santon nodded. "I sometimes wonder if this famous college ever amounted to more than Duncan and Gauvain. In any event, I don't doubt they controlled it."

"And now we have Leo. He's a good teacher."

The two of them stared at each other over the remains of their dinner. Neve wondered if Santon's thoughts were anything like her own. But it was much too soon to pursue where her mind had wandered.

Untrained men and women with some Auric access, but no path forward to develop their skills. A college controlled by an exclusive group. People like Santon and herself, powerful but not mages. No options.

Why not?

The noise at the other table rose to a crescendo. "San!" someone bellowed. "Get yourself over here."

"Five-card," someone else shouted. "Gimme a chance to win my money back."

"Dream on." Santon grinned and stood as Elin approached their table. "Chair's yours," she said. "I'm off to bed."

Neve liked Elin well enough, although their contact had been minimal. Her meaning was clear, though. Once she settled for sleep, she didn't want Neve stumbling in and waking her up. "You're right, I'm dead on my feet."

Both women gave a cursory wave to the other table, then Neve followed Elin upstairs to bed. A real bed, a real mattress. Neve could hardly wait.

Chapter 14: The Morning After

Santon groaned as he pried an eye open. Leo bustled about the small room they had shared overnight, humming to himself as he organized his few possessions. The tattered curtain covering the window did little to keep out a day much too bright with sun.

He rolled over, burying his head in his arm. It had been seasons, *years*, since he had tied one on like he had last night. At the time it had made sense, a friendly game of five-card, another jug, then another, the hour growing later as the group around the table became ever more convivial – okay, ever more drunk. It had been a long haul for them all, so finding this inn in an obscure hamlet, this chance for a break in the eternal routine of travel, stop, plan, build a road, repeat, had been more than welcome.

"Think you'll be alive again by, say, mid-morning?" Leo chirped. The old man was enjoying this.

"Water, caff," he managed. "Willow bark... my head." His voice sounded alien, but he'd picked up from somewhere that Leo had once been a soldier of fortune; he must know how it was for the troops when the pressure was released.

Leo rustled in his pack, then poked his arm with a stick. "Water's by your bed. Here's your willow. For caff, I'm afraid you'll have to get up."

How to balance the agony pervading his body against what he knew he needed? He stuck the twig in his mouth and chewed, but a willow stick would have negligible effect against the myriad assaults on his body.

"Your chamber pot's handy, should your stomach rebel... which seems likely," Leo said cheerfully. "Sorry, son, but I think you'd better drag yourself upright. I'll see you downstairs. I smell bacon."

The very word was enough to trigger a spasm in Santon's stomach. He managed to roll and lean over the bed before the inevitable happened. He was retching when Leo left, whistling and closing the door none too gently behind him.

Then, because no option seemed better, he hauled himself upright. He felt marginally better now that he had rid himself of the toxic ale and greasy food polluting his stomach. Enough, at least, to gulp down the mug of water and resume gnawing on the willow stick while he waited for his system to settle. Finally, shakily, he rose – almost putting a foot in the now reeking chamber pot – and managed to change into his cleaner outfit. He'd find time to wash out his clothing before they left. During the trip, Neve and Elin had rigged lines over the top of the second oxcart to dry their laundry; he'd make use of them.

Neve and Leo were heads-together over plates of ham, eggs, and potatoes. Santon had only a moment to acknowledge his annoyance at their collaboration – without him – before, once again, the smell of the meat threatened to undo the tentative peace he had negotiated with his gut. This time he was able to hold it steady, waiting until things settled down before entering the room.

None of the men from the previous evening were present, he noted with some satisfaction. He wasn't alone in his agony.

"Morning," Neve chirped. Why did women do that? Just because they had the sense to have a single, modest pull of ale and then go to bed didn't give them the right to gloat. "Caff's in a pot over there." She nodded over her shoulder to the serving bar.

"Thanks," he muttered, and slouched across the room to pour a mug. A double; the traditional caff mugs were tiny, nowhere near enough to quell his headache. Because of manners rather than a desire to be any closer to the aromatic plates of breakfast, he then joined Neve and Leo.

"We've decided not to work today," Leo informed him between bites. "Give everyone a day off. We'll rebuild the bridge tomorrow."

Might as well grant a vacation, Santon thought sourly, given that no one else had even made it for breakfast.

"Apparently there's a market, we can stock up on fresh vegetables," Leo continued. "Things can only get worse from here on."

There had been no reduction in his good mood, Santon noted. Sadist. "Great," he muttered, leaving it up to them to decide whether he meant the day off or the deteriorating conditions ahead.

Neve chimed in. "I thought you and I might explore the local area a bit, maybe practice some techniques. It seems to me there ought to be more points of overlap in our skills than we've found so far. The stronger we are, the faster this will be over and done with."

"Yeah. And hasn't that gone well." Was she out of her mind? After that horrifying incident in Vienne?

"A useful exercise," Leo said, leaning back and watching them. "As a mage, you mustn't deal in emotion. I know people consider Gauvain cold, but it's at least in part because he's aware of the risks."

Oh," Neve said, as if she had just received a profound truth.

Well, maybe she did. Santon thought back. Whenever Duncan manipulated the Aura, it was as if he had blanketed himself in ice. Cold and controlled. Had he ever taught this? Only by brutally suppressing anything that wasn't academic.

"Sure. Later."

The young woman who had served their meals last night came down the stairs, holding a covered, but still reeking, pot well in front of her. She glared into the common room as she passed, on her way to the midden no doubt. Santon watched with a pang of guilt. He should have carried the thing downstairs himself.

Neve stood and removed the plates, thank the Aura. She came back with two modest caff mugs, one of which she placed in front of Leo. They sipped, clearly relishing the beverage. For Santon, it was far past enjoyment; it had reached necessity. His oversized mug was empty already. He rose and refilled it but opted not to return to the table. Propped against a wall, he downed the bitter liquid. Then he headed for the door. "Later," he muttered as he went, hoping Neve and Leo had heard – and wouldn't follow.

Alone outside the common room, he considered. His plan had been to return upstairs, wash and shave, then get some much-needed sleep. But fresh air was pouring in through open doors at either end of the hall. However much the thought of returning to bed attracted him, there was no way his room, stuffy from one small window and two men overnight, would be tolerable. Gnawing on his willow stick, he exited by the front door, looked up and down the road, and turned west, toward the hills.

The land had grown rougher as they moved south. No amount of shifting east provided a smooth passage for the new road; they did better by remaining on the track, which now cut into the foothills. Bergen sat on the high bank of a river flowing briskly, with patches of turbulence, down from the mysterious range to the west. Even this close, the hills seemed more nebulous than ever; Santon never felt he could quite see them properly, as if they persisted in being shrouded in a light mist.

As he made his way along a narrow lane, he found small, planted fields and one paddock containing two cows and several goats. Beyond this evidence of habitation, the lane petered out. The land rose before him, intimidating in its bleakness. In the distance the beginning of the hills was marked by dense vegetation. His Aura-tuned senses hinted at the spells overlaying the hills as a cause for the unlikely lushness.

He picked his way carefully, paralleling the stony riverbank, noting the strength of the flow, probably the reason Bergen existed. Water, coupled with accommodation and supplies, would form an attractive rest stop – if there were any travelers.

Had there been traffic along here, once? They had seen no sign.

The sun was nearing its zenith, and he could feel sweat cutting rivulets through the dust coating his face. He was cursing himself for not grabbing a hat before he left the inn, when he stopped short. Both his mage training and his work as a surveyor had taught him to notice changes, and before him lay the mother of all anomalies.

The rectangular boulder was half the size of a man, with perfectly regular, hewn edges. Santon approached it, circled it, placed his hands on it and opened himself to it through the Aura. Nothing.

"Look at this one."

He jerked in surprise. The voice came from slightly ahead and closer to the riverbank. His eyes followed, to where a tall woman in a bedraggled tunic was waving.

Neve. Why had he hoped for a day alone? He shoved the willow stick into a pocket of his tunic – the headache was mostly gone – and picked his way to where she stood on another of the trimmed stones.

"Manmade. Has to be." She hopped down and ran her hand over the straight edge.

Like the other one, it was of a coarse, beige stone, likely sandstone. Several of the unnatural stones lay scattered in the field. "I wonder if there are more," he mused.

"There are." She indicated the far side of the river.

His need for quiet and his curiosity about the stones fought for dominance. Annoyed that Neve had seen more than he had, he looked. And saw...

It had been a tower, he guessed. Its base was still intact, but the top had been blown off, scattering stone in differing sizes across the land on both sides of the river. What was left rose irregularly, but never more than one man-height; from the quantity of stone, he suspected it had been several stories tall.

The remaining walls were black, not a match for the sandstone blocks they had been exploring.

A watchtower? Had there been a road into the hills here, once? The only tower he had ever heard of was Gauvain's, in Orlan.

"Can we get across?" Neve asked. She was already inching her way down the bank.

"It's not a light flow, and it eddies when it hits a block. Could be currents we can't see."

"Did you bring a rope? We could lasso that stone over there." She gestured, frowning into the sun. "Then fix it on this side and use it to work our way across."

"Why would I have a rope?" He hated the irritation in his voice, but honestly. Did she think he was a pack donkey? On the other hand, this tower... what had it been? His curiosity fired; who could resist an archaic building of no known function?

"No reason. But I want to get across. I'm a strong swimmer. I could—"

"No, you couldn't," he interrupted. "We go back and cross the river at the bridge. It's safer than risking an unfamiliar flow – and think of the source. You know better than to trust anything coming down from the hills."

"Good point."

Santon sighed a quiet breath of relief. Neve was sufficiently independent that she just might attempt the swim. He was in no mood to make a heroic rescue.

She picked up a piece of sandstone. From the regularity of the edges, it probably had broken off one of the larger ones. "I'll take this back for Leo. Perhaps he knows more about the history of this place."

Chapter 15: The Tower

Leo did indeed know more, Santon conceded, not from prior knowledge but from questioning the people he encountered at the inn and the marketplace. His arms full of last year's potatoes and a tired cabbage, he embarked on a history lesson.

"You're right in most of your conclusions. Once, this was a bigger town, servicing traffic along the road. Not much, but enough to support a stable economy – they charged a toll to maintain the bridge. The presence of the river was a bonus, because there aren't many water sources further south. As you can see, trade died out, the bridge fell into a state of disrepair, and the town itself shrank to its present lack of prominence."

"But the tower?" Neve asked, impatient.

Leo waited while Santon opened the door to the small carriage house, then dumped his load of vegetables into one of the donkey carts. "No idea. They know about it, of course. The local kids dare each other to spend the night there. But there are no legends, no mysterious happenings, nothing. Just an old tower."

"Someone built it," Santon said. "Someone saw a need. Who knows how old it might be?"

Leo dusted his hands on his tunic and headed out into the fresh air. "Not that old. Our people have only been here four hundred years or so, and the spells on the hills don't go back more than about three hundred. Perhaps it was only what it seems, a way for the village's inhabitants to see who was coming."

"It's not close to the road," Santon pointed out.

"True enough." Leo set the pace, heading back to the inn. "I took the liberty of ordering sandwiches," he said. "First we eat. Then you can take me to the tower site."

His stomach happily full of roast meat sandwich – goat, he guessed – dressed with a spicy sauce, Santon led the three of them across the rickety bridge and along the riverbank. Neve chattered nonstop behind him.

"There has to be something we haven't found. If San and I could just link our abilities—"

When had he become San?

"Which is risky," Leo cut in, likely assessing Neve's volubility as the result of excitement, coupled perhaps with frustration that she couldn't simply run a hand over one of the hewn stones and have an entire history revealed to her. "After the event in Vienne? I'm allowing this exploration as an exercise for the two of you to stretch your individual powers, but no more than that. I can't imagine the tower will benefit us unless you can use the stones to rebuild the bridge. Calm down, Neve. You'll miss your footing."

Neve made a noise that sounded like a scoff, but she shut up for a while.

The trio picked its way through low, struggling vegetation on the drier south bank. Far too many prickles and thorns, Santon thought as he disentangled his pants from yet another scraggly plant. A lizard darted from under a bush, almost causing him to trip. Other than lizards and a few importunate insects, he saw no signs of wildlife. A bleak place;

the fields on the north bank appeared healthy enough, but even with trade from travelers, it would be hard to forge an existence here.

Difficult to justify a tower of the dimensions his surveyor's eye suggested this one had been.

❖

"Here," Neve said.

They had circled the tower, entered the opening where a door had hung and crossed its dirt floor, once, twice. The heavily vegetated hills began perhaps five hundred paces to the west, but it was hard to get a bead on the landscape, as if the land were slightly out of focus. That didn't perturb Neve; even from Orlan she'd never been clear about the nature of the looming land mass dominating the western horizon.

The tower appeared just as it seemed, a dead artifact of some earlier need. She followed the wall, crossed the packed dirt floor, until... there. By some chance, she had picked up... something. She now stood in the center of the ruin, the tingling in her feet unmistakable. She had felt it before, on her own land, when an anomaly existed underground, whether a new rift or a water flow. This one felt different in one way, though – it seemed to be a single spot, scarcely extending to a body width. "Something's buried here," she said. "Whether it caused the tower's destruction, I can't say."

Santon frowned at the spot, otherwise undistinguishable from the rest of the dirt floor, which spanned ten paces across. "Anyone want to dig?"

"I could for a while," Neve said. "I can't judge how deep it is, or how big."

They both looked to Leo, who stood by one of the truncated walls, studying the joins. He glanced up. "You have today. Tomorrow we start on the bridge. Think of it as a recreational day off."

"Digging?" Santon sniped, but there was no ire in his voice. "What fun." He crossed the floor to the small pile of their supplies and extracted a spade.

"Wait." Neve frowned and paced a step or two forward, then back. "I've lost it."

"What do you mean?"

"I mean it's gone. I'm not picking anything up."

"Impossible."

Know-it-all. Neve bit down on her perennial irritation at his attitude as he came over and handed her the spade. She stood still and briefly closed her eyes. "Okay wait. It's back."

They looked at each other. "Oh, hell," Santon said. "Not again."

"Let me guess," Leo said. "You only sense it when both of you are near it."

Neve heaved a sigh of frustration. "I thought we were done with that."

"Are you kidding?" Santon retorted. "Whatever the energy is we create, there's no reason to think it'd just go away."

She took the spade and started to dig, carefully, because she didn't know what lay below. The ground was hard packed, but given the sandy nature of the soil, the work wasn't impossibly difficult. Santon kept his gaze outward, studying the landscape; were she not engaged with the spade, she would be sensing its strengths, soil quality, susceptibility to erosion, fertility – but Santon was probably daydreaming; he was no good at that kind of thing. At pacing back and forth, though...

"Would you stop that?" she snapped between spades full of dirt. "The way the energy comes and goes, it's making me dizzy."

"Sorry." He planted himself a pace from Neve's slowly deepening hole.

"Whenever you want a turn."

"Give." He held out his hand. Neve dumped her last load and passed the spade to him. They changed places and he dug in.

"It could be breakable, you know."

"Then maybe the energy will be broken, too. I don't know about you, but I'm not happy about this."

"No," she said. "Me neither."

When he unearthed the object, it was almost a disappointment. A single, oval stone, greenish with embedded white crystal striations, lay at the bottom of the hole. Neve estimated it to be the width of her hand. It appeared to be fairly flat, although she couldn't be sure about that until they extracted it.

"So?" Santon looked to Leo.

Neve spoke up. "I'm not sure I want to touch it."

Leo walked over and peered into the hole, which was as deep as Santon's shin. "I wouldn't recommend you both touch it at once, but I suspect it's all right for one of you. Do you feel anything?"

Santon shook his head as Neve said, "The tingling. Stronger now."

"Then perhaps we should ask Santon to extract it."

He bent down, balancing on the foot already in the hole, feeling around the stone with both hands. It proved easy to dislodge. He held it up. It was no more than a knuckle's width thick.

Neve backed away, her expression doubtful.

"Place it on the ground," Leo directed. "Then, Neve, I want you to approach it. See if it wants you to touch it. You've done this kind of thing before," he added, "so trust your instincts."

Neve stepped forward, aware of Santon scrambling out of the hole and backing away after setting the stone on the ground. The tingle faded as Santon moved out of range, but didn't leave completely.

Like healing animals, how I sense if they want me to.

Could she handle the stone the same as a wounded dog? It wasn't sentient. How could it tell her its needs?

She expanded her mind to encompass the stone, as Leo had taught her. The message was clear.

"This is mine," she said, focused on the sensations in her palm. "It's like it's saying so." She gazed down, feeling a tug in her heart.

For a stone?

Leo's hand was on her arm, giving her a gentle squeeze. "It's okay. We know already you have an affinity for things of the earth. When you're ready, touch it. Gently."

She gave herself a firm shake, as if snapping out of a daydream – grounding, she reminded herself – then knelt and found herself crooning as she reached out her hand, Santon hovering above her. With the touch of her fingers, something in the stone flared, a muted, greenish light that died almost instantly. Her fingers wrapped around it and raised it to her chest, where she cradled it as if it were a small animal. "It's mine," she repeated.

"Ours, I think," Santon said.

"No. It's telling me. Like it's been waiting for me."

She turned away from Santon, but Leo stepped forward. "One more experiment. Neve, place the stone on the ground for Santon to pick up."

She didn't want to. She wanted never to put the stone down again. But they needed to know all they could, and Santon... well, she sensed she could trust him. Grudgingly, she did as Leo instructed.

Santon picked it up, studied it, stroked it as she had. Nothing happened.

"Now," Leo said, "Neve, step back a few steps. Put a good distance between you."

She did, her eyes never leaving the stone.

At three paces... "*Ow,*" Santon exclaimed. The stone fell to the ground. "I think it bit me."

Neve moved toward him as he shook his hand and held it out. There was a faint red mark on the palm. "That hurt. But what the hell?"

Leo took his hand to study the mild wound. "Stung, more likely. There's a lot going on here we don't understand. This..." His voice trailed off as he gazed at the nearby hills. "This is magic beyond anything I've seen. We'll go back to the inn, to a neutral environment. We could all do with a tisane."

Neve picked the stone up. "This is crazy. It's giving me feelings as if it were sentient," she said. "I'd like to rinse it off, polish it."

"Crazy indeed." Leo led them out of the tower circle and toward town. "I need to contact Gauvain. I'd prefer if he were here to handle this. And..." He wheeled around to nail them both with his eyes. "Under no circumstances should you *ever* both touch it at once. Is that clear?"

"Very," Santon muttered. Neve nodded.

As the old man strode off, Neve held back, catching Santon's eye. "I don't want Gauvain anywhere near this," she said quietly.

"Neither do I."

An accord established between them, they hurried after Leo, the stone safely cradled in Neve's clasped hands.

Neve and Santon managed a more or less normal supper with Leo, one that involved not a mention of the tower or the stone. None of them wanted information to leak. The stone, washed, wrapped in a clean handkerchief, and safely tucked in a deep pocket of Neve's tunic, tingled periodically but mostly seemed quiescent, perhaps because Santon spent the meal well back from the table, the back of his chair propped against the wall as he nursed a beer.

Neve slept well that night, although more than once she reached under her pillow to stroke the stone.

The day dawned hazy, but promised more of the same, heat and dust. They got through it, beginning the preliminary steps for rebuilding the decrepit bridge as if nothing had changed. It was a credit to their mind training that they were able to focus on the task at hand.

After supper, though, Santon stated he'd be staying in the common room for a few hands of five-card, and watched Leo make his way to their shared bedroom. Neve went upstairs also, as if to bed. But Elin was a sound sleeper; Neve had no problem creeping out after the inn fell quiet, to meet Santon per prior, whispered agreement. The sun had sunk behind the hills to the west; the land was cloaked in obscurity. Keeping to shadows, they took the trail to the ancient ruin as being the best place either of them could think of for guaranteed privacy.

As they reached their destination, Neve asked, "Won't the guys miss you from the game?"

"Nah." Santon propped himself against the outer wall. "I led them to think I was meeting a bit of fluff – no offence."

Neve rolled her eyes and joined him against the wall, making a conscious decision to ignore the insulting comment. "As I see it," she said, "we have two main questions. First, it takes two of us to activate the stone. But what are we activating?"

"As a corollary to that, what would happen if we both touched it?"

She nodded. "And second, why is the tower here at all?"

"That one seems obvious, or at least I've been thinking about it all day, and I can't come up with any other reason. This is the start of an old path into the hills."

They were facing east, but Neve felt the looming power of the range behind her. The hills seemed to be not quite as tall as they were outside Orlan, but they still intimidated. "Why?" she asked.

Santon shrugged. "We only know of one route across the hills, not counting the way the Midlanders supposedly use down south. Perhaps this trail has some other properties? Different spells?"

"And the stone?"

"A warning mechanism?"

"Seems unlikely, given what it takes to activate it."

"True."

"When we were here before, did you spot anything about the tower itself? I was so caught up in the stone, I forgot to look around."

"Maybe." Santon lowered himself onto the sandy ground, then resumed his slouch against the wall. "I think there's evidence of a stair winding up. Just some faint markings. It would make sense – they'd want to get to the top if it's a lookout. And why build it if it isn't?"

Neve also sank to the ground, curling her legs under her. "The final question, I suppose, is what we do about it."

"Yeah. You know Gauvain's on his way?"

"*What?*" Neve sat straighter, a frisson of panic coursing through her.

Santon grunted an affirmative. "Picked it up in the Aura. He and Leo have a makeshift communication system. Ingenious, but fairly easy to tap into."

"Can we hide the stone? But then how can we study it? And it wants to be here, with us." Her words came out rapidly, almost falling over each other. *Stop it. Calm down.* Her self-talk didn't help much. The thought of Gauvain, close, still triggered near panic.

"Relax. Even with his power, he can't get here for two nine-days or more. We have time to figure out where to go."

Neve frowned. "Go?"

"You want to be here when he catches up?"

"No." Of that she was certain. By luck or destiny, the stone was in her keeping.

"We could continue south. If we didn't finish the bridge, the wagon train would be stuck here for a while. Give us time for a good head start."

"And break our contracts. I don't want to do that to Leo. I overheard him making this commitment to Gauvain."

"Ah, ethics." He sounded annoyed. "Could get in our way, you know."

"Do you think..." Neve paused, frowning. "Surely not, but do you think Gauvain could track the stone?"

"If I were carrying it, no. With you... maybe."

"That's what I thought." Her voice reflected her glum thoughts.

"There's another option," Santon said.

"I know. But it frightens me, especially since we don't know what the stone's purpose is."

"Have you ever been in the hills?"

"Never. We were taught to fear them. I suppose with an Auric connection, I'm safe enough, but still…"

"I have. Only one day in, then back out. Duncan sent me. It felt kind of other-worldly. Made me nervous."

Neve stood and walked around the tower's foundations to the west side, where she leaned on the wall. The hills stood out as a darker blot against the night sky. Santon joined her; they were silent for a while.

"We'd be crazy to risk that until we know more about the stone. And that means—"

"Yeah," Santon said softly. "But testing it could be risky. Deadly, even."

"I know."

"Let's get back."

They began picking their way toward the hamlet. "We have another five days, maybe, before we've finished work on the bridge," Santon said. "Then the wagon train goes on south. If we're going to do this, that's our window."

"Are we going to do this?" Neve heard the tentativeness in her voice.

"Hell if I know. At least it's all on the table. For now, we'd better get some sleep. We have a bridge to build."

Chapter 16: Escape?

Bridge planning and construction went altogether too smoothly for Neve's liking. After three days, the end was in sight; tomorrow they would do the first stress test. She and Santon were still in the hamlet, under Leo's watchful eye and with the ever-present threat of Gauvain's arrival.

Soon.

Leo had dropped the bombshell last night over dinner. The Aura alone knew how, but Gauvain had made remarkable progress and would arrive within a few days, less than half the expected travel time. No one was leaving the hamlet in the near future, no matter how stable the bridge.

The workers greeted the news of the impending delay with desultory cheers. Life in Bergen had proved to be pleasant enough, but they were all aware of encroaching time, the need to get this job done and get home before the weather turned. It wasn't yet Solstice, but they were no more than a quarter of the way to the place where they would construct the southern terminal, the beginnings of a town.

Neve met Santon's eyes, neither showing visible enthusiasm. Which Leo noticed.

"You do understand, don't you, that it's vital we have Gauvain examine the stone?" Leo's voice had an edge of sharpness, something Neve had noticed more than once in the last few days. "He's the only mage alive with the ability to tell us what it's intended for. Until then...," he shrugged, "... I'm sure you're keeping it safe, but we can't risk either exposure or exploration of its properties. That's the reality."

She and Santon had a decision to make, but for the moment Neve feigned indifference. "I get that. I just don't happen to like the man."

"And I'm not likely to forgive him," Santon mumbled under his breath.

"You're both adults," Leo said. "You'll cope."

The meal finished in a tense silence. Neve was sure, even without a chance for advance planning, she'd be creeping out to meet Santon after everyone was abed.

She found him along the road, staring at the bridge. It looked good. They had located a stand of timber to the east and recruited local men to help their own team. Stone was no problem; with practice, Neve had developed ways to shatter boulders into the sizes they needed. The roadbed was continuous, the supports solid.

"Nice job," Santon said without turning around.

She drew even with him. "Yep. We're good at this."

He shrugged and set off across the bridge, Neve keeping pace. "We have to come up with a plan. Now," he said.

At the far end they both stopped and looked around. They were alone.

"It scares me...." She sighed. "But I think we have to get it away from here."

"We could just rebury it." She felt Santon's eyes on her, although she couldn't see his face clearly in the deepening gloom. The stone tingled companionably in her pocket.

She shook her head. "No, that's what we can't do. Perhaps we could go a little way toward the hills and see if we can find a trail? See how the stone responds?"

At this point, the roadbed was elevated, the land sloping down steeply to the west before leveling out. Santon slid down the incline, Neve following. They huddled at the foot of the bridge supports, out of sight of the hamlet.

"When?" Santon asked. "At night? Even with magelight, that could be tricky, and might make us easier to track. And we don't know what effect the hills would have on light from the Aura."

"Leave just before dawn, then?"

"Bring water," Santon said as if it were all decided. "I'll meet you here. That way, if anyone sees us, it'll look like we're inspecting the bridge before the stress test."

"When?"

"No point waiting, is there?" Santon's voice carried a dictatorial edge, probably sensing her nervousness. "So... water, some trail food if we can get it without drawing attention."

Now that actual planning was needed, Neve was able to put aside her nervousness in favor of practicalities. "A change of clothes? Rain gear?"

"Yes," he said. "If this goes well, we don't know when we'll be back. We could end up in the Midland, for all we know. If we came back here, we'd walk right into Gauvain's arms."

Neve swallowed. "Borgonne's our home. We can't stay gone forever. Mostly, I want to keep the stone out of his clutches long enough to unravel its mystery ourselves."

"Do you think there's any point in both of us touching it before we head out?"

Neve shook her head. "I've thought about this a lot. Sooner or later we'll have to, but I think it will be safer if...

well, I'm guessing that in the hills it will be closer to home. It might not be as violent."

"Or might be more so."

"What do you think?"

Santon shrugged. "When the time comes, we'll deal with it."

Neve's gaze was far away, toward the blacker shadow created by the looming range to the west. "Are we... I mean..."

"Confident about this? No. But you're the one who attunes with it. If you think we'll be better staying here, then I don't have any argument."

She glanced up, toward the bridge. "Tomorrow, pre-dawn."

Santon paused beside her, setting off a burst of tingling from the stone. "I'll be here."

He scrambled up the bank and disappeared in the night.

Neve was as good as her word, appearing shortly after he slid down the bank from the road in the pre-dawn light. Neither spoke as they turned away from the hamlet and struck out for the tower. Santon had a strong intimation they had to get out of sight before the sun rose; against the scrub they would be visible, should anybody be looking for them. Leo, for instance. He set a brisk pace and found himself walking slightly hunched, as if the minor difference in height would serve to hide them.

Neve, he observed, did the same, coupled with anxious backward glances.

Santon was giving in to his curiosity. He knew it. He didn't care. The sensible route lay to the south, or perhaps doubling back and hiding out in Orlan. The spells peppering the hills made their chosen route risky; as well, there was no way to predict the effect of the stone, but he'd bet there would be one.

They didn't stop at the tower but continued west, separating to scout for any remnant of a path. At five hundred paces or so from the tower, they reached the green verge, which they now could see consisted of understory trees and shrubs higher than his head. The river, which had been their constant companion this far, cut sharply north, paralleling the verge until it disappeared from sight. There was no evidence of a way through the bank of vegetation.

"You finding anything?" he asked.

"Nope," she said. "You scout south, I'll take north."

He answered with a terse nod.

They set off in their different directions, but it soon became evident there was no entrance through the barricade. Back at the starting point, he accepted the inevitable; he'd have to cut a path.

Neve was perhaps fifty paces away. He shouted his intent, then set to work. First, he tried to push a trail through with Auric energy. No luck. Next, he tried fire, not, admittedly, one of his better skills. The vegetation remained impervious, so he resorted to old-fashioned muscle power, wielding his travel knife. The shrubs had a rubbery texture; he had to fight the knife to keep it from rebounding as he hacked his way through.

The sun was well up before his backbreaking labor paid dividends. The landscape abruptly opened out into a paradise – a green meadow, replete with wildflowers and birdsong, punctuated by random copses of fruit trees. Sun reflected off tendrils of morning mist that lay across the grass, blown by a light breeze.

It was altogether too perfect, especially given the dry conditions on the other side of the hedge.

Panting from his exertion, he swilled some water and wandered across the short grass, looking around to get his bearings. The meadow was bounded to the west by a rocky cliff; it would take much of the morning to walk to it. To the north and south he could see no end to the meadow.

A brook, no more than a long pace wide, emerged from a gully in the bounding hills and angled to the south. The thing actually made burbling noises. Despite the temptation to rinse his hot face, he didn't quite trust the water. At this distance and in the morning mist, the gully appeared more like a change in color and texture. He couldn't judge how rough it would be or whether it would be walkable. Still, it was a way in.

"Santon?" Neve's voice came from the far side of the hedge. She sounded anxious.

"Follow the cut," he called.

"Good luck on that."

He looked around. There was no sign of his path. Why was he surprised? This was the hills, after all. All rules were negated. Resigned, he began the tedious task of hacking back through. It was mid-morning before he emerged, not far from where he had first entered the foliage.

Neve was twenty paces away, poking at one of the bushes; when she heard him call, she turned and ran in his direction. "Thank the Aura. San, there's something odd about these plants. They're not..."

"Real?" he asked. "Try cutting through them and you'll change your mind in a hurry. But they're unnatural, for sure. From now on, we stick together. The way my path closed up, we could be in trouble if it happened in the hills."

"Like the tale my mother used to tell about a woman whose house was surrounded by brambles, and no one could get through."

"Exactly like that. Makes you wonder where the old children's tales came from, doesn't it?" As they talked, he could see the vegetation knitting into an impenetrable verge again. "This will take a while, so let's go." He gulped some water, gnawed a piece of fruit leather from his pack, then once again began hacking.

❖

It was nearly noon by the time they broke through into the meadow. Neve stopped short, looking around her in amazement. "This is miraculous."

"You could say that." Santon folded to the ground, rubbing his biceps. "If we meet many barricades like this, we aren't going to get far."

She studied the field, swaying lightly. "It's beautiful." She paused. "But... enchanted? Not real?"

He nodded. "It's the hills, or soon will be. Look over there." He gestured, indicating the gully piercing the towering rock face that marked the boundary of the hills proper. "Our way in, I hope."

She glanced back; the trail behind them had faded, the vegetation knitting up over the hacked trail. Soon it would be gone completely. "I'm starting to feel a little less real myself. Something about this meadow, like it's designed to bewitch us. Like we could sit down right here and never leave."

"And probably starve to death. The sooner we're through this, the better. I wonder if ordinary people would see what we do."

"My guess is no. And that they wouldn't be able to get through the hedge, however they see it."

Santon strode forward, Neve trailing in his wake. They followed the brook toward the start of the hills. The meadow was dry, although an odd mist persisted in tendrils over the grass. Neve's thoughts wandered; she couldn't focus. It was as if the meadow were her home, as if it were calling her to simply lie down and sink into the flowers, the mist.

She tugged at Santon's tunic. "Do you feel it, too?"

"They're already trying to deflect us. Keep going. Focus on where the stream cuts into the hills."

Santon's voice seemed to be coming from far away, although he was only a pace from her. There was grim determination in his voice; his eyes never moved from the cut. He reached back and grasped her hand, pulling her along in his wake.

Chapter 17: Gauvain Arrives

"What do you mean, they aren't here?"

Gauvain in a rare, towering rage was enough to terrorize anybody on the planet, other than the man he currently harangued. Leo replied in a voice that held only a hint of an edge – a warning – paired with a fair amount of weariness. Gauvain might rant all he wanted, but he'd never dare make his fury personal. They knew each other far too well. "I thought it best. In any event, I couldn't do much about it. With their combined power, they're well able to avoid whatever blocks I throw up. Besides, I'm too old to venture into the hills on my own, and I'd scarcely put the people of the hamlet at risk."

It being mid-afternoon, the common room was deserted. As Leo made his points, Gauvain looked around – for a server to offer him ale, probably – then returned his attention to Leo.

"How long ago?"

"Three days. They've got the stone, which may aid us in tracing them. If we choose to."

"As if that were a question," Gauvain snapped.

Clearly, in Gauvain's mind it was not.

The girl who serviced the common room came in with a pitcher and three mugs, which she placed before the men. Leo observed Gauvain as he poured a mugful with slightly unsteady hands. A coat of road dust covered clothing that hung on a body even more gaunt than usual. He had spared a minute, but a minute only, to splash water on his face, the insufficient wash only highlighting the lines etched there. He needed to be slowed down. The speed of his trek south had wearied him and probably sapped his powers.

Leo pushed his point. "I suggest we not rush We'll need your full strength in the hills. We'll never find them otherwise."

...or be safe. Leo didn't look forward to what lay ahead but accepted the impossibility of deterring his old friend. Even years ago, when they had first gone venturing together, Gauvain had been certain of his conclusions, rushing forward when he might have done better to regroup, seek second opinions or fresh insights.

Gauvain focused on the mug. Dehydrated, Leo speculated; on top of exhaustion, he was in no shape to take on the hills.

"Tomorrow." Gauvain interrupted Leo's musings. "We can't wait any longer."

"Of course we can. I've organized as much as I could, but for this? With so much unpredictable—"

"Hey, Leo. How are you doing?"

The young man bounded into the room and dropped his lanky body into a chair. Without waiting for a reply, he seized the remaining mug and poured himself an ale.

"John, it's good to see you again. How was the trip?" Leo noted the young man's healthy complexion, his energy and enthusiasm. Nothing could make it clearer how much the trip had cost John's master.

I remember Gauvain at this age. We're not getting younger. It would be the young ones to lead the world, soon.

"It was tough, but I learned so much. Wish we'd had time to see more of the land, though."

Gauvain grunted deep in his throat and ignored his apprentice.

"So, Neve's not here?" the young man continued, with barely a pause to inhale a gulp of ale.

Leo shook his head. "She and Santon disappeared three days ago. We're relatively certain they're braving the hills. You know about the stone?"

"Sure. But why go into the hills with it? Seems counterintuitive to me. Adding spells to spells."

"I don't know," Leo said. He wasn't about to admit his suspicion they wanted to keep the thing from Gauvain. Possessiveness or youthful pride, one way or another it wouldn't play out well.

John gave a dramatic shiver. "So, we'll be following them? That's exciting and scary all at once."

"That it is, boy. That it is." Leo signaled to the young woman hovering near the door, whose interest in the small group had increased measurably with John's arrival. This brother of Neve's had endeared himself to Leo early on in his training, not only by his obvious intelligence and capability but also by his willingness to pitch in. His farm training had influenced something natural in his personality; he saw what was needed and made it happen if he could. Now seventeen, he was well-grown with an easy laugh but flashes of intensity in his eyes – no wonder the serving lass had noticed. John had a solid future ahead of him.

Assuming they all emerged intact from the hills. Because John would take Gauvain and Leo's safety as his personal charge, most likely. Any severe injury, much less loss, would prove catastrophic to the young man's confidence. All the more important they begin well supplied and refreshed.

He ordered bowls of meat and lentils. If nothing else, he could assure his friend ate properly.

In the event, their departure date proved to be nondebatable. The next morning, Gauvain was unable to rise from his bed. Never sick, he didn't take the delay well, using up what little residual strength he had to harass anyone within berating distance.

Well, Leo sighed to himself, it was predictable. As long as Gauvain managed not to maim any of them as he recovered, all would work out as predicted. And perhaps – just perhaps – he would learn something.

Keep the kid humble. How many times he had thought that, in the old days. And, looking back over the years, how little success he had met with.

Resigned, he fetched yet another bowl of ox bone broth and set out for Gauvain's bedroom.

Chapter 18: Deserted

Neve kicked at a weed growing on the verge and mopped her forehead with a sleeve as she looked behind her. She had never heard any intimation that people lived in the hills, but a short, orderly group of cabins lined the path on both sides. None of the buildings showed any sign of age. Preliminary investigation had revealed solid wooden walls, doors that hung and closed properly. Windows without glazing let in only a thin veneer of dust. The houses shimmered in the heat, appearing slightly out of focus.

The path itself was well defined. Near the center of the identical buildings, where the road widened into a small square, the ground had been scorched sometime in the past. A lightning strike, perhaps? The thought made her shudder; she knew first-hand a possible source of lightning strikes, and didn't care to repeat the experience.

When she and Santon peered into windows on their way through the hamlet, they saw enough to conclude the structures were deserted, but not empty. Tables held roughly made dishes and carved wooden spoons. Cookfire enclosures contained ashes that looked far too fresh, given the absence of people. In small second rooms, beds were neatly made, although the coverings seemed spare. But there were no clothes or toys on the shelves. There was no recent sign of humans, or for that matter, livestock. Nary a footprint, a chicken scratch in the dirt.

Their walk to this place, once they had clambered up the gully and found a cleared path awaiting them, had revealed nothing unusual. Oddly, the prevailing sense of eeriness common in the hills had virtually disappeared as they passed the first house. That was unsettling in its own right, but it gave her pause – were there enclaves in the hills that were immune to the blanket of spells? Don't trust, she reminded herself, although the threat from the hills, if it existed here, seemed more potential than immediate.

The weather continued fine, which surprised her. She had assumed the drought extended only through Borgonne. Why would the hills suffer from lack of rain? Did the weavers of the spells not have enough sense to throw in a weather spell or two? Today, though, a hint of cloud brushed across the sky, merely some high cirrus, but it changed things, made the day seem slightly ominous.

A warning? She shivered, despite the heat.

Made curious by the seeming absence of spells, she made a small, familiar gesture with her hand, one that should create a light ball. Nothing happened. Was it possible the Aura itself had disappeared?

"How's the stone?" Santon asked. He had tarried in the center of the hamlet, his frown causing a crease between his brows. Catching up, he joined Neve at the far end.

"It's... oh." She put her hand into her pocket and fished out the stone. "Nothing. It's not responding."

Santon hovered over her open hand. "Still?"

She shook her head. "You're not triggering it."

"There's no Aura," Santon said flatly.

"It feels artificial. I don't like it."

"And where the stone's concerned, now there are three factors at play. You, me, and the Aura."

"We could have assumed that."

"Not really. Because we've never been without it." Santon gestured to encompass the homes. "Any idea what we should do about this?"

"Nope." Neve slipped the stone back in her pocket.

"Let's eat." Santon left the path in favor of a convenient, knee-height rock, where he sat and dug into his backpack.

Neve looked past the houses to the surrounding valley. The land resembled her home, rich, dark soil, gently rolling terrain. "These people were farmers," she said. "The land is made for agriculture. Look over there." She gestured toward the northern horizon. "Those trees are too regular to be wild. They were planted. Fruit or nuts of some kind, I bet. Want to go see?"

Santon had dredged a piece of dried meat from his pack and was munching. After a swallow, he said, "This is the first sign of anything different we've come across. I want to know more about it."

Neve pulled her attention from the distant trees to him. "Elaborate."

"I don't know exactly. Like the tower, you have to think it had a purpose. But what? Or suppose there never were people. Suppose it's just something like a prop in a play. Something to stymie travelers like us. Or maybe a migrant camp. People come and go according to the season."

"Don't think so," Neve said. "They'd be here now. Even in the hills, this is prime growing season." She sat next to Santon and pulled a chunk of bread from her own pack. "Take this," she said, ripping off a piece and holding it out to him. "We have to finish it before it gets moldy."

Santon took the bread and studied it, turning it over before risking a bite. "I expect it'll desiccate before it goes bad, given the heat and dryness. So far, it's just getting harder to chew. It's – what? – seven days since we left? I'm losing track."

Neve pulled out a small stick she had stuck in her pack on the first day and counted the notches, carved faithfully every evening. "Yep. Six marks. This is day seven."

"Think it's safe to split up? I want to explore the village more closely, but I can see you're itching to get into the fields."

She was. But... "No. This doesn't look or feel like the hills, but it is. We can't afford to forget that. I don't need much time on the land, just enough to sense how recently these fields were tilled, maybe what was planted."

"Let's do that first, then, while the weather's good. I don't like those clouds." He looked overhead, where thick stratus was overtaking the layer of drifting cirrus, driven by some air current that unfortunately didn't reach them.

Neve pulled her tunic from her body and shook it to create a tiny bit of breeze. "Funny. In Orlan, any weather that comes from the hills involves thunderheads."

"Yeah, funny. Let's go."

Santon stood on the edge of the largest field while Neve walked a few paces in. Even he could see it showed no signs of recent tillage, no stubble, no ridges from a cultivator. The land lay smooth and dark – he watched as she felt the soil, sniffed it, let it dribble through her fingers.

"Loam, more clay than sand, but not too heavy. I'd know more if I dared taste it."

"Don't."

She nodded. "Fertile, but if it was ever cultivated, it was a very long time ago."

He sighed. "Why am I not surprised?"

His job was to keep an eye on the weather and the village, as if it could disappear – it just might. He'd heard the stories about people becoming so turned around in the hills that they ultimately emerged where they started, rather than on the other side. Definitely best to stay alert.

"Ready to head for the orchard?"

She stood and dusted her hands on her tunic. "Sure."

There was a well-worn track to the trees, as there had been from the village to the field – and for that matter, from the gully to the hamlet. Tracks required travel to stay open; why were these in such good condition? The orchard was farther from the village, which made him nervous, but it might hold some answers.

The irregularities under Santon's feet proved to be nut shells. "Noisettes, I'd say."

"Mmm." Neve went straight in among the trees, reaching to pull down a low-hanging branch. She studied the leaves. "Healthy. Setting a good crop. Over there, the green's different." She released the branch and gestured. "Let's check out those trees, then get back to the village."

"We may not have time. The clouds are moving in."

"At this moment, getting rained on would feel good."

"At first, anyway." Santon wasn't easy about staying so far from the path, but he conceded and followed Neve around the orchard to the other end.

It took her less than a minute to assess the second part of the orchard. "Apples. These trees have been here a long time."

"Agreed. You can smell it." In fact, the air reeked of fermenting apples, no doubt from the windfalls, now thoroughly rotten, that littered the ground.

"In fact, I've never seen fruit trees this old," Neve said. "I can't even guess at their age."

Santon whistled. "Anything else?"

Neve backed out of the orchard and cast a glance over the entire agricultural area. "Also healthy, but beyond that I'm not sensing anything in particular. Let's get back."

They made it to the first of the buildings before a steady rain reached them. A place for shelter, yes... but for some reason, Santon thought he'd be more comfortable under their tarp, even if it meant getting wet. Silently, by mutual accord, they erected a protection circle encompassing the little building – although so far they had no proof a protection circle would do the least bit of good – then set to exploring the house.

The rain had been of short duration. At the first sign it was letting up, they fled the dead hamlet, Santon leading the way. Neither had unpacked, so they were out the door and heading up the trail quickly, having found nothing of interest in the house other than some suspiciously fresh pulses – dried beans, but dried recently, not shriveled to stones.

It was a relief to sense the Aura's presence again.

For once, the abnormal felt normal. As they exited the tiny town, the vegetation gradually came to resemble what Santon remembered from his brief foray into the hills farther north – unidentifiable plants growing with a tropical enthusiasm, vines climbing trees soaring skyward, understory plants so lush you couldn't see far off the track. The air felt thick with moisture, and little could be seen beyond the greenery hemming in the trail, although somewhere close he could hear water flowing. He was more uneasy about the sheer naturalness of the land they had crossed before reaching the dead hamlet than he was about the strange vegetation surrounding them now. At least this was, in a creepy way, familiar.

"I know you're curious," he said, "but I'd refrain from touching, much less plucking."

"It never crossed my mind, actually." Neve, who generally had walked several paces from him in the first part of their expedition, now clung to his heels. "They're not natural. I can feel it through the earth, the way they feed on some energy I've never experienced. I don't like it."

"I don't either, but I'd rather this than stay another day in that artificial town."

"Point taken." They'd discussed it briefly while they waited out the rain, both of them with low voices as if they feared being overheard. This deep in the hills, the normalcy of the hamlet had, contrary to expectation, felt decidedly abnormal.

"How's your little friend?" That the stone had grown quiescent when they entered the odd hamlet bothered him. It surely was spelled in some way, and the spell had something to do with the hills. The tower's location, its very existence, pointed to that conclusion. As they walked, he debated whether carrying the stone himself would waken it, but was forced to accept that it responded to Neve only. His presence was merely a catalyst, insufficient for whatever power it wielded.

They walked until twilight dropped over the hills. "Ready to stop?" he asked over his shoulder.

"More than. This is seriously uphill."

He drew to a stop. "I think we've reached the summit. Look."

A mist filled the valley below, obscuring much of the view. Above the mist, the trail was visible winding downhill. About halfway down, a clearing had been cut into the side of the slope. "We can make it before dark."

They did, just. Yet neither of them was in a hurry to set up their tarp and find kindling for a fire. In the dying light he could see his own puzzlement reflected on her face. This was no natural break in the vegetation.

He extended his personal field, sensing for danger. "Feels safe enough."

"We're not the first here," she said carefully. "But it's been a long time since the waysite was used. It's as if this was part of a regular route through the hills."

"Threats?"

"No, not that I can detect."

Santon quartered the small clearing, scuffing through forest detritus and sending out energy to detect anything that might put them in peril. Nothing was there but the layers of spells, which had been increasing all afternoon, he realized, so slowly he had barely registered them. But nothing posed an immediate danger. Satisfied, he started gathering downed wood for a fire. Living flora might carry all manner of hazards, but the dead stuff gave him no negative vibrations.

Neve pursued her own investigation. The space was small enough they were never more than seven or eight paces from each other, but Neve's report of lingering energies from other people kept him from being comfortable, even with that small distance.

She wandered into the center of the space and squatted, poking with a stick. "The fire circle hasn't been used in years."

Santon walked over, dragging a large branch behind him. He dumped his load and broke off one of the smaller branches to scrape away the accumulated litter. "Any idea how long ago?"

"Like the apples, too old to estimate." She gathered up a few stones and added them to the loose ring around the ancient remains of fires. "I'd lay odds this was a regular route. What's strange is we didn't see any waysites before we got to the hamlet. Was that the end of the road?"

Santon finished scraping the litter from the fire circle and began to break up the branch and lay the wood. "What's sure is, there's something ahead."

He looked up. Neve met his eyes in the rapidly encroaching gloom. What he read there reflected his own uneasiness. "We'll feel better with a fire and food," he said.

"Which we're almost out of." They'd been on reduced rations for a couple of days. "We're going to have to hunt and forage," she added. "John's friends, the ones who crossed the hills from Orlan, said they hunted all the time and it was fine, as long as they stayed close to the path."

"Hang on." He channeled his energies and lit the fire. Its warmth gave him immediate comfort. More exhausted than he had realized, he dropped to the ground, leaning back on his arms. "We're only doing this to try to figure out what the stone is for. I say we've gone far enough. If we don't come across anything tomorrow, we experiment. Both of us have to touch it, sooner or later."

Neve sat next to him, staring at the fire. "We could turn around. Try it once we're out of the hills."

She looked tired and grubby, her hair lank, face with a layer of grime, tunic and trousers just plain filthy. He was sure he looked no better. "They're about four days behind us, no more than that. We can't get out without meeting them, and then Gauvain claims the stone."

"We don't have to give it to him."

"True. But do you want that kind of confrontation here, in the hills?"

Neve compressed her lips, but she shook her head in agreement. "I still don't like it."

Santon shifted his arms and stretched out full length on the ground. "I don't either. But those are our choices."

She stood. "I'll see what I can put together for supper. It won't be exciting."

Santon reflected briefly on the excellent stew served at the inn in the village. "Anything will do, thanks."

He forced his body to relax and stared overhead, spotting a star or two through the overhanging trees, aware of Neve bustling around the waysite. They'd eat, they'd sleep. They'd walk another day, adding the search for food to their routine. And then they'd play with the stone.

Please the Aura, let it not be malign.

Chapter 19: The Chase Party

Gauvain drew to a halt, ostensibly to glare at the landscape. His senses quivered under the barrage of spells emanating from the hills.

"Problem?" Leo asked from behind him.

"Yes." Leo ought to know he wouldn't have stopped if he wasn't concerned.

John was somewhere up ahead, a fact Gauvain didn't like, both because it emphasized his own age and relative weakness and because he'd rather keep his small troop close together. But the young man's energy was irrepressible.

The old man caught up, the younger one strode back toward them. His little band intact, he once again surveyed the land. "We aren't welcome here," he told them.

The land itself offered no obvious clues as to the source of his uneasiness. The trail had been well marked from the beginning, leading from the ancient tower. A thick hedge blocked the entrance to the hills, but the remnant of a trail coupled with a little muscle from John had allowed them to hack their way through. On the other side lay a struggling meadow, weeds overpowering the grassland. There had been evidence of recent passage when they climbed up a dry gully into the foothills. Now they traversed a hilly land of low scrub, gradually climbing. Ahead of them loomed the hills proper.

Inwardly, Gauvain cursed the impulse that had seen him expend so much of his power to get to Leo as quickly as possible. The challenge ahead promised to tax every trace of strength left in him.

What was the source of his uneasiness? Were the hills implanting doubts in his mind? What difference did the stone make, anyway? Except that in untrained hands...

"They aren't children," Leo said calmly, with the unnerving ability to read his thoughts that, over the years, had proved to be sometimes a lifesaver, sometimes a curse.

Gauvain grunted and plodded forward, not rushing, conserving his energy.

"This isn't anything like I expected the hills to be," John observed, not for the first time. "It looks like the land is suffering." He squatted and ran a handful of dirt through his fingers. "This should be fertile, but where's the vegetation?"

"Drought," Leo said. There had been clouds overhead the day before, but no rain.

"Or illusion," Gauvain interjected. The state of the land didn't interest him. He wanted to catch up with that impudent woman and Duncan's apprentice. The boy might have abilities – probably did, given the amount of time Duncan had invested in him – but his training was incomplete. There was no way to predict the damage they might do should they take it into their heads to experiment with the stone.

"What on earth?" John, who as usual had galloped fifty paces ahead of them, stopped dead in his tracks.

Gauvain and Leo caught up quickly. In a shallow valley less than half a day's walk away was a village of a dozen houses, which was strange enough. Worse though, Gauvain sensed an emptiness ahead, as if the hamlet and the land around it had been hollowed out. It was more than merely the absence of the spells common in the hills. The place hovered on the edge of time itself, not real but not an illusion either. A place that didn't – couldn't – exist. And yet it did.

Probably.

"Do you sense danger? Should we continue?" Leo looked around, studying the land, the town.

"Not danger, no." Gauvain frowned, sorting out the admixture of impressions flooding his nerve endings. "It's deserted, but not in a common way. As if the buildings are unaffected by the spells but not free of them either."

"Odd," John said. "I'm not sure I understand."

"Odd indeed." Gauvain dropped his pack. "I suggest we take a break and have something to eat. We should have time to get there before sunset."

"If it's really where we want to be," Leo muttered. Leo always favored caution.

Mildly annoyed, Gauvain said, "I see no reason why not. There's nothing malevolent, and freedom from the spells might be just what we need to get a good night's sleep."

Leo shot him a look that plainly said he didn't agree, but shrugged off his pack and began rummaging for dried meat and waybread. John stood still, studying the distant hamlet before turning to join them, making his own attack on the supplies in his pack. More weary than he was willing to admit, Gauvain lowered himself carefully – not even Leo knew about the creeping pains in his knees. He was silent as they ate, pondering the mystery of the buildings, and even more the mystery of the absence of spells.

Chapter 20: Campout

The trail wound through a wonderland of valleys and meadows, jungle and tumbling waterfalls. Neve would have reveled in the beauty of it, were it not – to her – so obviously artificial. Whenever she focused on the land rather than simply admiring the scenery, the unreality was blatant. But she couldn't force through the illusion to the underlying truth.

She had said as much, back at the first waysite. Santon agreed, although he didn't connect to the land the way she did. His was a logical conclusion – tropical vegetation had no place this far north, much less in the higher elevation of the hills.

There had been another waysite after the first, each conveniently placed exactly where it was needed, leading Neve to wonder if the sites themselves were real. The current one, deep in a primeval forest, featured a bubbling spring of clear, delicious water, and a patch of edible greens atypical of the prevailing vegetation, almost as if they had been planted there for her to find.

"These may not be hills at all," he'd said, idly drawing patterns with the toe of his boot in the forest detritus covering the ground. "They could be mountains. Duncan used to say there are so many layers of spells that it's impossible to disentangle them now. It seems Borgonne and the Midland didn't get along," he added in classic understatement.

"You have to think this is overkill. It's lovely, but all this just to keep the two countries apart?"

"Seems crazy, doesn't it? I'm going hunting."

She had just added a handful of greens to the pot bubbling over the fire when she heard Santon coming back from his hunt.

"Got one." He squatted by the fire and commenced to skin and gut the carcass of the small animal, a type she had never seen before. Like her, he was efficient at the work; in no time, his meat joined her greens. "Does it occur to you that this is too easy?"

She shrugged. "The spells here are as prominent as ever. It's not like the hamlet."

"No, but it was nice of the spell-makers to provide for travelers." Santon stepped out of the waysite to dig a hole and bury the remains of the animal. He poured water over his hands, scrubbing them clean before returning to the fire.

"I'll tell you what it feels like," Neve said. "It's like there's a permanent protection circle over the waysites. Whoever set up this route wanted travelers to be safe and cared for."

"I guess we should be grateful." He bent down and stirred the pot before settling on the ground near the fire. "But how far should we push it? What are we trying to prove? Are we going to go all the way through the hills just to avoid Gauvain? Is it worth it?"

Neve's hand went instinctively to the stone in her pocket. She had started to think of it as a sort of pet, she realized, checking on it regularly, testing for reactions. Soon after they left the dead hamlet, the stone had resumed the faint tingling that amplified when Santon was close. "I don't know anymore. I feel like I want to move forward – almost like I *have* to move forward. I don't feel threatened, we're finding food, the weather's good."

"It's an adventure."

"So was joining the expedition, at least for me."

Later, relaxing after they cleaned up from their meager supper and cast a protection circle – despite Neve's sense that the waysite *was* a protection circle, both felt more secure using their own methods – they talked it over yet again.

"It's not doing anything," Santon complained. "We chose this route to see if it would trigger the stone. It hasn't."

"And because the only other routes led to dead ends."

He stretched out on his bedroll, cradling his head in his hands. "If we experiment with the stone now, then we have no reason to run from Gauvain."

"Or more reason." Neve leaned back on her arms, enjoying the way the fire's warmth radiated down from the dome of the circle. "If we blow something up, we'll be in trouble. If we discover something worthwhile, he'll claim it. You know he will."

"I don't actually know much of anything about him," Santon said, "and neither do you, except hearsay." He raised a hand when she started to interrupt. "One cruel encounter when you were a little girl doesn't count."

At some point during their hike into the hills, she had told him about that initial interview, the way she still reacted to Gauvain viscerally. Sharing such tidbits helped relieve the homesickness that washed over her occasionally.

"Anyway," he continued, "Leo's a good guy. How awful could Gauvain be if Leo's stuck with him for so long?"

"Father?" Neve ventured.

"Father figure, more like. I'm sort of inclined to think Gauvain hatched rather than getting born the usual way." He grinned; Santon was enjoying their discussion. "A day or so ago, I was ready to call a halt. But now I'm curious to see what's ahead. The alternative being more road repair."

"We were doing okay with that. We've got a good system."

"Yes, but suppose we do come out in the Midland. How cool would that be?"

"But the stone..."

The sun had dropped behind the hills ahead of them, and night was falling quickly. "Let's discuss it tomorrow," Santon said. "I'm flat out of energy." He turned away, back to the fire. Within minutes she caught a soft snore.

This was typical of their conversations over the last two days. Bring up the subject of the stone, question what they were doing, then one or the other of them would defer any decision. Deferral, to Neve, felt like the better option.

But she wasn't ready for sleep, not yet. The unlikelihood of her being here at all instead of shielding the barley from pests, helping her mother in the kitchen, still challenged her mind. Long she sat in the dark, gazing at the dying fire, listening to the eerie silence and caressing the stone, safe within her deep pocket.

Chapter 21: Near Miss

The next day, the path grew steeper and more winding. As they eased along a steep mountainside, a mist-filled valley far below them, Neve found herself fighting both the grade and a stiff breeze that threatened to push her far too close to the undefended edge of the path. "Just charge on," she called ahead to Santon, who seemed to be unconcerned by the challenges. "Don't wait up for me or anything."

From the set of his shoulders as he stopped and turned, she concluded he was irritated. "What's the problem?" His mouth twitching into an annoyed grimace, he walked back toward her. "Got a stone in your boot?"

She scowled. Her boots were fine, thank you very much. But the combination of altitude, something she had never experienced in Borgonne, and the gusts pummeling the path had made her less sure of her footing.

Besides, neither of them had woken in a good mood. More spells?

"I'd rather stay close together, that's all. You seem determined to reach the Midland before lunch."

"You've never had a problem keeping up with me before."

"Well, maybe today I do. I suppose you never have an off day, being so perfect and all."

Santon dragged a hand through his hair, which he hadn't tied back in the usual tail. "I don't recall ever claiming perfection," he said, his voice dangerously quiet. "Only competence. Which you might learn from. What's got you dragging your heels today?"

The stone let loose a powerful vibration just as an unusually strong gust of wind forced both of them to grab for handholds. Beneath her feet, the ground trembled, sending rubble skidding down the slope above them. Clinging to an overhanging branch, Neve assessed the chasm at their feet, then shot a glance at Santon.

Horror and guilt warred in his expression as the awareness of what they had almost done swept over them both. "Oh, hell," he said.

"Yeah." As the wind dropped, she left her handhold and passed him, walking a little way to a place where the trail opened out into yet another waysite – far too conveniently to be natural. She crossed the clearing and sank onto a log.

After a minute, Santon joined her. Glaring down at her, he said, "Okay, let's talk."

"About...?"

"Why we're both in bad moods, for openers. Why you're moving more slowly today."

"And why you're moving like every spook in the hills is on your tail," Neve interjected sourly.

He ignored her. "How much longer this trail is going to wind uphill before we find something else that isn't explainable. Like this clearing, which I'd swear wasn't here just before I turned around."

"Like a million things," Neve said. "What are we talking about, anyway? How close we came to triggering another tear in the Aura? That's what we should be concerned with."

Santon sat next to her on the log. "True. We haven't fought in a couple of nine-days. Why now?"

The stone gave a buzz – a stronger vibration that Neve now recognized as a signal Santon was nearby – then reverted into its usual mild tingle. She was silent, taking in the clearing, the near absence of movement in the air – was the wind confined to the path? – and the verdant, unnatural vegetation surrounding them. Idly she brushed a tendril of a nearby vine from her shoulder, keeping her gaze resolutely ahead, refusing to look at the man slouched next to her. "There's a little plantain cake left from supper," she said, a peace offering.

"Thanks, not now." Santon did turn, looking straight at her. His gaze bored into the side of her head. "It's time we were honest with each other. Are you sure you want to go on? We could experiment with the stone right here, see what happens, and turn around. There's no reason to be foolhardy, and frankly, trekking through the hills with no reason and no destination is dumb."

Neve sighed, a deep, full-body sigh that shook her from head to knees. "I guess I'm just not ready to try the stone – I'm more than a little afraid of what might happen. Any idea how far behind us they are?"

Santon went into the weird, disconnected state that she knew meant he was accessing the Aura. "Two and a half, maybe three days."

Neve stood with a suppressed groan; the persistent uphill climb had taxed her quadriceps. "Let's keep it that way, shall we?"

She had moved twenty paces along the trail before Santon left the clearing. He caught up with her and passed her. This time he didn't charge in front but continued at their previous pace. Not quite companionably, but the flare-up of hostility had been blown away.

Chapter 22: Upper Wem

After taxing Neve's legs all morning, the trail began a downhill plunge not long after their lunch stop. By mid-afternoon, it leveled out into a wide, sunny valley. In itself, that was sufficiently strange; the valleys they had traversed since the deserted hamlet had been mist-shrouded, damp and dense with vegetation. Odder still was the presence of cultivated fields and fenced-in meadows. Neve stopped to rub a handful of soil through her fingers. "Loam. Should be great cropland," she reported. "It doesn't feel dead like the hamlet did. Someone is working this land."

Ahead of them, a range of steep hillslopes bounded the valley. A stream cut through them and followed their path a ways before meandering to the south, bisecting a meadow of grazing sheep. The trail ahead appeared well traveled. "The farmers must live the other side of that," Santon said with a gesture. "It's easily defensible, which makes it dangerous for us."

"Perhaps we could climb one of the hills and see what's on the other side? Or swim the river?"

Santon ignored that, frowning. "What we don't have is weapons, beyond knives."

"Weapons?" Neve echoed. In her life, she'd never once felt herself to be physically threatened, even by the hills. Surely these people, whoever they were, wouldn't be dangerous.

"Couldn't you do a binding spell? Or make them drop their weapons?"

"In the hills?" Santon retorted. "Anything I tried would likely rebound on me. I'd rather not test the Aura right now."

They stood silently by the stream, studying the bucolic scene around them. Neve shuddered, despite the mild weather, struck by the impossibility of this place's existence in the middle of the hills.

"That might be a toolshed over there," Santon said, gesturing across the fields north of the trail. "Maybe we could scavenge a pitchfork. Or an axe if we get really lucky."

So peaceful. So much like home, in a way... Neve shook off her gut reaction. Santon was right. This was the hills, and preconceptions held no weight. "Let's go," she said.

Santon gave a curt nod and left the path, following a verge dividing two fields. Neve stayed as close as she could, one hand convulsively clutching the stone.

They didn't make it far.

From the gorge, furious voices tore at the air. It took a moment for Neve to sort out that the rage was not directed at them.

A deep voice, male: "...goin' anywhere, young lady. You get yourself back home this minute."

Higher pitched, furious: "You and all of 'em. You haven't a clue, have you? *Get your hands off me!*"

Two figures emerged. At a distance, Neve was able to make out an elderly man, bearded, barrel-chested and clearly fit in the way typical of men who worked the soil. And a girl, perhaps mid to late teens, dark hair swirling loose around her head as she struggled to free herself. She wore a long vest over her tunic in a fabric Neve couldn't readily identify, but not the usual linen so common among the working classes of Borgonne. She bore a small pack on her back.

The girl was dragging the man behind her, so frantic was her desire for escape.

The man dug in his heels and jerked the girl backwards with a roar. "You will *not* disobey the rules."

The girl stopped fighting and turned on the man, who let go. Arms akimbo, she shouted, "The rules never prohibited a trip to Little Wem."

"They do now, as far as you're concerned."

The girl's attitude changed to wheedling. "I'll *die* if I have to stay cooped up here. You can't imagine, no one can. I want to see—"

"Oh, girlie." The man appeared to sigh; Neve sensed this wasn't the first time the two had had this conversation. Their voices grew almost too low for her to hear. Only her Aura-augmented senses and the quiet of the valley allowed her to pick out occasional words.

Beside her, she realized abruptly, Santon stood still as a stone.

The man's voice was low and reasonable. "You think we all haven't been plagued by those selfsame dreams? This is reality, Tess, nothing more or less. I'm sorry for you, girl, I am. But you're old enough to put your imagination aside. We're going nowhere, any of us."

"Nor is anyone ever coming here. *Ever!* And I'll be..."

"As you are," the man said placatingly. "And that's fine enough. And as for no one coming here, what do you make of those two then?"

She cast a glance across the fields and froze. "Oh..."

The man's gaze followed the girl's, locking on them. Neve felt the strength draining from her knees, but she held up a hand in acknowledgment.

Look friendly. Look non-threatening.

Santon still didn't move.

At first, the girl stood stricken, as if an apparition had appeared in the field. The man seemed more relaxed, almost as if their appearance hadn't been unexpected. After a frantic glance back at the gorge, the girl reached for the man's hand. First reactions over, the two parties eyed each other.

Neve gave Santon a little shove. He shook her off but began to walk, mechanically, out of the fields. Neve stayed on his heels, wary.

By the time they reached the main path, the man and the girl were moving in their direction. They came within five paces of each other before stopping.

Neve took a half step forward and gave their names. "We... well, we set out into the hills from Borgonne. We didn't expect to meet anybody. We don't intend to interfere with your lives in any way. We mean no harm," she added a little desperately. "We just want to pass through, that's all, honestly."

Stop babbling, she lectured herself. But it wasn't as if she was getting any help from Santon, who once again was frozen in place.

The girl, Tess, was as still as Santon. Neve looked from one to the other, puzzled. They had fastened eyes on each other, and it was as if whatever they saw had hypnotized them.

Neve addressed the elderly man. "I see we speak the same language, or nearly."

Say something. She couldn't keep a one-sided conversation going forever.

Whether or not he picked up her internal plea, the man spoke. "Not in my lifetime. Nor my da's."

Neve cocked her head, sorting it out. "No one's been here in that time?"

"True enough. No stories of passersby in generations. And then you're there standing by the barley."

"It's no mystery, really. We're just... it's hard to explain."

"You've been touched," the man declared. "Only those as are touched can go through the hills, or so they say. I suppose that's still true?"

Touched. The Aura. "Yes, it's true. Look, is there somewhere we can talk? I'm a little shaky. We didn't expect to see anybody."

"And yet here you are." The man seemed to be loosening up; perhaps he was warming to them, or intrigued by the situation. "But we can't know, can we, if you mean harm. We'll take you to the village, right enough, but you'll be giving up your travel knives. And we'll be watching you, every step."

"But we can't be certain of you, either." Neve thought a moment. "Our knives... It seems unlikely you could mean us harm, but—"

The girl Tess interrupted. "Who's she?" she asked, gesturing at Neve.

Santon woke up. "Just someone I know."

Ah. Neve's eyes met the man's. They'd both come to the same realization. Without words, before even a brief introduction could be made, some recognition had occurred between Tess and Santon. How it would play out, she couldn't begin to guess, although given the girl's determination to escape...

And what would *that* mean for their expedition?

Without further discussion, and perhaps recognizing the futility of stripping them of their knives, the man led them through the gorge, his hand once again firmly on the girl's arm. Neve and Santon followed. Neve didn't attempt to break through the strange fog that seemed to have gripped her companion; whatever was going on, he would have to navigate it on his own.

Chapter 23: Lower Wem Hosts More Newcomers

Gauvain's nose twitched. Odd. After a lifetime of acute sensitivity to the Aura, to be in a place with no auric awareness troubled him. He looked at Leo, standing beside him as they paused in the center of the deserted hamlet. His old friend was frowning.

Summoning his resolve, Gauvain strode to the nearest building – not that there was anything to choose from. Each structure exactly mimicked the others. A dozen tiny residences, and no sign of life.

Leo addressed what they both were aware of. "Makes no sense, does it? A pocket in the middle of the hills with no trace of the Aura. Defies everything we know about its reach."

"I wonder how long it's been this way," Gauvain murmured as they entered the house. The place was immaculate, nothing out of place. He made a cursory survey of the second room, but found only a straw mattress, the linens folded neatly at the foot.

Nowhere a footprint, a sign of cooking. "I suppose we should check the fields. I'd like to know how large this bubble is."

"I for one wouldn't mind taking advantage of those chairs and sitting at a table like civilized folk," Leo said. He placed his pack on the table and rummaged, producing his interminable dried fruit and several strips of smoked meat from a catch John had made two days before. "We could even use plates. And we are low on water."

Gauvain's attention was elsewhere. "I expect there's a well somewhere," he said absently.

"A safe one?"

"No idea." Satisfied the house held no secrets, he prowled out the door and further along the street.

John caught up with him. The boy had lingered behind, poking at an outbuilding behind the second house in the row. "An old latrine," he said. "They were farmers, by all appearances. But where are their implements? Did they pack up their tools and flee? I don't get it. More though – I tried to create a light ball to see in the shed. Nothing. It doesn't just *feel* like the Aura's not here. It truly isn't."

John's words confirmed Gauvain's suspicions, but the boy's boundless energy was an irritant. "It seems to be safe enough. Could you go check the fields? You might find fresh fruit – that seems to be some sort of orchard over there."

"Sure." As he had hoped, John set off at his usual loping pace.

"Is that wise?" Leo, always cautious, appeared at his elbow.

"Why not?" There were times for caution and times for boldness. Leo, the career soldier, seemed never to have learned the distinction.

"Because we haven't the first idea what's going on. We're probably best off staying together."

Irritated, Gauvain said, "He was getting on my nerves. There's nothing happening here. He'll be fine."

"I was actually thinking more of us, two elderly men on their own. We might need his strength."

At the notion, stated so bluntly, that he was now elderly, Gauvain merely huffed and turned away. But there was little else to explore. They had stumbled upon some kind of Aura-free enclave in the hills, but other than defining its boundaries, he could think of nothing else to do about it.

Leo, indefatigable in his rationality, touched his elbow. "I suggest you come in and eat something. If nothing else, the absence of the Aura seems to allow more intense sunlight to penetrate. I suspect we should get under cover before we both suffer sunburn."

Made increasingly ill-tempered by the presence of a mystery he was failing to penetrate, Gauvain accepted the advice and trailed after Leo back into the tiny house. At least some meat would revive his energy, although the thought of more dried fruit... ugh.

Chapter 24: Meeting the Town

From her place near the bonfire, feeling more human with washed hair and a clean, borrowed tunic, Neve watched. There was certainly a lot to see.

In sharp contrast to the hamlet she now knew was called Lower Wem, the Aura was fully present, and Upper Wem pulsed with life. She estimated the populace sorted into upward of forty families, with ages ranging from one babe in arms to a significant contingent of elders. Almost all of them were in the town square, some hovering around the cookfire a little distance away, others chatting or simply relaxing near the fire. The children scampered and danced to the driving beat of a drum, and she noticed more than one young couple disappearing into the shadows.

The sun was approaching the high horizon formed by the hills to the west. An uneasy time, neither day nor fully twilight. Transition, a time of possibility and threat. Neve involuntarily shuddered. Despite the general friendliness, she couldn't quite forget that she was in the hills, in the midst of what amounted to a lost civilization, people who had been out of contact with Borgonne for generations.

She and Santon had been assigned one of the tiny cabins, built to the same plan as the ones in the dead town called Lower Wem. At her request, an extra pallet had been provided. Did the residents assume they were lovers? Given what was going on under all their noses between Santon and Tess, how was that even possible?

Santon wasn't in evidence, although Tess was over at the cookfires – held there by the will of a woman anyone would be afraid to defy. She had met Tess's formidable mother when they first arrived and had stepped lightly ever since. The woman's opinion of the chemistry that had seized her daughter and the stranger was expressed by tightened lips and a glare whenever her gaze fixed on Santon.

Poor Tess.

So far there had been no interrogation, nothing more than pleasantries such as anyone might exchange with a traveler. The weather, the state of the trail, food preferences. But no mention of conditions in Lower Wem, the world outside the hills, or what they were doing here at all. She fretted about what to tell them, as she might worry a sore tooth, including whether to reveal the stone. Half of her wondered if these people knew its secret, the other half feared it would be taken away from her.

Her hand stole into her pocket and was rewarded with the comforting tingle.

Without admitting to possession of the stone, how could they explain their unlikely presence? She wouldn't mind a quiet moment to talk it over with Santon. Again she surveyed the crowd, trying to pick him out. He blended right in, with hair tied back and a twelve-day beard. She spotted him a little distance from the fire, chatting with a group of younger men. Since their arrival, he had been largely oblivious to her presence, leaving all the details of their accommodation to her. It was the worst case of infatuation she had ever seen, but at least he was getting in some male bonding time.

Probably pumping them for information about Tess.

As the early twilight deepened, the community gathered around long trestle tables for the evening meal. Neve ate a familiar dish of lentils and barley flavored with a hint of meat, said little, and continued her observations. She saw nothing abnormal at all. A hard-working farming community – she might have been at home. Those near her at the table asked more of the expected questions and shared tidbits about their lives. Again, nothing unusual, but she was able to engage with their comments about weather, soil, what to plant and when, and discovered, somewhat to her surprise – because nothing could genuinely surprise her anymore – that some of her hard-discovered techniques for encouraging the crops were well known here and practiced regularly.

Was this, then, a community in which everyone had an Auric connection? But the way they spoke of being 'touched' suggested otherwise.

So many mysteries, and a need, more intuited than observed, to be cautious with how much she revealed. She wondered if Santon, installed at another table, thought the same.

She volunteered to help with the cleanup after their meal, and as soon as that was done she was escorted to their little house – with apologies and the weak explanation that because the buildings all looked the same, it was easy to become confused. So, they were keeping an eye on the travelers; wandering would not be tolerated.

Santon came in shortly after. Warm water had been provided, and although they had washed before joining the town at the bonfire, they both took advantage of it, stripping down for a more thorough bath. After so many days on the road, modesty was no longer an issue between them.

"We need to compare notes," she said, rubbing her short hair with a towel.

He grunted as he sloshed water over his head and down his chest, rinsing off soap. "They haven't asked us anything so far. I doubt they will. We're being treated like conventional travelers."

"Even though there clearly haven't been any others in – how long do you suppose? Generations, according to Tess's grandfather." Refreshed after her sponge bath, she shrugged into her borrowed tunic – theirs had been taken to the communal laundry – and sat cross-legged on the bed.

"It's as if we're a responsibility," Santon said. "Tending us is a protocol passed down from parent to child."

"I like it here. It's comfortable. But...."

"Hmm?" His back to her, he continued his rinse, scooping the water up again as it landed in the large, low-rimmed basin.

"Well, to point out the obvious... your reaction to Tess was pretty extreme."

Santon didn't reply, devoting his attention to the towel. When he finished, he draped it over the rack provided, donned a tunic matching her own, and sat next to her on the bed. His face was troubled. "It was worse being inside it. I felt as if I'd lost touch with reality. But I didn't sense any outside control. She just... I don't know. It happened to her, too."

"Have you talked about it? Maybe it's natural here."

"I don't think so. She was rattled. When we were walking back to the village, I wanted to ask, but she was shutting me out. I think it frightened her. Or I did."

"The Aura trying to get your attention?"

Santon's face twisted into a wry grin. "That was my thought. I was meant to notice her, and the Aura was making sure I did. But I've never heard of such a thing."

"The hills."

"The hills. I'm going to bed." Santon rose and picked up the spare pallet, giving it a shake as he rolled it out.

"Wait," Neve said. "They haven't asked why we're here. They may. Do we tell them about the stone?" She fished under her thin pillow and brought it out. Given Santon's proximity, it vibrated enthusiastically. Idly, she stroked it as she might a cat. Now that she thought about it, the vibration was similar to a purr. "Given this," she said, holding it up, "you seem to be some kind of magnet. The rent in the aura back in Vienne, the stone's intensity, and now that weird fugue state."

"Let's hope that's not true. As for the stone, we may have to tell them. It's the only reason we have to be here. Furthermore, what about Gauvain and Leo? Having two sets of travelers landing on their doorstep in the space of a few days is going to make an impression."

"We could be gone by then."

"Could we?" Santon stretched under the sheet and burrowed into the pillow. "That – thing – with Tess. I've got to find out what it was telling me, what we're meant to do about it. I don't think we'll be leaving here any time soon."

Neve flopped back on the bed. "You're probably right. But..."

"I suspect we won't have a choice. For now, don't volunteer any information. We'll see how things unspool."

Full night had descended as they spoke. Neve hadn't lit a candle or bothered with a light ball, so the room had faded rapidly into darkness. She grunted an acknowledgment and turned, seeking a comfortable spot on the mattress. Tomorrow would bring its own challenges; best she be rested and ready.

Chapter 25: What the Heck Happened?

Neve had already left the cabin when Santon woke. No surprise. Despite the fog in his head, he sensed her instinctive bond with the people of Upper Wem based on their shared farming heritage. From the moment they entered the valley of fields and meadows, she had attuned, commenting on the pasture layout, sampling the soil with her hands – he had reminded her again not to taste it – watching the weather. This was her specialty; he would do well to pay attention to her instincts.

Assuming he could clear his head.

He rolled off the mat and gave himself a full body shake before splashing cool water on his face. The mental fog lessened once he and the girl Tess weren't close and weren't paying attention to each other, but didn't dissipate completely. Rather despairingly, he wondered if it ever would. Awareness seemed to be part of the equation. That first eye-lock had triggered it. From then on, if he was aware of her – or presumably, she of him – the fog came back. Neve assumed he was in the grip of some primal male fascination, but he knew better. This was different, and he was glad Neve was around Because she was the only one in the village he trusted.

Breakfast had been served in the one building, other than barns, that was larger than the others, a sort of town gathering place. Most of the residents had already dispersed to their day's work. The damn fog had knocked him for a loop, but he was grateful he'd been given the time to sleep. He'd needed it. They had saved him a bowl of barley cereal, with syrup and a handful of dried fruit, all topped with cream. He sat at the end of one of the trestle tables, now reconstructed inside, and dug in, wondering if caff was an option.

Neve stuck her head in the building. Spotting him, she strode over. "You okay?" she asked, a hint of doubt in her voice.

He swallowed. "Have a seat. Do you have time for a chat? I want your impressions."

Neve glanced around before sitting across from him and leaning forward over the table. "On the surface, this is a typical village. But there's something...."

Santon could have done with a second serving, but it didn't appear anyone was left in the building, or any food, so he sighed and pushed the bowl away. He lowered his voice and leaned toward Neve. "About yesterday, what happened – that wasn't normal."

She knew instantly what he was talking about. "Infatuation, is what I thought."

"No." An emphatic head shake accompanied his declaration. "I'm attracted – what man wouldn't be? But this felt like something more."

"The Aura getting your attention." Neve's voice held flat certainty.

"But why? What am I supposed to do? Or I guess I should say we, because I'm pretty sure it hit both of us."

"Have you talked to her?"

He snorted. "With that dragon of a mother guarding her virtue?"

Neve shot him an answering grin. "We can go around her, or just tell her what happened. Maybe it's not unheard of around here. Maybe she, or someone else, can explain what's going on." Neve hesitated. "How do you feel about Tess?"

"Hell if I know." Santon straightened and ran a hand through his unbound hair. "My head's still hazy. I'd like a chance to find out."

She nodded. "I'll try to divert the mother. You find Tess. The two of you sort it out."

Time to change the subject. Whatever the current messed-up situation, he wasn't one to delve too deeply into personal matters. "How's the baby?"

"Tingly. Likes it here, I think." Her hand slipped toward her pocket, then she stopped and folded her hands on the table. "No point anyone suspecting I've got something in there."

"It's possible they have our answers."

"Could be. It all must tie together somehow. But I'm not ready to risk it."

"I reckon we're going to be here another day or two."

She nodded. "So, they'll catch up with us."

No need to say who 'they' were. "Probably."

They were silent, thinking about adding Gauvain to the mix... Santon didn't know the man except by reputation, but wished there were some way to avoid the inevitable collision. At least they were in civilization of a sort. The townsfolk would be a buffer.

Neve squeezed his forearm. "I'll go find dragon mother. You track down Tess. Let's try to get one answer today."

"You're a pal."

Santon carried his bowl to the deserted kitchen and washed it out. Neve was gone when he returned to the dining hall.

Chapter 26: Santon finds Tess

Despite the presence of more people than Santon had been around in a couple of nine-days, Tess proved easy to locate. A group of women gathered around a loom pointed him toward the barley field, where he found her working a pointed hoe fashioned from wood, probably hardened over a fire. Yesterday she had worn a brilliant vest, unlike anything he had ever seen; today, she was dressed in a linen tunic to her knees, the same as everyone wore, even in Borgonne. What set her apart was her hair, long and lifting gently in the breeze, medium dark but aglow with sun-lit blond highlights.

Hans, the elderly man who had thwarted her flight, whom he now knew to be the girl's grandfather, worked at some distance from her, but he looked up regularly, keeping his eye on the girl. For her part, she fixed her gaze on the hoe.

As if sensing his presence, she straightened, looked around, and spotted him. They both froze, the familiar fog descending over his brain. But this time he was ready for it. He did his best to ignore the perceived loss of clarity and followed the track between rows into the field. She, for her part, stood stock still, waiting. The man, noting the interaction, began weaving his way through the barley toward them.

Santon clasped his hands behind his back, sending a signal: *I am harmless, I bring no threat.* He stopped a little distance from her and kept his voice neutral. "Hi."

Her eyes reminded him of a cornered wild animal. She said nothing, but her grandfather gave him a short nod. "Young man."

Santon shifted his focus from Tess, relieving the fog slightly. "Sir." Involuntarily, he found himself blinking, as if rapid eye movement might clear his head.

The three of them stood in a rough triangle, the grandfather in a different row. The awkwardness of the moment triggered something irreverent in his mind – *It's as if I were telling the offended family I'd got her pregnant.*

What if he had? What if the blasted hills had perverted the Aura to the extent—

Whoa. Stick to reality.

"I'm hoping you can help me. Something's strange here. I don't understand what's happening." He addressed the man only, as Tess remained unresponsive. "I've never experienced anything like this. It's like my mind's in a haze...."

The man nodded. "We've seen it, years ago. Didn't think it would happen again. *Tess,*" he said sharply. The girl jumped and turned to face the man. "Girl, get to your ma. You can finish your hoeing later."

Tess dodged around him, stepped over a row of barley and bolted for the main path. Santon watched her go, puzzled. Yes, whatever had hit him was unexplained, and a little scary, but he was functioning at some level. She was surrounded by family and townspeople who clearly cared about her welfare. Why was she so spooked?

He turned back to the man. "I'm sorry if I've frightened her. I didn't mean to."

With Tess gone, the fog lessened, and the man relaxed. "Well, besides the binding, you're the first man not born in the village to come through here in her lifetime. That'd be enough to unnerve any woman of a certain age."

Binding?

Oh, hell.

Santon was silent, thinking it through. "I assume it's the same for her?"

The man gave a curt nod of his head.

"Tell me what you mean by binding."

They were both silent, the man as if he were debating whether to speak, Santon waiting for whatever came next. Because the old man's words would carry his fate, of that he was sure.

After the pause became awkward, he said, "Please. Just tell me."

"This tale needs to be shared," Hans continued. "We'll go back, round up the elders. That way, you'll get a more complete picture of what you're up against."

His gut churning from the ominous direction the conversation had taken, Santon followed Hans back to the path where Tess waited, having obviously ignored her grandfather's command. No surprise – the mother was hardly the comforting type, and Tess clearly sought comfort. She whimpered, and Hans put an arm around her. "We'll make it work, lass," he murmured. The girl, far from the firebrand of yesterday, turned to her grandfather and buried her head in his shoulder.

Santon met Hans's eyes over her head. "I have a bad feeling about this."

"No need." Tess in tow, Hans began moving back to the village. "You'll handle it, once all the information's gathered. Understand," he said as they reached the gorge, "nothing like this has happened in generations. For Tess's sake, we need to devise the best strategy. Safeguards. I hope you aren't planning on going anywhere anytime soon."

"I am, actually. Neve and I, we're on a quest of sorts."

"And she seems a capable woman. She'll manage on her own."

Or with two companions, who should get here tomorrow.

His head swimming with the fog and what little new information he'd gleaned, he walked behind Tess and her grandfather toward a meeting that he knew with every fiber of his being would be the harbinger of his fate.

The elders, Hans and three others, sat on two facing benches in the village square. The rest of the community gathered around, accompanied by some nudging and shifting for position. Clearly Santon wasn't the only one with a stake in the story.

Hans cleared his throat, and despite the ambient noise, everyone heard and settled down. Children darted through the circle; no one restrained them. Sitting on the end of a bench, Santon spotted Neve across the gathering, keeping track of the crowd. Tess sat beside her grandfather. Her mother stood behind her, one hand on her shoulder.

"The situation is, the fog's come back," Hans stated baldly into the quiet. Santon sensed an increase in alertness. "This time it's bound Santon here, and our Tess."

There was a gasp. A threat to the newcomers was interesting; involving the girl made it personal.

"Now, I'm gonna say what I know about it. Then you all get your chance. It's been so long, I'm not sure how much is real and how much just got made up over the years. We need to get to the truth. Agreed?"

Riding over a soft murmur of assent, Hans continued. "Near as we can figure, the fog afflicts people in pairs. You feel as if you can't think clear, according to legend. When the couple are close together, the fog is worst. Gets thinner – better, you might think – as you move farther apart. Thing is..."

There was a pause that Santon read as ominous. The people around him fell into a dead silence. Even the children stopped their chasing game, waiting.

"What the Aura's saying is, you're bound. With no escaping we've ever found. And, if that distance stretches too far, the consequences—"

"Just say it, Dad. Blurt it out. We all know anyway," Tess's mother interrupted. Santon noted a whiteness around her knuckles as her grip on Tess's shoulder tightened.

Hans swallowed. He twisted on the bench to meet Santon squarely. "You get too far away, you go mad. Or some say die. One way or another, your life is no longer in your keeping."

Tess came to life from the near-catatonic state she'd been in since he had met her in the field. She twisted free and looked up at her mother. "Ever think I might want to go with him? See what the real world's like?"

Her voice it was deep, melodic, bearing no hint of harshness. It shocked him and set something vibrating in his chest. It bore no hint of the high-pitched squawking of the previous day.

Her mother merely sighed. "It's not for folks like us to leave here. You've heard the risks."

"Supposed risks," Tess retorted.

"The Aura's fragile hereabouts, we believe," Hans said. "The spells on the hills – oh yes," he added at the quizzical expression on Santon's face, "we know all about them spells. That's why we're here in the first place, to make sure travelers get through safely. We were guides, back at the beginning. Because it's dangerous. Can't predict how they'll react. The hills or the travelers."

"Some say the hills eat you up," someone in the crowd put in. "Nothing left to find but maybe a boot."

"You hush," an elderly woman on the opposite bench said. "That's hawking fear. It was one person, an idiot who wandered too far from the path. Could've been anything, even some wild animal."

"Could've been supernatural forces," the man in the crowd rebutted. "You can't say."

"Can't gainsay either," Hans said. "But returning to the fog, folks, the point is, we can't trust that the Aura, or the hills, are gonna behave as they ought. There's reason to believe the spells mutate over time, interacting in ways we can't predict. So, we need to fill in all we know about the fog, but not rely on it too much. Because it may have changed."

"Remember the story about the traveler who stayed? Ended up inventing a new way to roof the houses. Had a dozen children, they say. Fog made him brilliant."

"Virile, too," someone chuckled.

"Might have been the love of a good woman."

"Assuming she gave a fig about him."

"Mama, what's a fig?" a child demanded.

"And that story was two hundred years ago," Hans said.

Interesting, but not immediately relevant. "How do you know about the madness?" Santon put in. "Has it happened?"

A woman on the opposite bench spoke. "The last couple the Aura claimed, seems he couldn't take the isolation, and she wouldn't budge, so he set off on his own. She bided well. But another traveler – last one through before you folks, in fact – knew him and said he sat rocking and moaning, couldn't be budged, no matter what they tried. That was – how long ago, Hans?"

"Seventy, eighty years?"

"What direction did he go?" Neve asked. All heads turned to her. "Through Lower Wem, or the other way, to the Midland? Perhaps we could find out more."

"Borgonne," Hans said. "This was before Lower Wem was evacuated."

"Is that another aspect of this?" Santon asked. "Lower Wem?" All eyes turned to him. "We couldn't understand it. It's a place where the Aura doesn't exist, or so it seems."

One of the elders, a pipe dangling from his mouth, said, "Happened forty years ago or more."

"But why? Was it anything to do with the fog? And where were the people evacuated to?" Santon felt as if he was drowning in questions, far too many things he didn't understand. Suddenly, their mysterious stone seemed like a minor inconvenience given the scope of new information.

The woman took a breath. "Aura's gone. How were they supposed to live without the Aura supporting them? Place grew hollow feeling. No one was comfortable."

"They moved here," Hans added. "No one goes there now, other than to check on things periodically. It's not a popular job, though."

"Why check, when there's nothing there?" Mysteries upon mysteries.

"One example, there's farmland and perfectly good houses. Suppose you'd stayed there, squatting on our doorstep so to speak. Place is in decent shape, so it'd be tempting. We don't need renegade mages so close."

"So," Santon said into the murmurs of assent that met Hans's last statement. "The Aura's capable of disappearing, and who knows what else, and Tess and I are bound together for eternity. Tell me, are you all 'touched' as you put it? Do you sense the Aura? Work with it?"

A younger man, probably in his thirties, chuckled. "Not a bit of it. We know it's there, we can use it to support the crops, but that's it." His tone turned dark. "Magic's something best left to travelers like you two."

"No one comes through here who can't access the Aura?" Santon asked.

"No one comes through at all anymore. Until the pair of you." There was an accusatory tone to the man's voice, as if the place should be on a prime route across the hills.

"And your reasons for being here aren't exactly clear, are they?" That came from a woman standing by the antagonistic man.

Hans stood. "This isn't relevant. For the moment, we need to assure our Tess is safe. For that, Santon needs the facts as best we can say them. Anything else?"

"They say when you've got the fog, the sex is fine." It was a younger woman, judging by her voice. Santon turned, but she was hidden in the crowd.

A ripple of laughter rode over the gathering. Hans grinned. "They say, with no hard evidence beyond that couple with the dozen children. Anything else?"

Comments flew. "There was talk about a pair earlier, both men they were. Lived here, kept their own houses and women, didn't interact much. Seemed neither of them liked the muddle-headedness."

"Can't say I blame them," Santon said, occasioning a chuckle from the crowd. Good. The populace was on side.

"Longer lived," said a hunched elder on the opposite bench, a cold pipe jutting from the corner of his mouth, triggering a stream of comments from the crowd.

"Better able to fight off the agues and such."

"Strong."

"Good looking."

"Good cooks."

"Mean," someone said, putting in a dissenting comment. "Didn't tolerate any back talk. Thought he knew it all."

"That was one of those men," Hans said. "But he was like that before the fog, or so they say."

"It sounds like it's all myth now," Santon said. "And..." He hesitated, but it might as well be said. If he'd learned anything from his lessons with Duncan, it was that the Aura couldn't be denied.

"Does it always involve somebody who is 'touched', as you put it? Who has Auric access?"

Santon's eyes roamed the crowd, but it was Hans who answered. "Not as far as we know. Sometimes it's two from the village. Not aware any of them were touched, but it was so long ago we can't be sure."

Neve spoke up, addressing the townsfolk. "If one of you left, went to Borgonne or the Midland, would you be okay? Are you able to leave the hills?"

A question Santon hadn't thought to ask. He felt a chill cut through the warm day. He could literally be trapped here.

If the myths were true.

Hans said, "One of us did just that, left here maybe twenty years ago. Went west. He came back, said he didn't like the culture there. Doing fine, as far as anyone can tell. Joey, you here?"

A middle-aged man stepped forward. "It was nothing special. A long trek for not much reward. I wouldn't do it again."

"But health-wise you're okay?" Santon persisted. "Your mind's sharp?"

Joey let out a guffaw. "Sharp as it ever was. Never was much in the brains department, my wife says."

The townsfolk joined the hilarity. Joey clearly was a favorite.

Hans rapped his cane against the bench, calling order. "Anything else?"

Into the ensuing silence, Santon said, "So, Tess and I will have to forge our own path. Figure out for ourselves how to live with it." There was no point kicking against fate. He just hoped the town would give them time and space.

Could he possibly stay here forever? Would Tess be willing to follow him out of the hills? Could the townsfolk bear to let her?

Would the spells on the hills let her?

Was this something he'd want?

Sensing the fun was over, the crowd began to fray at the edges as people made their way back to the barn, the fields, the kitchen.

Santon crossed the square and sat the other side of Hans. He leaned forward, trying to connect with Tess. "Do you want to go for a walk?" he asked. "I guess we'd better get to know each other."

She stood, tossing her mane of hair. With a glare in his direction, she followed her mother toward the cookfire.

Hans leaned onto his knees, sharing a look with the other elders. "Never one to be tied down, our Tess," he said. "Give her a while to get used to the idea. Likely she blames you."

Santon sighed. "With reason. If I hadn't turned up, none of this would have happened."

Neve materialized behind him and put a supportive hand on his shoulder, an unusual gesture. "Or could have, maybe with someone else. We can't predict. A merging of energies, a particular pattern..."

He looked over his shoulder at her. "Any or none. Lately, every time I think I'm getting a grip on the Aura, it trips me up."

Hans clapped him on his thigh and rose. "Come on, lad. I could use some help in the barley field. I doubt Tess will be coming back."

Santon patted Neve's hand and stood, releasing her. "Talk to you later?"

She nodded. "This is scary."

His voice dropped. "I know. We'll get through."

He stood still for a bit, as Neve trailed off toward the cookfire. Then he accepted his immediate fate and joined Hans, walking back to the fields.

Chapter 27: Confab

"I reckon we have one day at the most before they get here." Watching the townspeople as they moved about, Neve joined Santon on one of the benches in the square.

Lunch in the hamlet had proved to be casual in the extreme. As the day before, after the discussion with the village, she had found an assortment of leftovers, flat bread, and dried fruits laid out on one of the trestle tables in the community hall and cobbled together a meal.

"It's good," Santon said with his mouth full, waving bread rolled around leftover lentils.

"Barely a day," she continued. "As if we weren't in enough trouble." Neve wielded her own bread wrap and took a healthy bite.

He swallowed. "This place has some advantages. It's peaceful. Hard to imagine things going bad, even with Gauvain on our tail."

Neve took her time. Lentils could get old in a hurry, but it was better than their last few meals on the trail. Adding the fruit made the whole mess tastier. "You're stuck here, or at least stuck with Tess – not that that's bad, necessarily, but scarcely of your choosing. And with Leo and Gauvain turning up tomorrow... I'd say things could get worse in a hurry."

"More complex for sure."

Neve did her best to keep annoyance out of her voice. Santon was unrealistically cheerful, given what they faced. More specifically, what *he* faced. Irreverently, she wondered if he would be quite so perky had the binding paired him with a dour, forty-year-old male instead of the nubile Tess.

Not fair.

"Hey." Santon put his free hand on her arm. "I'm not all that thrilled about things, either, but we've made it this far. Anyway, it feels good to do physical work. What did you do all morning?"

Neve applied herself to the lentil-fruit mixture. After dispatching another bite, she said, "I went to the abricoe orchard. Abricoes are a good choice here, they'll thrive in cooler climates. The trees are healthy, well tended. As you'd expect, I suppose. It isn't like people have anything else to do."

"It's all about survival. No time for taverns or theater performances."

"Mmm."

"So, to get to the point I know you're dying to make..."

Neve grinned. "The stone."

"Yeah. It's okay?"

"Wide awake and tingling like mad, with you so close. Another example of the Aura deciding who should be united, wouldn't you say?"

Santon grimaced. "What I don't like is being the focus of two different spells. I haven't seen or heard any reason to think they're connected, but it is strange."

Santon had been cheerful through their makeshift meal, but now he was serious. "To be honest, I've got almost more than I can deal with right now. Getting out this morning, working in the field helped, but...." He slumped slightly, his gaze going far away, across the cold fire pit toward the track west. "I need some time alone this afternoon to work with the Aura – if it'll even let me. Try to find some answers." Abruptly, he turned to her. "I'm scared, Neve. The fog... and there's something about that girl. She's almost fey, like she isn't quite real. And all that emotion." He shifted his gaze away again. "I'm a little afraid to be around her, even apart from the fog."

She shifted on the bench, a tiny move toward him without touching or impinging on what she now realized was a self-defined isolation, a little Auric space keeping him apart. She had used that type of isolation once or twice herself, when the world threatened to overwhelm her. "Like she might turn on you and claw your face? I know what you mean. But I guess you'll need to talk to her sooner or later."

"Later, by preference. On the surface, I love it here. But at times I find myself itching to get out, get back to Borgonne."

"Come find me if it all gets too much. At least you know me, we were raised in the same world, we've both got an Auric connection. I might be able to help."

Santon shoved the last of his bread and lentils into his mouth and chewed slowly. When the bite finally went down, he wiped a hand across his mouth, then smiled. "Thanks. Never thought I'd say this a few nine-days ago, but you're a pretty good travel companion."

She smirked. "You're not so bad yourself. Be careful, that's all."

"You, too."

They parted, Santon heading for the trail to the goat field and Neve returning to their small cabin. The night had not been peaceful for her, and a nap would be an amazing, rare luxury.

Chapter 28: Who is He, Anyway?

The next day dawned overcast, with impending rain in the air. Neve turned her face to the sky, opening farmer-trained senses. Rain would feel good about now. She hoped the weather hadn't been so dry farther north, and her parents and John were having a successful season.

Hoped, but doubted it. Although she was now some distance south of home, and in the hills to boot, she wasn't *that* far away. Even in a land of numerous microclimates, the weather didn't vary much from place to place.

She walked to the hall alone, enjoying the cloudy day and moist air. Santon was nowhere to be seen. In fact, she had barely laid eyes on him since their talk yesterday. Occasionally she had spotted him at a distance, working on the land or integrating himself into the young men's culture of the village. From what she could see, he appeared to be perfectly content, which made her wonder if he would stay here and she would find herself going back to Borgonne with Gauvain and Leo.

She had adjusted to the rhythm of the village and wasn't running late. All around her the villagers were breakfasting or beginning the working day. She nodded her thanks to the woman doling out a thick porridge, added a handful of chopped, dried abricoes, and seated herself on a bench against the wall. Unlike Santon, she was content to be alone, to watch.

Before she could take a bite, her solitude was interrupted. The woman she privately thought of as the dragon mother, whose name she now knew was Elsa, sat uninvited next to her.

Elsa looked weary; she slumped, just slightly, compared to two days ago. Neve reminded herself to be compassionate. After all, her daughter had been struck by a bizarre spell, courtesy of the Aura, one that could result in her loss should it prove to be impossible to keep Santon in Upper Wem.

And she also had to control Tess, a challenge Neve was coming to appreciate. When not working in the fields, the young woman had spent yesterday flouncing around the village and its environs, radiating defiance. She had said little, however, so Neve wasn't certain whether the attitude was directed at Santon, the village, or her mother.

Elsa said nothing as she ate her porridge, but there was *that* in her manner that suggested Neve had better not move away. Accepting the inevitable, she joined the other woman in their silent breakfast. Elsa finished first – no doubt more accustomed to downing the gummy mixture – and took her empty bowl back to the kitchen before sitting again – positioning herself, Neve thought, for battle.

But her approach was anything but dragon-like. "Tell me about the young man," she said simply, her neutral tone somewhat at odds with the grim set of her mouth.

"Oh." Neve should have predicted this. What else would the village care about, and especially Tess's mother? "You understand, I've only known him for four or five nine-days, traveling as part of a caravan or working at road improvement. We've spoken little of personal matters."

"Ay, but how a man comports himself over days of tedium, or when given a job of work, is a fair marker of his character, or so I believe."

Neve snorted. "I always thought the better marker is how he comports himself after an evening in the tavern."

Elsa nodded, allowing a hint of amusement to cross her face. "A fair point. We have no tavern here, although we have heard of them in tales. The beer comes out, though, on occasion. Some can handle it, and some not."

"The only time he drank to excess, he was miserable with a headache the next day. A beer or two after work is more his style."

"He handles his power fairly?"

A question she had not contemplated. What constituted fairness, where the Aura was concerned? "Let's say I've never seen him use it to compel someone or to cause damage." Not on purpose, anyway. The catastrophe they mutually had caused didn't count. "I can't say he goes out of his way to use it for good. For him, it's more academic. He explores the Aura, tries to understand what it can do."

"So, the fog will intrigue him but not frighten him?"

Neve allowed herself another bite while she thought that over. "I haven't seen him to talk to since yesterday, but he seems content to me. Wouldn't you agree?"

"Aye." Elsa's voice took on a hard edge. "But that could be the possibility of bedding my girl. Men have been trying for her since she turned fifteen."

This time Neve allowed her mouth to quirk in amusement. "I imagine so." Then, remembering who she was speaking to, she added, "Raising her must have been a challenge."

Elsa's snort confirmed it. "And family? Is he good to them?" Elsa leaned forward. This mattered to her, more than the other questions.

"His parents live in Orlan, but I don't think he sees them often."

Elsa frowned. "I thought everyone lived in Orlan. Why shouldn't he..."

Neve shook her head, reminding herself that whatever these people knew of the world outside the hills was based on information years, possibly centuries, old. "I live on a farm northeast of the city. Santon works as a surveyor. He's from Vienne, a small town a couple of days south of Orlan. Many people live in the city, but far from all." She thought it just as well not to mention his training with Duncan and that mage's unexpected demise.

"I see." Elsa took this in. "The young man is not yet attached, then?"

Neve paused. They had never discussed it. Based on the mild flirtation she had observed back in Vienne, not to mention the years Santon had spent in Duncan's compound, she supposed not. "I don't think so. He's never said."

"That's a relief. As much as can be expected, anyway. I can only hope he proves to be honorable to my girl. She's tempestuous, our Tess, but hasn't much experience."

"And you're worried," Neve completed the woman's thought. "We don't know yet what he will do, stay or go. I wish I could tell you more. Amazing, really, how little it's possible to know another person, even after spending most of a season with him. This business has shaken him, I think, although he hasn't said much since that first day. He's a man grown, and I'm sure he has a history of some sort, but he's a good worker. He can be impatient, but he doesn't demand what can't be given. And he likes it here."

Neve paused to take a breath. For her, that was a long speech. But the troubled look on the other woman's face had drawn her out, wanting to make it better.

As if you could.

Elsa nodded a terse thanks and left, presumably to resume her day's activities. A farmer herself, Neve understood the imperative. Because she had inserted herself seamlessly into the rhythm of the village, she deposited her nearly empty bowl in the kitchen and left the common room also, heading for their cottage to tie back her hair before accompanying a team to the vegetable gardens.

Before she could step through the door, a figure standing by the opening to the tiny bedroom whirled and stalked toward her.

There was next to no light in the cottage; the window on the back wall faced north and was heavily shaded by an overhanging conifer. It took Neve a moment to sort out what was happening. By then the figure – which, in the light from the door, resolved itself into Tess – had arrived, because of the step up into the cottage, to loom above her.

"I want you out," the young woman hissed, with enough vitriol that Neve involuntarily stepped back. Tess in her turn moved forward, placing herself solidly in the doorway, one hand on each side of the door frame. The girl's hair was wild, her eyes unfocused.

Horrified, Neve focused on the immediate... yes, threat wasn't too harsh a word. Tess looked ready to physically drag her away if she failed to disappear.

But the town had made her welcome and assigned this cottage to be hers and Santon's. Not Tess's right to dictate. Furthermore, the young woman's histrionics, which she had had time to view first-hand over the last couple of days, had worn thin. "I think not," she said, stepping forward with every intention of charging right through Tess if she didn't get out of the way. And she could do it, too. Years of farm work had built her strength, enhanced, she suspected, by her Auric connection.

Tess backed up, her glare mixed now with uncertainty. Neve strode across the front room to the tiny table and sat, making an abrupt gesture indicating Tess should join her. The young woman slowly approached and perched on the other chair, watching warily. The hostility hadn't burned itself out, though, despite her restrained demeanor.

"I suggest you calm down," Neve said. "You're not making yourself clear. I'm no threat to you."

"So you say." Tess sprang up and began pacing the tiny space. "You live with him, you sleep with him. But that's *over*." She wheeled to face Neve. "Time you get used to that."

By now Neve had sorted out what was going on. "Time for you to take a dose of reality. I don't know where this fog thing is going, or what it will mean to you or Santon. But frankly, that's nothing to do with me, except to the extent he chooses it. Right now, I'm the closest friend he has." She made her voice hard. A touch of cruelty might just get through to her. "If you want him to think of you as more than a hot lay, don't try to control him or decide who his friends are."

It didn't work. *"Friends!* You think I believe you can keep your hands off him? Every night alone here, and all those days hiking the hills? *He's not yours!* He'll never be yours. You'd better get that through your head, or—"

"Or what, Tess?" Neve interrupted. "I'm telling you now, don't try to tie Santon down. He's his own man, and you've barely met him. And for the record, getting to know him will take nine-days. Seasons even. He's a grownup, not a child. He keeps to himself, and he's resentful of any effort to control him. As I said, you can choose to be nothing more than a sexual partner if that's enough for you. Or you can risk driving him away, whatever that would mean for the fog. If you want anything like an adult relationship—"

"You have congress with him!" Tess screeched.

It took Neve a moment to sort out the archaic word. "No, I don't."

"You're lying." Tess sat back down at the table, her fingers clutching the edge so tightly that her knuckles were white. "No woman could lie next to him night after night and not..."

In the gloom, Neve suspected Tess was blushing. She sighed. Their arrangements were basically nobody's business. But if nothing else, she could see Tess was genuinely upset, and probably frightened by the future. "We aren't lovers," she said, "and never have been. He sleeps on a pallet on the floor. Usually we barely see each other, morning or evening. We've talked about his situation, but right now I'm not even sure how I'm getting back to Borgonne."

"Oh." Tess released the table.

"You want some advice?" Sensing Tess was about to flare again, Neve barged on. "Seek him out and talk this through – like adults. He won't appreciate you behaving like a brat. Find out what he's thinking, whether he'll go or stay, whether he's open to considering your opinion." Privately, she guessed he'd dismiss her wishes unless she proved herself to be a rational adult. Santon wasn't used to dealing with temperamental children. "You two have become a couple, albeit a strange one. Only you can work it out."

Tess visibly sagged. "I want to leave, and I don't. I want it to be my choice. This is like an arranged partnership or something."

"Yeah, I get that. Prove you deserve his respect if you want a say in your future. Otherwise..." Her thoughts went back to the superior air he'd brought to that first interview with Leo. "He can be arrogant and stubborn. It's possible to be partners, but if you're going to throw tantrums, don't bother."

That hit the mark. While Tess probably had allowed her frustrations to dominate throughout her life, it wouldn't work anymore.

"I still want you out," she muttered. "It's not appropriate."

"Now that may be a fair point," Neve conceded. "But first, if anyone's leaving this cabin, it's Santon, not me. Second, is there anywhere for him to go?"

Clearly, Tess hadn't thought it through. "Bunkhouse, maybe. Some of the guys built it, didn't want to live with their parents."

"Then it comes back to Santon again, and the others. Not me."

Their eyes locked in the dim light. Neve's Aura-enhanced senses told her she had been heard, but the girl would struggle to admit it. She privately thought someone should have put reins on her much sooner, but it didn't matter now. What was, was.

And good luck to you both.

With nothing more to say, Tess stalked out, her back rigid with dignity. Neve counted to twenty to be sure she wouldn't whirl around and reappear, on the attack again. Then, feeling wearier than before, she hauled herself into the bedroom to track down a hair tie.

In the back of her mind, she wondered how Santon would cope. And how Gauvain and Leo would affect the mix.

Chapter 29: Arrivals

Santon sat on one of the benches on the edge of the village square, grateful for the respite. He and a couple of the other men had been off in one of the far fields, hoeing with fire-hardened sticks, treating the crops to techniques related to the Aura if not exactly touching it – a brand of earth magic alien to him – and checking for insect infestations or the presence of larger herbivores. Even in the hills the crops weren't immune to disease and predation.

The people of Upper Wem worked hard, in ways he had never experienced, but he was grateful for the opportunity to learn from them and exercise his body.

In a few minutes he intended to raid the lunchtime buffet. For the moment, he was content just to sit in the shade. Even the new aches in his muscles pleased him.

Across the clearing, Tess stood shaking bits from her skirt. She had been in the weaving hut, probably carding wool. Discovering her location wasn't difficult, in fact he could hardly avoid knowing her whereabouts with every helpful person – especially the younger men – keeping him informed. Sometime soon he'd have to talk to her, start to get to know her. His hesitancy met an equal reluctance in her; it was evident in the way her gaze skittered away each time their eyes met. They needed to get past their mutual distrust if they had any hope of surviving the binding.

As if to remind him, the now familiar fog invaded his thoughts. Tess was drawing closer.

Well, he chivvied himself, no time like the present to improve their acquaintance. He had just risen and begun to cross the square when a shout stopped him in his tracks.

Neve.

He spun in time to see her bolting from the square toward the trail to Lower Wem, where a young man had appeared. His brain caught up; she had shouted a name.

John? Her brother? Here?

The entire village watched as Neve threw herself into his arms and the two hugged, spinning around like mad things. Despite her obvious joy, Santon felt his heart sink. Because the only conceivable reason for John's presence was that he had been traveling with Leo and Gauvain. Right on schedule.

And wasn't this going to be interesting.

Neve was a woman of the earth, however, not given to flights of rapture, so before long she had dragged John across the square to the buffet tables, most of the town flowing in their wake. As he watched, she equipped them both with bread trenchers full of spiced beans. They joined him at the edge of the square. "Santon, this is my brother," she said, speaking loudly enough for everyone to hear. Dropping her voice, she added, "You know the rest. They'll be here soon, probably before midafternoon." She and her brother plonked down on the bench.

Up close, John was seen to be a tall youth, gangly but strong, with an unruly shock of dark hair, all of him stained by the rigors of travel. He grinned, nodded, said, "Glad to have caught up with you at last," and took a healthy bite of the bean mixture. Appetite came first at that age, Santon thought with a hint of amusement. His Auric senses suggested there was no menace in the boy, none at all. He was young and on an adventure.

Odd he should be one of Gauvain's students, but at least it proved normal people could survive contact with the Black Mage, whatever his reputation.

Matching John's smile, he said, "I'll just grab some food." He left brother and sister alone on the bench. Let Neve have her reunion – or as much as possible as the village elders, rallied into a posse, descended on them.

By the time he returned, the town had established John's credentials as Neve's brother, another one 'touched' by the Aura, and had gleaned the tidbit that two more were on their way. As he approached the elders, he sensed consternation, which resolved quickly into a concern about where they would stow all these newcomers. It seemed the cabin he and Neve occupied was the only guest accommodation available.

He touched Hans' shoulder and nodded to a peaceful corner away from the gathering that had formed around Neve's bench. "The ones coming," he said. "They've been following us. We know one of them, the other's the most powerful mage in Orlan."

"And they bring trouble." Stated as fact rather than question. The man looked worried, as well he might, given Santon's forced attachment to Tess.

"No, nothing like that. We..." How to put this? "We have some knowledge they want. Nothing of significance, but we'd prefer to keep it from them."

Hans ruminated for a moment. "Will you be placing the village in an awkward position. Needin' to take sides?"

Santon shook his head. "No, nothing like that. It's nothing nefarious, I promise. A curiosity concerning the Aura, or maybe the hills. That's the trouble, we don't know much more than they do. We're agreed, though, we don't want Gauvain, the mage, to get his hands on it."

Hans nodded. "I understand."

"I doubt that. But I daresay you will."

"The townsfolk have come to like you, young man. You'll have our support."

That was a boon beyond what he had expected. "Thank you," he said formally and reached out.

The two men clasped arms. Santon wasn't quite sure what it would mean, but he knew an agreement had been struck.

In the meantime, Neve and John were the center of attention. Neve said little, Santon observed, but never took her eyes off her brother, who seemed to be delighted by the company and more than happy to regale them with his adventures on the road. From a distance, the family resemblance was obvious, something in the shape of their mouths, the way they both spoke with their hands flying. Clear also was the deep affection they felt for each other. John's loyalties just might be challenged before the day was out.

Santon's mouth quirked into something that wasn't a smile, nor yet a grimace. More a statement of determination as he watched the crowd, which seemed inclined to share in Neve's happiness, and speculated on what kind of reception the next two visitors would receive.

When Gauvain and Leo appeared on the track along the river, the village was still celebrating John's arrival – which, for some reason Santon couldn't readily discern, was considered cause for a party. Almost everyone had gathered in the village square. Food flowed from the cooking huts, and the noise... well.

The young man was lapping up the attention, and Neve hovered close by like some kind of mother hen. They were well looked after, so Santon worked his way around the edges of the crowd toward the notch. The village would notice the newcomers soon enough, but he needed time with them to judge their mood.

Even from a distance, Leo and Gauvain appeared footsore and bedraggled, showing none of John's resilience. Santon followed the trail from the outskirts of the village, pacing his movement to meet them halfway.

Leo saw him coming and gave a tired acknowledgment with his hand. Gauvain merely plodded forward.

As they neared, Santon could see that Leo leaned on his walking stick, easing a limp. His glower, however, overrode whatever trail-induced discomfort he experienced. No question why. In his view, he and Neve were undisciplined children who had caused him and his boss untold inconvenience.

Too bad. Leo knew why they had fled.

"Sorry about that," Santon said with an attempt at casualness as the men pulled into range. He expected an angry reply from Leo and cold fury from Gauvain, but to his surprise neither man spoke against him. Instead, as they drew abreast Leo held out a hand to grasp his arm.

"Help him," Gauvain said, with *that* in his tone which denied any possibility of not being obeyed. "He's injured his foot."

"I noticed." Santon studied Leo top to bottom. "At least you're ambulatory."

"Everything in me wants to give you a clout upside the head," Leo growled, but his free hand tightened on Santon's arm.

Santon nodded, determined to show no remorse. "No doubt. But you can't deny it's been an adventure. Let's get you into the village."

By now their arrival had been noticed, and several villagers were approaching. Gauvain stood a little apart, staring along the track toward the welcome party, then left the other two behind and strode down the path with every appearance of renewed energy.

He still had said nothing beyond the instruction to assist Leo. Santon read that as ominous.

Neve watched the unfolding drama. It couldn't be said that Gauvain received the quality of welcome her brother had. Did they sense the same threat in his forbidding demeanor that she did? John greeted his master cordially but with no particular warmth, and the village, taking precautions, formed a circle around the newcomers. Only Hans, newly arrived from one of the barns, dared to break the uncertain silence.

"You will be the renowned mage, I take it."

Gauvain rewarded him with a nod.

"The Black Mage."

Neve's attention was piqued; had Santon referred to him so? For that matter, had he mentioned they were being followed? Where was Hans getting his information? The hills, always spooky, suddenly felt spookier.

"A pointless epithet," Gauvain said dismissively.

"Well, I'm not so sure." Hans spoke with a folksy country drawl. Neve allowed her curiosity free rein. Hans was anything but an ignorant bumpkin. In fact, in their occasional interactions he had shown an astuteness and depth of understanding that sometimes amazed her. Disguise, then.

Letting Gauvain think himself superior while they took stock of him.

Supported by Santon, Leo had joined the outer ring of spectators. When his gaze swept her, it carried a wave of disappointment, as if she had let him down. But what did he expect, given her need to protect the stone? Nobody forced them to follow. She managed a half smile and shrugged.

Santon eased the elderly man toward a bench and helped him take the weight off the injured foot.

"Well," Gauvain said, addressing Neve. "I certainly didn't expect a deserted village, much less an inhabited one. I suppose it could be argued that you have led us on a path of discovery. I trust you, or someone, will illuminate us regarding the purpose for this settlement."

Hans spoke up. "Begging your pardon, Mister Black Mage, but the reason is simply that we live here. Whatever the purpose three hundred or more years ago, so things stand now. Our home, and not deserving of disparagement."

Neve grinned. Hans was putting on a show, a backcountry attitude coupled with the occasional big word by way of warning. The village wouldn't tolerate any attitude from the mage.

"Could we get a healer over here?" Santon said. "We've an injured foot."

Two of the village women broke away from the crowd and descended on Leo's bench. The rest remained grouped around Gauvain.

"Accommodation is available, I assume?" the mage queried in a tone that made the request more of a demand.

"We'll come up with something," Hans said, his tone suggesting the proffered accommodation might be anything from a place in the barn to an overnight by the fire. Neve pinched her lips to forestall a grin at the indignant expression flashing across Gauvain's face.

Chapter 30: The Main Event

Night had never felt so ominous.

Reflecting on the day, Neve had nothing to complain about. Leo's foot, which proved to suffer from a mild sprain, had been poulticed and bandaged. The elders had evicted a couple from their home to make space for the two older newcomers, who emerged from their cabin only for a largely silent supper. Neve suspected they both had indulged in a long, much needed nap. John had been bunked in with a few of the younger men.

As she worked through the afternoon in the barley field, she had debated whether to hide the stone where Gauvain wouldn't find it. Finally, she decided against the idea. There was little to be gained now; one way or another, the stone's location, if not its purpose, was soon to be revealed.

Her brother had found instant friends among the younger people of the village. A group of them had trooped off toward the pastures, where John spent the afternoon happily tending the goat herd. He had given her a full report over supper before disappearing, pursuing his own social life.

An interesting day.

Twilight came early as thick clouds moved across the sky, cutting off the last light from the sun. Random gusts buffeted the fire in the center of the square, causing dancing shadows that merged with the surrounding darkness. Neve involuntarily thought of ghost stories her father had entertained John and her with, back when they were children.

She had seen Santon around, but they hadn't spoken since lunchtime. He spotted her as she emerged from the hall after supper and waved her over to the bench he seemed to have claimed for his own personal use. He was just outside the ring of firelight and in an ideal position to watch the comings and goings on the square.

As she sat beside him, he said, "What's the story? Is he always so silent?"

He meant Gauvain. "Not in my experience, but I suppose it's a tool in his arsenal. Another way to be threatening. Did they say anything I should know?"

"No. It's puzzling. I expected them to attack. Instead, they ate and drifted off, scowling all the way."

Hans and Elsa wandered over. "You've not spoken with her," Elsa stated, her gaze spearing Santon. "This can't go on. She's becoming distraught, not knowing."

Neve expected Santon to get his back up, but instead he looked down as if seeking a pattern in the beaten dirt. "I know," he said quietly. "It's just... when she's close, I can't even think. The fog's so dense I can hardly see. I don't know how to do this, what to say."

"You've no thought about whether you'll go or stay?" Hans asked. Neve was impressed by the neutrality in his voice. He might well have been hostile at the thought of losing a loved grandchild.

Santon shook his head, still looking down. "This isn't any easier for me than it is for her. I'm not sure what I have to give her right now."

Elsa released a sigh into the wind. "Something you might work out together?"

"Might," Santon conceded. Then he looked up, stood, and took Elsa's hands. He focused only on her, his voice intense. "I don't want to hurt her or harm the village in any way. As for the future…" His voice trailed off as he turned his gaze to the fire. "Truly, I wish I knew. You'd all prefer I stay, I assume. She seems to long to go, to see new places."

"Not completely," Neve put in. "She's torn."

"This is her home," Santon conceded. "and people here love her."

"Not a reason to avoid getting to know her," Hans said. "You're bound to a stranger, as things stand."

"The fog's a reason."

Santon stood a full head taller than Elsa, but the older woman exerted a dominance over the conversation even Neve could sense. "Stay or go, there are expectations. Time you lived up to them."

"To be fair," Neve put in, "the day Leo and Gauvain turn up isn't the best time to make life decisions."

Elsa dropped Santon's hands and turned to her. "Those men, they're after the stone."

"The…"

Elsa made an exasperated sound. "We're no fools, young woman. Time to decide who's the legitimate possessor."

Neve's voice sounded in her own ears as if it came from far away. "You know about… it?"

"Entirely possible we're not like the people outside the hills," Hans said. "We've developed an affinity, see. I can't claim to know how different we are, since we don't get much chance to compare. But the stones, oh yes. We know about them, and we know you've got one. What happens next, that's the question."

"Oh." It was feeble but all Neve could think to say. Her hand automatically went to her pocket. Given Santon's presence, the stone fizzed with energy.

"What do you recommend?" Santon asked.

Before either Hans or Elsa could answer, the atmosphere around the fire changed. Neve, who had already been mildly freaked out by the looming darkness, shuddered as the gaunt figure of Gauvain stepped into the circle of light, his cape flaring around him in the wind. In that moment, there was no question, none whatsoever, who wielded the power.

Neve fully expected thunder. Although atmospheric pyrotechnics failed to materialize, the effect of Gauvain's arrival directly in front of her was no less fear-inducing. She stood, hoping to lessen the intimidation factor, and swallowed, hard.

"This game has gone on long enough," Gauvain stated, his voice flat. "You know why I am here and what I want."

Neve might be struggling to channel strength to her knees, but the same couldn't be said for Elsa. She elbowed herself between them and faced him, glaring upwards, hands on hips. "What makes you think we would permit you to take it?" she demanded.

Whoa. Neve stepped back until her calves hit the bench, then shifted to the side as subtly as she could. No one paid her any attention. All eyes were focused on the confrontation between the haughty man and the fierce woman.

Ice and fire. Which would prove most powerful?

"I fail to see what business it is of yours." Gauvain drew his cloak closer around him as if to avoid any risk of its hem touching Elsa's linen dress.

"Anything that affects the hills is my business."

"Our business," Hans corrected, shifting to stand next to Elsa. "The village's business."

Santon stepped close to Neve. The two couples formed a rough line in front of Gauvain. Neve was reminded of a game she had played as a child, in which one of them had to break through the chain formed by the others.

"I see." Gauvain whirled and gestured at the fire, which flared to twice its height, sending sparks flying against the dark sky.

"Your point?" Hans asked.

So much for intimidation. Neve did her best not to sputter with laughter.

Next, Gauvain pointed at the ground, which shook, knocking her sideways into Santon. A rift opened at their feet. It wasn't deep – they weren't going to be injured should they tumble in – but a point made.

Hans and Elsa both squatted down. Hans reached into the split in the earth and prodded the dirt with his fingers. "Evidence of drought, for sure. Techniques like that, *properly controlled,* could help us with irrigation. Perhaps you could teach Santon here?" From his squatting position, he shot an innocent glance up at Gauvain.

The mage whirled and strode to the far side of the fire. Neve caught a glimpse of a clenched fist as his cloak tossed in the wind. Then he came back, his face noticeably more relaxed, almost conciliatory.

Change of tack, she thought. Now what?

Gauvain addressed Hans, businesslike and reasonable. "I beg your pardon. I admit I am, shall we say, mildly surprised that the inhabitants of a village so deep in the hills would be interested in a simple stone. Please understand, it was stolen by these two, and I consider it my duty to retrieve it."

Stolen? Triggered, Neve took a step forward. "We didn't—"

Santon put a hand on her arm, drawing her back. "It may be wise to adjourn to the hall," he said.

Elsa and Hans straightened. Elsa turned to a handful of villagers who had gathered around, keeping their distance while straining to see the rift in the ground. Neve spotted Tess, her hair wild in the wind, staring at Santon. At Elsa's gesture, they all backed up another pace or two.

"Yes," Hans said into Gauvain's face. "Santon speaks well. Come."

Gauvain, having lost the initiative, swelled with indignation, but before he could say anything, Hans brushed past, Elsa at his elbow, leading them toward the greater privacy of the hall. Santon followed, keeping Neve in tow. He stopped briefly in front of Tess, where he leaned in to whisper something. The girl reluctantly joined onlookers who melted away as silently as they had arrived.

Santon and Neve disappeared into the hall, and Gauvain stood abandoned by his audience as the first hard drops of rain exploded on the bare ground.

Chapter 31: No Meeting of Minds

The day had been hot, but night and rain had lent a chill to the air. Elsa went into the kitchen to make tisane. Neve followed her, distancing herself for a precious time from the confrontation to come. Leo settled onto a bench, resting his injured foot, and Santon helped Hans set up a trestle table. They all grouped around the mugs of tisane, joined belatedly by Gauvain. The mage, Neve noted with a hint of amusement, chose to bring over a single-person stool and place himself at the head of the table.

Overhead, the storm grumbled, rain deafening on the roof, a wind whipping around the corners. A single tallow lantern on the center of the table did little to dispel the encroaching gloom. Neve was grateful to be safely inside, no matter her companions.

Gauvain made a show of swirling his cape before finally sitting. "The stone is worthless in the hills, I daresay," he stated, commanding the conversation, "but given its purported energy, it mustn't be left in untrained hands."

"Oh?" Elsa cocked an eyebrow. "Has it come to harm? Do you have any notion what to do with it yourself?"

Gauvain shot her a none-of-your-business look and spoke with exaggerated patience. "As I said, it requires study. By someone who knows what he is doing," he emphasized, shooting a glare at Neve. "Not an untrained wildling."

No thanks to you.

"With earth-based skills that you lack," Santon interjected. "As do I. The stone won't respond to you, I'd wager. It doesn't to me, either. It's nothing short of a miracle that Neve was around to discover it."

"Where is it?" Gauvain's question was a command.

"In my pocket." Neve's hands curled around her mug of tisane, relishing the warmth spreading through her fingers. Nonetheless, she itched to reach down and cradle the stone, which tingled comfortably next to her thigh.

Gauvain extended his hand across the table, palm up.

A shaft of lightning struck close by, the thunder instantaneous and deafening.

Hans waited until the reverberations had died out, then gripped Neve's arm, as if she might be inclined to accede to Gauvain's demand. "Don't," he said, and looked directly at her. "Tell me, are you here, as I conclude, in flight from these men? Do you fear them?"

Gauvain slowly retracted his hand.

She got an encouraging nod from Santon, then said, "Fear them, no. But we believe that it is up to the two of us to explore the purpose of the stone. We found it, and it seems to respond only to us."

"What's it doing now?" Leo asked. He had been quiet, almost absent from the discussion.

Neve, her earth-grounded senses alive, put Leo's silence down to fatigue. She smiled; she liked Leo. "It's fizzing. It's always more active when Santon's close, but lately its reactions are more intense, as if it's responding to Upper Wem as well."

Gauvain glanced at Leo, hastily suppressing a flash of puzzlement.

"The town. We're in Upper Wem." There was an edge of irritation in Leo's voice, as if he was annoyed that his more active companion hadn't managed to unearth this simple fact.

"I've heard of Upper Wem," Gauvain mused. "Somewhere, something I've read... You've been here for some time, I conclude?" he asked Hans. Elsa, being both female and without an Auric connection, he ignored.

"Three hundred years, give or take," Hans said.

"And this woman has told you about the stone." His tone suggested Neve, having violated one of the College of Mages' deepest secrets, now stood on trial before him.

Pompous ass.

"Oh, no." Elsa chuckled. "Not she nor Santon either. But we know about 'em."

Gauvain's brows shot up. "More than one?"

Hans grinned. "Don't know how many, exactly." He glanced at Santon, then at Neve, as if asking permission to speak.

Santon shrugged. "Might as well get all the facts. Have you seen other stones? And how did you know about ours?"

"One other," Elsa said. "We found it ourselves."

"In Lower Wem," Hans said.

Neve stilled. "And that's why..."

Hans nodded. "When that stone lost its power, it took the Aura with it, or so we concluded. And it's pretty hard to survive in the hills without protection from the Aura."

"So, they left," Neve murmured, remembering the otherworldly, exposed feeling of the abandoned village.

"Leaving behind those things travelers like you might need, as it's a logical stopping place on the trail. It seemed most sensible at the time," Elsa said. "Possibly they could have continued on there, but it didn't feel right. You've been there, so you know."

Neve felt a shudder capture her innards. The four of them were 'touched', as the locals put it, and she suspected Lower Wem had affected Leo and Gauvain the same way it had Santon and her.

Gauvain steepled his fingers in front of his face, a gesture Neve remembered. "So, your stone controlled the Aura in that village."

"And by extension," Santon said, "each stone is responsible for something about the hills. The spells on the hills."

"The spells, yes. It seems so." Gauvain's voice was faint, as if his thoughts were far away.

"How was the other stone deactivated?" Santon asked.

Hans and Elsa exchanged a look. Hans sighed and said, "It was my mother. Our line seems destined to be entangled with the magic in the hills, even though none of us has ever been touched. She was a little girl, poking around in Lower Wem's orchard as children do. She unearthed it. Knew there was something strange about it, so she brought it into the village."

Elsa picked up the story. "The elders passed it around, but it seemed like an ordinary stone, only oval and polished."

"Green?" Neve asked.

Elsa shook her head. "Reddish, with brown veining. We've still got it, if you want to see."

"I do," Gauvain said, a command. Hans swung his legs from the table and left the room, letting in a blast of storm-tumbled air.

"Anyway," Elsa continued, unfazed, "nothing happened, and they assumed it was some artifact left over from when the trail was built. Until the village healer took it."

She let a pause drop among them. Once again Neve got the feeling Elsa was toying with Gauvain, forcing him to wait. On the other hand, Elsa certainly knew how to command her audience.

"And?" Gauvain prompted.

Elsa shrugged. "The thing flared. Healer got nasty burns on her hands. She's gone now, but about those burns, they healed lickety-split, no scarring even, but she had twinges from where the burns had been for years after. Like as if it was caused by something that wasn't ordinary fire, you know? The villagers, they got her hands in water – the well in Lower Wem's really cold, but the water's tasty, did you try it? Anyway, they got her hands in the water—"

Neve suppressed a giggle. The expression on Gauvain's face...

Patience at an end, he roared, "What happened, Woman?"

"Oh." Elsa turned innocent eyes on him. "Well, she dropped the stone, and it burned the earth, didn't it, right in the road. The scar's still there, maybe always will be. And...they weren't sure what happened. The place felt different. Sort of empty."

Nobody spoke. Neve glanced at Santon, remembering the scorch mark on the road back in Vienne, the atmospheric tempest triggered by their own heightened emotions, the burn on his arm. His thoughts had gone there, too; she saw it in his eyes as his hand strayed to rub his injured forearm.

Hans slipped back into the room, struggling to close the door against a wind that wailed around them, causing the lantern to flicker. Neve shivered. The earth did not lie peaceful this night. She wondered what devastation they would find in the morning.

The door secured, Hans returned to the table in time to say, "Later we worked it out. It had to be the Aura, gone."

"You're right," Santon said grimly. "There's no trace of the Aura around Lower Wem. Even our stone stopped responding."

Gauvain sat up straighter. "How?" he demanded. "How does it respond? Leo says it's a tingling—"

"We'll get to that," Santon cut him off. "The first stone – did it change?"

"Not that any of us could detect." Hans placed a small, reddish polished stone in the middle of the table. Quick as a snake, Gauvain reached over and claimed it. He turned it around in his hands, seeming to be lost in thought.

He's using the Aura to explore it. Neve expanded her senses toward the stone and felt nothing. Whatever energy it once had possessed was depleted. Gauvain's frown suggested he had come to the same conclusion.

Hans and Elsa sat back, sipping the tisane and watching with mild interest. The room had grown chilly as the storm's fury penetrated the crudely constructed walls. A cool current danced around their legs, causing Neve to curl her toes in her boots.

Gauvain slapped the stone down on the table. "While it's interesting to know more than one of these exists, it's hardly relevant to the current situation. You," he growled, pointing with a hard finger at Neve. "Turn it over, before more harm is done."

Hans stood and shifted to stand between Gauvain and the door to the outside. Elsa planted herself by the door to the kitchen. The old folks might not have much chance against an enraged Gauvain determined to escape – or then again, Neve reflected, perhaps they would; the inhabitants of Upper Wem continually surprised her. While this felt like the most ordinary village on the planet, despite its improbable location, there was something just a little – uncanny, she decided – about the whole situation, as if the very ordinariness were a sham. Still, whatever happened next, she suspected it was unlikely she would lose possession, with four of them aligned against Gauvain, and Leo seemingly uninvolved. The stone tingled in her pocket, as if encouraging her.

Santon gave her a tiny nod. The time had come. She slowly extracted the stone. Gauvain's gaze followed her movement hungrily; he seemed to tremble with anticipation. Neve set the stone in the middle of the table near the other one, gave it one last stroke as one might a favored pet, and released it.

It lay there, innocuous.

Gauvain reached for it, his fingers moving cautiously across the table, until at last he touched it, wrapped his hand around it, and drew it to himself. In the heavy silence that filled the room, he studied it, stroked it, frowned. "There's nothing here."

"I told you," Leo said, sounding tired.

"No response?" Santon asked.

Gauvain ignored him, going deep into trance, both hands now wrapped around the stone. When he emerged, the hard edges of his voice gave ample evidence of his displeasure. "You have perpetuated a fraud and cost me vastly in terms of time and energy expended," he said. "I won't forget it."

Neve held out her hand.

"No," Gauvain said, drawing the stone closer to his chest. "I think I will keep this for further study. A souvenir of sorts to remind me to avoid the folly of gullibility."

"I don't think so," Santon said.

Neve rose to her feet, heart pounding, and stepped around the table to Gauvain's side. Assuming a mantle of indifference, he held it away from her. "Or perhaps I won't bother. It's nothing special, is it? Merely a dull green stone. But I see no reason why you should reclaim it."

Neve darted behind Gauvain and lunged. Their hands met on the stone.

A pulse of energy filled the room, briefly turning night into midday. The stone blazed with searing heat, forcing a cry from Gauvain – a cry quickly cut off. He dropped the stone as if scalded. The pulse faded to nothing.

"By the Aura." Suppressing a groan, Gauvain barely got the words out through clenched teeth. All color had fled from his face; his hand, red and clawed, almost glowed in the lanternlight. He cradled the injury close to his chest, covering it with his other hand as if to protect it.

Elsa slipped into the kitchen.

Neve held her hand up, flexing her fingers. The flash hadn't burned her at all. She wrapped her hand in her skirt and lifted the stone from the floor before realizing the padding wasn't necessary. As quickly as it had flared, the heat had disbursed. The stone tingled in her hand as she returned to her seat, dimly aware of Gauvain's quiet moan.

Santon placed himself behind her and put his hands on her shoulders. She leaned her head back against him, eyes closed, fighting shock. She had expected a reaction when she and Santon finally touched the stone together, but this stunned her, as did the injury to the mage. A quiet rustling told her Hans had returned to the table. She wrapped both hands around the stone, squeezing gently as if to comfort it, not to mention confirming ownership.

Elsa returned, carrying a large bowl of water. "Need to kill the heat," she said. Without further preamble she plunked the bowl down in front of Gauvain, seized his arm, and forced his hand into the water.

He gasped, then was silent.

"It took the two of you, in combination, to trigger it," Leo said. "I've long believed it controls the spells at the entrance to the trail. We won't know exactly what it did, if anything, until we get back. But it's clear," he added with a glance to the end of the table, "it doesn't like you. I think I'd avoid any further contact."

Gauvain answered with something that sounded like a low growl but might have been a whimper of pain.

"That makes sense, and we need to go back," Santon said. "Our stone is a long way from home."

"There's Tess," Elsa said, feet sturdily apart, arms akimbo.

"And that's beyond my understanding, but I won't let harm come to her." Santon sighed.

Whatever benefit the water might have conveyed, Gauvain was shaking and had broken into a sweat. Burns were bad enough, but this burn... well, it wasn't natural. And from the look of his hand, it must be agonizing. Nonetheless, he bridled. "More mysteries? What are you playing at now?"

But his companions showed no appetite for further discussion after the drama of the last few minutes. "Not now," Hans said, dismissing the Black Mage as if he were no more than a recalcitrant child. "You can wait until the morrow." A silent message passed between him and Elsa, and he stood. "We're retiring. You are welcome to talk as long as you want, but the crops won't wait and we've a day's work ahead."

"As do Neve and I," Santon said. "We earn our keep here."

Didn't get much more pointed than that. Neve sent him a silent look of appreciation.

Gauvain wasn't budging despite the assault on his nerve endings – not to mention his prestige. "We've come far to find you. I demand to know what—"

"Demand all you want," Santon said. "I'm ready for bed, and I'm sure Neve is, too. Good night to you." He offered a hand, assisting Neve to her feet. "Come on," he said gently. "We'll see how things look in the morning." He led her to the door. Outside, the air lay peacefully over the village, and a few stars showed among the scuttering clouds. The storm had blown itself out; tomorrow would be a day of sun and steam.

"I'll drop some salve by your cabin," Elsa said to Leo as she stood. "Might help."

No one was exactly tripping over their feet to aid the mage, Neve noted. She slipped the stone back into her pocket, where it had lived for many nine-days now, and silently accompanied Santon into the night. Elsa and Hans followed close behind, leaving Leo to deal with Gauvain's injury and fulminations.

Chapter 32: A Chat with Leo

Neve slept surprisingly well, waking only once to seek the familiar tingling from the ever-present stone. Sleep proved to be a decent way to hide from its violent reaction to Gauvain. Despite last night's shock, she kept it close, clutched in her hand or tucked under her pillow.

The morning dawned clear. Later, the infusion of moisture would make the day steamy and uncomfortable, but for the moment she drew a deep breath, enjoying the freshness, before rolling off the narrow bed. As she readied herself for the day, she slipped the stone into her pocket as always.

Santon wasn't there. She concluded she had slept late. Something about Upper Wem scrambled her time sense, but she didn't want the people of Upper Wem to think her lazy.

She found Leo on a bench in the square, presenting his foot to the healer who was smearing it with a greasy salve. "Come," he called to her. "Sit. I want to talk to you."

At least he didn't sound hostile, Neve reflected as she crossed to him. But first things first, and that meant breakfast. "Can I bring you a bowl of porridge?" she asked.

"Lovely, yes." He turned twinkling eyes on her. "I've no wish to go inside. I haven't experienced a morning after rain in a long time."

"Not since before we started the trek south," Neve confirmed. "It feels good. I'll be right back."

The healer manipulated the sore foot, evoking a sharp *Ow* from Leo. Neve smiled as she turned away. Whatever she thought of his boss, she and Leo had forged a friendship of sorts during their shared travels. He had expanded and structured her knowledge of the Aura, proved a useful sounding board for their construction ideas, and generally served as a stabilizing influence on the whole expedition. A father figure, she reflected as she ladled the gummy mess into two bowls. She added handfuls of chopped, dried abricoes and returned to Leo's bench.

The healer was just finishing, wrapping the ailing foot with an encouraging pat. "Walk as little as possible today," she cautioned as she rose with a creaking of knees. "Or you'll be living with this for a while yet."

"Thank you." The old man shared a smile with the old woman, who set off across the square with her salves and bandages, leaving Leo and Neve alone on their bench.

"I'm curious about your plans," he said as he dubiously attempted to stir the glutinous mess in his bowl. "Are you ready to return to Borgonne? I assume you fled to keep the stone from Gauvain, but that problem seems moot now."

"I think the stone's safe enough. I wonder how close we are to the Midland." Neve took a bite, which effectively prevented her from saying anything more until she managed to swallow.

"I talked to some of the residents yesterday. Most of them experience the village as being a little closer to Borgonne. The spells on the hills distort things, and it's never the same for two people in a row, so it's impossible to say for certain. You're tempted to go on?"

With difficulty, she forced the porridge down, making a note to take a smaller bite next time. "Aren't you? I've never seen the Midland. They say it's a completely different culture. But I haven't forgotten we have a road to finish. I sense we're approaching Solstice, but does time pass at the same rate in the hills?"

Leo shook his head, fished out a chunk of abricoe, and ate it. "I don't know. Maybe. Gauvain's earlier crossings seem to suggest it does. We'll be going back. You're more than welcome to accompany us."

"Both of us?"

Leo frowned at her. "Why not? Santon – has he other plans?"

"The fog. It might—"

"That was mentioned yesterday, but no one has explained. Can you tell me what it means?"

Neve nibbled at the porridge, which, with cooling, had become more solid. "It doesn't affect me, but he has some decisions to make." Briefly she explained the bond between him and Tess.

Leo was thoughtful. "So, he could stay, go forward, or return, but always with the lass," he mused. "Any thoughts about what is most likely?"

She shook her head, once again finding her mouth gummed up. The new bite dispatched, she said, "He's avoided talking to her. Says it makes his head even fuzzier when they're close. I've been speculating it may be more than the fog, as she's a bewitching young woman. And tempestuous. The two of them could prove to be a volatile combination."

Leo grinned. "And the girl – does she want to go?"

"When we met her, it appeared she was running away. Hans, her grandfather, caught her just the other side of the notch. There was a lot of yelling."

"So, your appearance was fortuitous, from her perspective."

"The town doesn't want to lose her, and given that she's never known anything else... I suspect she might find the so-called 'real' world less exciting than she expects." Neve, following Leo's example, began digging out the chunks of abricoe and popping them in her mouth.

Leo put a hand on her arm. "We'll talk later." He nodded across the square. Gauvain stood in front of the hall, clearly trying to decide whether to venture in. The mage's left hand sported a loosely wrapped bandage, the pale linen in sharp contrast to his habitual black attire.

Fair enough. Leo either wasn't ready to share or would prefer to do so on his own terms. "I have to get to work," Neve said. "I'm expected out in the livestock sheds today. we want to see if some of the earth-based techniques you taught me will help a donkey with an infected hoof. We always used poultices, as they do here, but maybe I can add some kind of boost."

She stood, Leo rising with her assistance. "I'm sure you've always added a boost, as you put it, but you probably weren't aware of it."

"Good luck," she said in an undertone, as Gauvain, rejecting the hall, strode across the green toward them.

She got a guffaw out of Leo. "No worries, lass. I'm an old hand."

Neve collected the bowls and headed for the hall, nodding to Gauvain in passing.

Chapter 33: A Chat with Tess

Santon found Tess behind the main buildings, outside a nondescript laundry shed surrounded by some of the least inspiring scenery he had seen in the hills. Useful to situate monotonous tasks here, he supposed, but depressing to work in. The land around had been thoroughly trampled; more dirt than grass, low shrubs outlining the yard – and, he discovered, providing places to drape the drying linen. At this time of year, almost everything was linen.

The sun had emerged from the last of the night's clouds full and hot, and the boilers in the shed created a steamy atmosphere. Before he'd been in the yard to a count of ten, Santon could feel moisture condensing on his skin, swirling around his head. A miserable place to work.

Two women and one man labored over wooden wash tubs, scrubbing tunics. Tess's face was red and dewy in the steam. She maintained a constant chat with the other woman, even as she swiped back a lock of her luxurious hair with a forearm. None of them seemed to mind the heat.

Santon minded it, a lot. Borgonne was hot enough in the summer, but without the addition of such humidity. When coupled with his reluctance to spend time with the girl, he found himself growing more irritable the longer he stood on the periphery watching.

The fog didn't help. His carefully rehearsed words vanished in the steam as he watched Tess.

Finally, the other woman looked up and noticed him. "Oh, hey," she said. "Tess, your man's here."

Tess carefully finished scrubbing a tunic, saying nothing, before she so much as glanced at him. She had to have known he was there; the fog affected her as much as it did him. So, she was making a point.

The tunic finished, she handed it over to the man for rinsing and rose from her stool, shaking out her skirt. "You're looking for me?" Her gaze was skeptical, her tone far from welcoming.

"I am. Take a break."

Tess spoke quietly for a moment with the woman next to her, then skirted the wash tubs and crossed the yard. "About time," she said, not caring if she was overheard. "You're making plans and not including me."

"No plans yet. Let's walk." He hadn't meant to be abrupt, but the heat, the fog, her hostility.... Santon turned on a heel and strode away, leaving Tess to follow or not, as she wished.

She didn't wish. After twenty paces or so, the lessening of both heat and fog sank into his thought processes. He stopped. "Look, I'm sorry," he said without turning. "This is tough."

She came up to him and threw the words at his back. "Yeah, and you're such a brave, strong man and all."

He turned. "Well, what do you expect? I didn't choose this any more than you did. And frankly, I'm not ecstatic."

Her flashing eyes penetrated the fog just fine, along with her ire. "And I did? You think you're going to control what happens? Think I'll just trot along behind you – like now? Think again."

She whirled and would have fled had he not grasped her arm.

Her bare arm.

Oh, hell. The magnetism was there. Whether natural or spell-induced... he just didn't know. He carefully moved his hand away and swallowed. "Walk with me, Tess. We don't know each other. We should, before either of us makes a decision."

She stared at him, not quite meeting his eyes, then gave a short nod and moved ahead of him, leading the way back to the town square. He let her go, careful not to crowd her. She cut through the village and took a path he hadn't explored, down toward the river.

The place she took them to was cool and sylvan. A refreshing breeze touched his sweat-dampened skin. The river here flowed steadily, deep and quiet. Santon would give a lot to jump into it. Instead, he sat beside her on a ledge of rock. She kicked off her boots and let her feet dangle in the water; he did the same. The relief, after the appalling heat of the laundry, was visceral.

Tess spoke first. "I want..."

When her voice dropped off, Santon looked at her. As he suspected, she didn't know what she wanted. Up close, it was evident how young she was. Leaving the hills, especially with an older man who was essentially a stranger, couldn't be in her plans, but missing a chance to see the world outside the confines of the village – that scene back when they'd first arrived made it clear she wanted more than Upper Wem provided.

He risked an observation. "Outside the hills isn't that different, you know. Villages, farms, people working, some nice, some not."

"More'n I've got here," she muttered.

"What interests you? If you stay, are you likely to be forced into a life you don't want? Marriage and children, for instance? Or is that what you want? Dammit, Tess, I don't even know where to start. We're bound together…," and the damn fog made every sentence a challenge, "… and we're not even from the same cultures. Tell me how you want to do this."

Tess slipped from the ledge into the water, which came mid-calf, and waded a short distance downstream. The branches of a willow draped around her; she ran first one withy, then another, through her hands, staring out across the water. "I've never even been to the far side of the river, except to the beach over there. We never go beyond. The farthest I've been is Lower Wem. We're warned against, from the day we can walk. How'm I to say if I want to leave or not?"

"From what we're told, you're wise not to explore too far. The hills aren't safe, but no one can say quite where the danger arises." As he slipped off the ledge and followed her through the water, he kept his voice low, forcing out the words he'd said to almost no one else – because she deserved to know. "I was taken from my family when I was twelve. They were happy enough to lose me, since there was money involved. I spent years in an isolated compound, only my teacher and me, a handful of servants. I had a day of freedom twice in a season, when I could go into Vienne, the closest town. But my family moved away soon after they got the coin. I haven't seen them in fourteen years – since he *purchased* me. I guess they didn't care enough to seek me out." The bitterness crept in; he couldn't help it. "Duncan, my teacher, was killed a couple of years ago. I've worked as a surveyor since then. My point is, being out in the world may not be as wonderful as you think."

Tess was quiet, but she regarded him, a small vertical wrinkle between her brows. He was about to speak again when she said, "You're angry. I don't like that."

He shook his head and, following her example, began playing with one of the trailing withies. "Not so much anymore. Bitter, perhaps. I'm old enough to know I can't get the years back."

Her voice dropped to almost a whisper on the breeze rustling the sheltering tree, nearly drowned out by the fluctuating chorus of birdsong around them. "I'm not even seventeen yet."

He closed his eyes. The damned fog had paired him with a child. She was so young... and frightened. To be faced with a decision of this magnitude, despite her bravado, would be a lot, probably too much.

"We've got to get to know each other," he said cautiously. "Understand each other. Figure out what's possible, what isn't."

At his words, she made a rude sound in her throat. "You don't get it, do you? You really think there's a choice?"

He smiled, ignoring the intensity in her words. "Of course there is."

"You're a fool." Her grip on the branch intensified into a chokehold, crushing the leaves. "It's like fate," she spat. "I'm expected to be here, and here I'll be. And now it's the same for you."

What happened to a logical flow of conversation? Stay calm, he lectured himself. Voice of reason. "Not if we choose otherwise. I've talked to your mother and your grandfather. They don't want you to go, but no one's ever said they wouldn't let you."

She yanked the withy with enough force to strip its leaves as she turned to face him, fury and pity warring in her expression. "Are you blind? Look around. How many do you see?"

Santon frowned, confused. "Many? Many what?"

"People," she screeched. "We've under a hundred now. They can't afford to let me leave. I'm prime breeding stock, aren't I? Nice wide hips, pretty enough any man in town would bed me, and willingly."

He let the silence build while he thought this through. "You're saying," he said slowly, "that without you, without young women like you, the town will die."

"Exactly what I'm saying." The full force of her frustration turned on him. "They want babies. Need 'em. And you're saying you'll leave and let my village die out, all for your own lusts."

"I'm saying no such thing," Santon said, grasping for rationality despite the tension seizing his muscles as the implications of her words sank in, "They can't possibly keep you prisoner here if we choose to go."

She reared back. "And now you're asking me to sneak away without so much as a blessing from my mother? How *dare* you?"

"Whoa." He took a ragged breath. "I'm not asking anything of you. That's the point. We don't know what we want from each other."

"I know your wants," she hissed. "I see it in your eyes."

Heat crept over his face. He'd thought he'd masked his desire well. "Any man would want you," he said, infusing his voice with every bit of dispassionate reason he could muster. "As you've just acknowledged. It doesn't mean I'll act on it, now or ever."

She whirled and scurried up the bank where she stood above him, wringing out her skirt. "You'll go and leave me with no choice if I'm to live and not lose my wits. Maybe I want to stay here. Maybe I don't want to be your *woman*." The last word carried a full burden of contempt.

Well past mere annoyance himself, he thrust the withy away and joined her on the bank, brushing the trailing branches aside. This emotional, illogical dialogue had reached its end. "I've never heard so many contradictory statements in one conversation in my life," he said, not even trying to keep his frustration hidden.

Her fury departed abruptly, leaving her drained of energy. "We're not leaving. No point thinking otherwise."

And this wasn't the right time to argue, although her words had kindled a fear inside. He'd already spent too much of his life confined, subject to another person's demands. But he said only, "Let's go back. We both have work to do."

In a segue so abrupt it left him reeling, Tess said, "Not sure how I'm going to live with the fog," as if they'd just had a perfectly normal, sensible conversation.

"Me neither." He left her side to scoop up his boots, her sandals from the ledge. "We'll learn to work with it. Even if it means living at either end of the village. That is, I don't want to imply we'll be... you know."

Well, that was brilliant. But if nothing else, he was absolutely certain that this child-woman would never grace his bed.

Her lips had tightened into a stubborn line. Much like some donkeys I could name, he thought – and wondered how they would ever manage to live in the same village, whether Upper Wem or somewhere in Borgonne.

Silently, he followed her, still barefoot, up the path to the village. Neve could help him disentangle the mess his life was in, he was sure of that. Over the nine-days, he had come to rely on her common sense, her calm in the face of challenges.

Chapter 34: Facts about the Fog

But Neve was nowhere to be found. On inquiring of a man passing through the square, Santon was told she had gone into the animal pens with John, the two of them exploring ways their respective Auric energies, hers earth-based, his of the air, might aid the herds. He didn't manage time alone with her until they both had retired to their cabin that evening.

Already in his sleeping tunic, Santon sat on the edge of Neve's bed, waiting as she washed. They could be siblings, so little modesty was left between them. It had been nine-days since he had really looked at her; perhaps he never had. Neve was a colleague, sturdy and capable, and not in the least his usual preference in a woman. It was odd, then, that tonight he found his gaze caught on the curve of her back, the long muscles of her thighs. There was nothing soft or alluring about her, which had contributed to the physical ease between them. Still...

Enough of that. He spoke without prelude. "We have a problem. Or at least, I do."

"Something new?" Her voice was partially muffled by her towel.

"It's bigger than we thought. Tess says they won't let us leave."

She frowned and wielded the towel vigorously. "There hasn't been a single hint of forcing you to stay. Not one."

"How many would you say live here?"

Neve turned to rummage in the small stack of clothing at the foot of her bed. She pulled a clean tunic over her head before speaking. "A hundred, maybe a few more."

"And how many children?"

"About... maybe seven or eight?" Her face froze as the implications hit her. "They're below the number they need to survive."

"Exactly." Santon heaved a sigh and leaned forward, elbows on his thighs. "And Tess is at a prime age to produce more. I am too, I suppose. So, she says they'll force us to stay here. How, I don't know."

Neve nodded and worked her wet hair with the towel. "This fog... perhaps it's designed to guarantee there'll be enough adults of child-bearing age to assure the town's survival."

"Makes as much sense as anything. But there's something else." He paused. "They've told us about the fog and how Tess and I can never be far apart. But Neve... what if it isn't true? What if they're using this fog to bind me here?" His voice dropped – awareness of his own vulnerability kept him cautious. "What if it's a lie?"

"You mean you might not be bound to her at all? You might be able to walk away? Would you want to? Would it be fair to Tess?"

"Perfectly fair, if it's all deception."

"What does Tess want?"

"No clue. I tried to talk to her, but I've never had such a confusing conversation. All I can figure is, she's really young. I remember when I was her age, wanting to train with Duncan, at the same time wanting to run."

Neve tossed the towel onto their pile of dirty clothing on the floor. "What do you suggest? Would you leave her behind?"

"Not unless we're sure."

"Is there any way to test it?" Neve sat beside him, their shoulders touching. She was solid, Neve was. Physically, but in her mental habits as well. He couldn't have a better ally.

A light tapping sounded from the door. Santon jerked upright, then chided himself. The whole situation had him on edge. Since he couldn't imagine anyone seeking him out, he looked askance at Neve.

"Of course we answer it," she said lightly as she stood.

She formed a light ball as she passed through the main room and opened to the door to – who else? – Gauvain, a dark stain against the dusk, wrapped in that infernal cloak.

The Black Mage stepped in without waiting for an invitation. Santon took his time about joining them in the main room. In the dim glow from the light ball, the three of them eyed each other.

Santon wasn't in the mood for Gauvain's posturing. "What do you want?" he demanded.

"A word," Gauvain said. "I believe I have discovered something that might be of interest to you."

"I find that hard to believe." Santon gestured at the small table; Gauvain commandeered one of the chairs with the air of a lord mayor preparing to address the populace.

Neve took the other chair. Santon leaned against the wall, staring at the mage.

As if he were speaking to himself – in other words, ignoring them – Gauvain said, "I have been doing some research on this fog of yours. I believe it is possible to split it, if not dissipate it altogether."

Santon's focus became more intense; he leaned forward.

Neve's brows raised. "Wouldn't others with Auric abilities have discovered this before?" she asked. "Someone would know."

Contempt replaced pride on the mage's face. "I daresay some of them did. There would be little point in sharing such knowledge outside this benighted town. What is more surprising is that neither of you sought to free yourselves from the spell."

"Only Santon," Neve said. "It hasn't touched me."

The mage rolled his eyes. "A quibble. You choose to involve yourself, although your powers are hardly compatible with the problem."

"Granted," Santon said. "I've sensed from the beginning that this is magic of air, or possibly fire. Neve's earth-based skills won't help much."

"You've tried to manipulate it?" She shot a look at him.

"Of course. Not with any success, but then I haven't had much idle time." The last words were emphasized, a dig at their guest and his failure to contribute to the welfare of the hamlet.

Gauvain ignored the comment. "Are you interested or not?" he demanded. "I assure you, I have more productive uses for my time than assisting failed apprentices—"

Santon cut him off. "Don't you dare!" he growled. "You're the one responsible for my master's death. I was within months of qualifying as a mage when he made that ill-fated visit to your blasted tower."

"And was stabbed by an intruder. I know better than you what happened." Gauvain stretched, as if working out a kink in his back. "The energy in my study was disrupted for weeks.

And I certainly haven't seen you coming to me to finish your training. If you truly were committed—"

"Your reputation precedes you," Santon said sourly. "Go ahead. What have you learned?"

Outside, a bird shrieked and wings beat the air. Neve sighed. Now that the mage's shield of intimidation was slipping, Santon had to agree his antics had become tedious.

"Patterns in the fog, which you would have noticed had you been paying attention." By now, Gauvain focused solely on Santon.

"You try living in the midst of it."

Gauvain made a dismissive gesture with his healthy hand. "There is a wave pattern. The wavelength compresses when you and that girl are close together, while the amplitude increases. The combination leads to the appearance of greater density."

"I see," Santon said slowly. "And to split the fog..."

"One possibility is to stretch the wavelength to breaking," Gauvain said.

"Which leads to madness," Santon mumbled.

"Another is to provide a counter wave. One whose amplitude cancels out the one creating the fog."

Neve sighed and stood, gesturing for Santon to take her place at the table. This, he knew, would be far beyond her understanding. She settled against her pillow, listening through the door as they tore into the problem.

When Santon next glanced in her direction, she was fast asleep.

Chapter 35: A Light in the Dark

Neve saw little of Santon over the next few days. He spent all his spare time huddled with Gauvain and John in Gauvain's cabin. Occasionally they would venture out past the barley fields, as if they were testing the strength of the fog as it stretched. The thrust of their experimentation seemed to be how to break apart these wave things and free Santon from the spell. The purported waves in the fog were completely invisible to her, and only her own mage training prevented her from scoffing at their very existence.

The villagers were curious. She concocted a story about ongoing training. Santon agreed to it, although he wasn't happy being demoted to student.

The real question, to her, was where the spell originated. Was this some mischief from the hills, or – more sinister – did Upper Wem itself control the fog? But if the point of the fog was to keep Santon in the village for his expected breeding value, they were unlikely to tell her. Hans and Elsa were unfailingly polite and welcoming, as was everyone in the village, but when she thought about it, their discourse held little substance, and her questions were politely ignored.

Leo was her ally. She met him on a bench tucked against the edge of the square where some tree-based shade was available, over a lunch of lentils.

"I think," he said gravely although his eyes twinkled, "if I have to face another day of this, I'll rebel and set out for Borgonne on my own." He gestured with the bowl. Today the lentils included some bitter greens, but little seasoning otherwise. Neve wondered if her body was getting enough salt.

"Do you understand what they're doing?" she asked. "Santon's given up trying to explain. I guess it's like me trying to explain the stone. At some level, I understand it, but I couldn't begin to tell how it works or what it's intended for."

Leo poked morosely at the lentils. "The stones control aspects of the spells on the hills. The evidence of the red stone proves that. Even if you and Santon activated yours here, we probably wouldn't know what it did, if anything, since its purview most likely is the hills near the tower ruin."

"That seems so long ago," Neve murmured. She forced down another bite, guiltily aware she should be grateful for any food at all.

Leo sighed a little as he stretched first one leg, then the other. "I'm glad for the extra rest," he admitted. "My foot's still aching a little. I don't look forward to the walk back."

"I do." She dropped her voice. "The longer we're here, the more I'm ready to leave. There's something about this place that just doesn't sit well. I can't explain it."

"I know what you mean. Something's niggling at John, I think, but Gauvain doesn't seem to notice, perhaps because he's so caught up in their research."

"A different energy? John has touches of earth, I think, but not Gauvain or Santon. I should have realized, working with John, that having different affinities means different ways to access the Aura. I always assumed it was preference, not something innate. And another thing – Santon told me he couldn't actually do half the assignments you set me."

"A source of frustration for him. Our system of mage training tends to emphasize air magic at the expense of the others. I've never known anyone with developed abilities in water."

"Mages. Odd creatures."

Her dry assessment provoked a chuckle from Leo. "So true." He leaned a little closer, speaking quietly. "Do you ever feel you're in danger?"

Neve's eyes widened. "No. Not at all. Do you?"

He shook his head. "Not exactly. It's just this feeling, as you said, that things aren't as they seem. That I'm missing something." He stared out over the quiet square. "I've always been the soldier, the one who makes sure our environments are safe. Even as a boy, Gauvain was wrapped up in his mysteries. He likely would have walked off a cliff or two if I wasn't acting as our eyes and ears."

"I love the image, thank you." Neve stood, shaking out her linen trousers and picking up the bowls. "I'm due in the barley."

"And I shall hobble to the kitchen. They've discovered I'm handy with a knife, and something involving many carrots is planned for supper."

"In that case, you can drop these off in the dining hall." Neve handed over the bowls. She felt a momentary urge to kiss the elderly man on the cheek. Instead, she waved as she crossed the square to the trail leading to her cottage and the barley field.

Neve was restless that night. Tomorrow would be the day; Santon was ready to execute their working and wanted to meet with them all at the river the next morning – a secluded stretch south of the barley fields – for a planning session.

Because a lot could go wrong, and even if it worked, the implications needed to be recognized and prepared for.

The impending experiment weighing on her mind, she finally gave up on sleep. She quietly unfolded from her bed. Outside the cabin door she slipped on her boots and set out along the road toward the village.

The night was crystalline, the air with a hint of crispness never noticed during the day, the stars rampant across the firmament. In the square, Neve stopped and stared up for a while, mapping the stars she knew, judging their positions – not for the first time – now that she was so far from home. Seeing those familiar landmarks was comforting, a reminder that the hills, however odd they were, still formed part of her world.

As she lowered her gaze, she became aware of a faint glow behind the cabins along the trail on the far side of the square. Near the laundry? But surely no one would be washing at this time of night, and why would anyone be guarding the ramshackle boiler and tubs?

Using her earth-based Auric abilities to move silently, a technique she had mastered many years ago, Neve ducked behind the hall and watched the scene unfolding two cabins down. Elsa and Tess stood in the laundry clearing in the faint glow of a shielded lantern. Tess appeared to be practicing an intricate hand movement, coached by her mother. Both women were intent on their work. Neve couldn't hear their words but did pick up a rhythm in the quiet voices.

Tess let fly with a growl of frustration, and whatever they had been doing stopped. Elsa stepped forward and landed a slap across the girl's face. "Concentrate," she snarled – that, Neve heard clearly.

But then things changed in a flash. Neve froze, almost afraid to breathe. Where Tess had stood was a thin, defeated-looking girl with lank, dark hair. A vision? It only lasted a split second, then Tess was back, and the two women resumed their hand motions. Elsa lectured as they worked. "You know your job."

"I told him we weren't leaving," Tess protested.

"Now we've got that mage interfering..."

Tess continued to protest, but it seemed half-hearted.

A hint of fog condensed around the girl's hands. Spellbound, Neve watched as Tess stretched the wisps.

So. Neve blinked a couple of times to clear her vision and very slowly, very carefully, made her way back around the hall. No pausing to admire the stars this time; she didn't stop until she had shut the cabin door behind her. After casting a small light ball, she put a hand on Santon's shoulder.

He woke immediately. As if the slight quiver in her hands was sufficient to alert him, she felt him tense, but his voice was quiet. "What?"

"We have to get out of here," she whispered. "It's all a lie. Even Tess. Everything."

His brow furrowed. "The fog?"

"They control it." Neve left her crouch beside his pallet to perch on the edge of her bed. "I just watched Tess create it."

"Oh, hell."

Sotto voce, she told him about her restlessness, her decision to step outside, the odd encounter she had witnessed between Tess and Edna. "It's a glamour of some type, I think. She's not what she seems."

"So, it's all staged to keep us here, or me at least. They probably knew we were coming as far back as Lower Wem."

"Not all, I don't think. That first day, Tess trying to run away, that was real enough. I suspect Hans saw a solution when we appeared in the field, and he made it happen." Neve was looking around the cabin, inventorying their possessions, calculating how long it would take to pack. "How they'll react if you break the fog tomorrow..."

"At least I won't feel guilty about it," Santon said. "If there's a rebound, we could be injured. Given what you've told me, I won't blame myself."

They discussed their departure briefly, but there were too many unknowns to plan. Finally, Neve curled onto her bed, her hand wrapped around the stone. "Sleep," she announced, "as much as we can with whatever's left of the night. We'll need it."

Unusually, Santon leaned over and placed a hand on her forehead, easing her eyes closed. "Air clears the thoughts," he said. "Sweet dreams."

Her mind fought sleep in favor of planning the morrow, but it was a lost cause. Her last thought as she drifted into unconsciousness was whether it would be possible to commandeer or scavenge provisions for the trek without anyone noticing.

Chapter 36: Quake

After breakfast, when the citizens of the hamlet were engaged in their workdays, Neve stood with her colleagues in a circle at the isolated spot by the river. A narrow path had led them through dense, high scrub to the riverbank. Several upright willows lined the water, but there were few other trees.

Neve's nape tingled, although she had taken the precaution of casting a protection circle. She couldn't let go of the need to scan the environs, convinced they were being spied on. But really, what difference did it make?

Santon relayed the information Neve had passed on the night before, allowing her to keep a watch on their surroundings.

Leo stated the obvious. "After today we will no longer be welcome here."

"If harm comes to Tess, they'll probably lynch us," Santon said.

"We will execute the working this afternoon from the trail to Lower Wem," Gauvain decreed. "It would make sense anyway. The further away we are, the less risk to you."

Santon nodded.

"We'll need supplies."

"We can hunt and forage, the same as we did to get here."

The look of distaste on Gauvain's face suggested he had done no such thing.

"We need a ruse," Leo said. "A picnic or something that will let us take more than our share at lunch."

"Be sure you have plenty of water," Santon said. "Gather what food you can without raising questions. Dry stuff. Waybread is perfect."

Gauvain made a disgusted snort.

"It's nutritious and calorie rich," Leo said.

"Guys my age are always hungry," John contributed. "I always stock up anyway, so a little extra won't be noticed."

John was slightly on edge, Neve noted, and eager. This was probably the biggest working he had ever been a part of – the realm of the mage made real. She shot a smile at her brother, who grinned back.

With nothing more to be said, the group fell silent. Santon and Gauvain stared at each other. "Ready?" Santon asked.

"The sooner we do this, the better," Gauvain confirmed.

Neve caught a falter in Santon's voice, though she doubted anyone else did. From that more than anything else she gathered the extent of the risk he'd be taking, and how much he was worried about it. But it was going to happen. The two men spoke quietly, as if rehearsing. She began to remove the protection circle.

There was a permutation in the atmosphere. She and Gauvain looked up at the same time. "We're not alone," he said, very quietly.

They had made their circle on a flat piece of land near the river. Without further spoken agreement, they drew it tighter. Overhead, a bank of dark clouds had gathered to the north, spreading rapidly over the sky. Within seconds the bright day turned to twilight. A small wind danced between them, cooling the air to the point of discomfort.

"Intimidation," John said with a chuckle, but his voice was pitched slightly too high.

"For the moment, ignore it," Leo said. "Are we all clear about our next steps? Pack, including water. Eat well and select provisions for the trek. Meet at Santon's cabin midafternoon and be ready to leave."

"And tell no one," Santon added. "Make it look like a casual hike."

"Gauvain and Santon will complete their preparations this morning – not you," he said with finality as John started to interrupt. "You're not sufficiently experienced." At Gauvain's nod, John subsided.

Santon stood and wandered closer to the river, staring downstream. Planning the assault on the fog, Neve speculated as she finished dismantling her protection circle. She knew him well by now; he would spend the time before they attempted the rending in rehearsals, going over the steps again and again to execute the spell as perfectly as possible.

Leo was about to say more when the ground rumbled beneath them. "Not another one," Neve moaned. Earthquakes were common throughout Borgonne. In the hills they had occurred occasionally, mostly mild shivers like this one. But then she was quiet, listening to the earth. "No," she said. "This is different. This is—"

The earth heaved, throwing them all off balance. A sharp crack filled the air. The ground once again buckled.

"*Neve!*"

Before she could work out what had happened, Santon tackled her, shoving her bodily to the side and landing on top of her. A rustling that started out slowly, then built into a crash, contributed to the shaking. She found herself pinned face down by both Santon and a second impact an instant later. While the earth continued to shudder, she managed to turn her head. Where she had been, one of the willows now lay. She and Santon were tangled in its branches, but at least had missed the force of the trunk's fall.

"Hey," she said quietly.

"Are you okay?" Santon's voice was shaky.

"I think so. You?"

"Don't know yet. Something hit my back."

"Fingers? Toes?"

A pause. "Seem to be working."

She heard the others shifting around, accompanied by curses. "Help me here," Gauvain commanded. The branches around them shifted.

"Gently. We don't know if they're hurt." Leo's voice. He squatted near her head. "Santon? Can you move?"

She felt shifting, then Santon said, "We're pinned – by a branch?"

"We'll get it off." John's voice sounded dazed as his boot appeared in her field of vision. "We'll need to lift and drag it over there. Be careful it doesn't fall back."

"It won't," Leo said grimly, and began assigning places.

In the end, moving the tree without risking further harm proved too complicated, so they removed individual branches. With only their trail knives, it was time consuming. Neve lay still and waited, more than conscious of Santon's warm weight above her. Funny, she hadn't thought of him as a human male at all during their tumultuous relationship. He was adversary, colleague, companion, but... man?

Something to consider another time.

Finally, they were freed from the branches pinning them down. John was on the ground beside her immediately. "Sis? You okay?"

Santon started to move but stopped. "Hurts," he reported. "Just bruised, I think. I'm kind of shaky. Someone give me a hand?"

"Wait." Leo knelt. Based on Santon's grunts, Neve assumed he was running his hands over him, seeking injury. Lying under Santon was a new experience for sure, and she decided she wouldn't mind it in another environment. But the ground was hard, and he was getting heavy. "Finding anything?" she called.

"He's okay." Leo stood. There was some more shuffling, and Santon's weight lifted as he was assisted up. Freed, she rolled enough to see him sitting next to her – and sending her a look surely the others weren't supposed to see, one compounded of fear and... interest?

She reached a hand, and he grasped it. Their eyes met. His very clearly conveyed they had a lot to talk about, but not now.

Leo scanned their horizon. "No sign of our visitors."

"You sensed them, too?" Neve asked.

He shook his head. "Saw ripples in the scrub that shouldn't be there."

To her disgust, Neve found she was trembling. It wasn't as if she hadn't experienced numerous quakes before, but something about this one felt wrong, as if the earth fought the vibrations rather than rolling with them. She couldn't quite put it into words, but Santon picked up on her uneasiness.

"Change of plan," he said. "They knew about this meeting and did their best to disrupt it, so I think we'll to have to leave surreptitiously. Tonight. We have to go back to the village now, although I don't want to, because we need our water containers, cooking supplies, clothing..."

"Agreed," Gauvain said. "Your energy is too scrambled to attempt the rending any sooner."

"Also," Leo said, "we couch this morning's events as an unfortunate accident. Agreed?

He was met by grim nods. The implications of what hadn't quite happened were beginning to sink in.

Santon turned toward the barley field and groaned low in his throat. "Sorry, back's sore. I'd also like to try for some healing before we set out. Neve?"

"Sure, if it's just bruising." She stood, using Leo's hand as a support, and took a tentative step away from the downed tree, toward the road.

The others followed. No one said a word.

The villagers had caused an earthquake, and almost killed her. Neve didn't know how to absorb this information, other than to shelve it and get on with ordinary tasks. Working healing techniques for Santon would be grounding, just what she needed.

Chapter 37: Getting Out of Here

Santon spent the afternoon flat on his stomach while Neve applied poultices and unguents and waved her hands in some way that made no sense to him, but did impart pain relief, at least temporarily. Nonetheless, he was concerned about his ability to walk any distance, especially with a pack slung over his shoulders.

John had volunteered to carry the pack. He'd declined the offer, then cursed himself for a fool, letting pride get in the way. He supposed he could grit his teeth and bear the pain, but wasn't looking forward to it. Neve had rolled her eyes when he shooed her younger brother away. She wouldn't provide a sympathetic ear for male foolishness.

By late afternoon, when she took a break from her incantations, he tried a few of his own, simple air-based spells that had helped back in his youth, when bruises were a way of life. They didn't seem to do much; he wondered, with hindsight, whether Duncan, perhaps through guilt at having caused the bruises, had augmented the spells to give him some relief. If so, the mage had never imparted the secret.

Probably it would be better if he got up and moved around. Neve had brought him lunch, but he should be able to make it to the dining hall for supper. Refusing to groan again, he struggled to his feet.

Damn tree.

He'd have to move carefully, but... yeah, it would give him time to think. *Solo* time to think.

The awful truth was, he had *liked* lying there on top of her. Liked the feel of her robust body, muscle with just the right amount of softness. Come to think of it, he'd missed her company over the last few days while he worked on the fog with Gauvain and John.

But come on. He'd known a woman or two. Slender, flirtatious women who understood about men and their needs. Not stubborn, or argumentative, or, heaven forbid, a mage with power equal to his own. Not someone he'd constantly be tested against.

He reeled in his thoughts. It wasn't a competition. Neve had never challenged him, except to get his best ideas, his best magic on the table. Between them, they were building a damn fine road.

Suddenly, that idea of working on the road felt like heaven, the best place in the world to be. All they had to do was survive the hills.

After walking around the limited confines of the cottage for a while, Santon made his way to the dining hall, praying that no one would slap him on the back. He helped himself to a piece of barley bread and a bowl of stew, made with an unknown meat and – surprise – lentils, and found a seat against the wall next to Leo. The two men eyed each other, each gave a terse nod, and they ate in silence. Across the room, Neve and John chatted with Hans and a few others. There was no sight of Gauvain.

"Meditating," Leo said quietly, reading his mind.

"Should be eating. Strength." It was as if they were communicating in code.

Leo surreptitiously shifted aside his overtunic to reveal a healthy supply of foodstuffs. As well, he openly carried a bowl holding several pieces of the barley bread soaked in gravy from the stew. If he took supper to Gauvain, it would go unremarked, but Santon silently added thievery to the man's skill set.

No one approached them during his meal, which was in itself unusual.

Tess entered and eyed him from across the hall. Santon felt his mind go numb, but by now he was almost used to the fog. Sometime tonight he'd be free – or so he hoped.

He waited until most people had left, detouring by the serving tables where he helped himself to handfuls of barley bread and dried fruit. Jerky would have been a nice addition, but meat appeared to be in short supply and carefully rationed. Ah well, he was a good hunter. They would be fine.

Back in the cabin, where he was at sufficient distance from Tess that the fog was barely noticeable, he arranged his supplies on Neve's bed, then carefully wrapped the food in wax-impregnated linen and stowed it all in his pack. He dropped his few possessions on top. That done, he sat and waited impatiently for Neve to return. His back needed more attention before they left.

They met Leo's party in the middle of the night and inched their way to the outskirts of the village. Their exit had been uneventful so far, which made Neve nervous. The sky had cleared from the heavy cloud bank that accompanied the quake, and the path was visible by starlight without resorting to light balls, or what Santon called magelights. The five of them walked speedily – and yes, Leo had no trouble keeping up – but with care toward the gap in the range separating the two valleys.

As the path joined the river within sight of the pass, a group of seven men materialized, seemingly from nowhere. Magic, Neve thought, and uttered a silent curse for not paying closer attention. By now they all had a good idea of what the villagers were capable of.

"Nice night for a walk," Hans said. He stepped out in front of the others, the anointed spokesperson.

"Very," Santon replied agreeably. "In the ever-changing nature of our pilgrimage, it seems we are now needed elsewhere. We must thank you for your warm welcome."

To her right, she heard Gauvain shuffle impatiently, but he said nothing, thank the Aura.

"Not mannerly at all, leaving without so much as a fare-thee-well. In fact, it just might give rise to a notion you're sneaking away." Behind Hans, a couple of the men advanced until they stood shoulder to shoulder.

"Events transpired to make it necessary for us to depart. Naturally, we had no desire to disrupt the village at this late hour. Please convey our kindest regards. Your hospitality has been peerless."

Under cover of darkness, Neve rolled her eyes. Santon was laying it on, his voice unctuous, almost syrupy. Did he really think they'd be able to get past these men, who obviously had been on the watch for just such a break, without a struggle?

No, she realized. He was buying time while they all had a chance to assess. John stepped slightly away from her. Gauvain shifted closer to Santon. Leo hung back, to her relief. However surprising his capabilities, his age would render him a liability.

"Thing is," Hans said, "that's not how we run things here. We have expectations about our guests. That they'll behave in ways that don't raise suspicions, for instance. All in all, we think it best you turn yourselves around and return to your cabins. In the morning, we'll discuss next steps."

"I'm sorry," Santon said calmly. "We can't do that."

"I'm afraid you have no choice," Hans countered, just as calmly. "We have our ways of conducting matters in the village. You're stepping afoul of 'em."

"And I must tell you there is no choice, for you or for us. You've provided respite, and now your job is done."

One of the men behind Hans shouted, "There's the matter of Tess."

Neve was certain no one present had forgotten about Tess, but before Santon could reply, the air around them became denser, more opaque, as if the fog bedeviling Santon had expanded to envelop them all. Gradually – but altogether too fast for Neve's liking – the figures confronting them faded into the obscurity. Hans could be seen, barely, with his two supporters, but the others swiftly became invisible.

The fog swirled, seeming to catch shards of starlight, creating a dizzying array of light and shadow. Neve had to shield her eyes to avoid being hypnotized by it. Santon had days of experience with the fog, Leo was an old campaigner and was unlikely to allow himself to be ensorcelled, and Gauvain brought years of experience with Auric mysteries. But her brother? She glanced to her left. Sure enough, John stood as if entranced, his head moving slightly as he followed the hypnotic patterns dancing in the air. "Don't look," she whispered furiously to him, but he showed no sign of hearing.

His voice pitched to carry no further than Santon, Gauvain said, "If we intend to try our cutting technique, I suggest now would be a suitable time."

The fog failed to mask sound. The men confronting them were spreading out, creating a loose semicircle large enough to prevent any of them from shifting far off the path. In effect, they were to be herded back to the village, if the townsmen had their way.

Santon stepped back, reaching Gauvain's side without incident. Facing each other – each watching the other intently – the two men began actions that made no sense to Neve but were obviously well rehearsed, involving close coordination of their three hands – for Gauvain kept his burned hand carefully at his side – and muttering, in unison, words she couldn't understand. Around her, the fog swirled more quickly, and a strange tension gripped the air unlike anything she had ever experienced. It seemed to penetrate her viscera, pinch her brain so that thoughts were forced out to merge with the dark morass around her.

Everything froze, the men, the landscape, everything except the constantly swirling darkness surrounding them. Time became meaningless; to her dying day Neve couldn't say whether they were all in stasis there for a minute or a nine-day. Only Santon and Gauvain seemed able to resist the drugging fog.

Then she heard more footsteps, closer this time. Quietly, so as not to disrupt the spell, she whispered, "They're coming."

There was a nerve-wracking pause as the quiet chanting wound down and silence pervaded the landscape. Then Santon let out a guttural cry, and both mages made downward slashing movements with their hands. As quickly as it had appeared, the fog dissipated, but with a rebound force that knocked Santon and Gauvain from their feet and left Neve staggering.

When she regained her balance, she took stock. Santon and Gauvain were picking themselves up. Leo had fallen and remained down, whether from weakness, injury, or prudence she couldn't tell.

Two of the villagers were missing, the others were staggering to their feet. And there was no sign of John.

Chapter 38: Cabin Fever

They were placed in Neve's cabin, and a guard was posted at the door. Leo had been allowed the single bed, where he collapsed, although she couldn't detect any injury. Shock, she concluded, and emotional overload.

From one of the chairs drawn up to the small table, his forehead on his hands, Santon muttered, "At least now we know what we're up against."

"Unfortunately, so do they," Gauvain countered. He had commandeered the other chair and turned it so he could rest his head against the adjacent wall.

Santon straightened and stood. "Sit," he commanded, his gaze on Neve.

She started to protest, then gave it up. In truth, she had nothing left, and wondered a little how Santon and Gauvain were remaining upright. As she sank into the chair, Santon propped himself against the wall next to her. "They won't hurt him, will they?" she asked. A stupid question, but at least she had been able to mask her anxiety. Gauvain already had little enough respect for her, a mere untrained earth mage. They didn't need a sniveling female to add to their problems.

"I doubt it," Santon said, and gave her shoulder a quick squeeze. "I think they have other uses for him."

"What?" Need to know was clear in her voice. Gauvain also turned a sharp gaze on Santon.

"We've agreed they need breeding stock," he said. "John's a better choice then me, being younger."

"And less experienced, more malleable," Gauvain added. "But he's not without resources. One of my best students, in fact. I'd like to know his whereabouts."

"He's okay," Neve said. "They've got him in your cabin. They gave him water and some seasoned ground nuts."

Her statement was greeted by a stunned silence. After a time, Gauvain said, "You know this, how?"

In the other room, Leo rolled onto his side, his face toward the wall. Still worried about shock, Neve stood and draped a light wrap over him before returning to the other two. "John told me. We've been sending messages back and forth for years. Not always perfectly, but I could—"

Gauvain sprang to his feet. "I don't believe you," he barked. "He would have told me."

They were interrupted by a stranger, who came in without knocking and dropped two thin pallets on the floor at Gauvain's feet. "Sleep well," he muttered as he turned and left, slamming the door behind him.

Neve shrugged and suppressed a smirk. "Why? We both assumed it simply came with our other abilities. He's much better at it than I am, probably because of his air affinity. He checked in right after they dumped us here. I've been reluctant to try to reach out to him until I discussed it with all of you, since we still don't know how much our captors can do. If they knew..."

"They wouldn't like it," Santon said with masterful understatement. "And you're right. We shouldn't try to contact John again until we know better what we're up against."

"I don't think I could right now anyway," she said. "I'm too drained."

"As am I," Gauvain muttered. "In the Midland, they've perfected the ability to send messages over the Aura. Despite extensive experimentation, I've yet to be able to do so. It may be that I have no trained colleague to receive what I send."

"Duncan told me you had a way of communicating with the mages in the Midland," Santon said.

The pause stretched almost to breaking before Gauvain finally spoke. "A different matter altogether. There are always untrained yokels with just enough Auric capability to protect them crossing the hills, and enough gullible people to spread the rumors. I've seen no reason to disabuse them. Leo maintains my network."

"So, you've been running messengers over the hills. Interesting," Santon said with just enough dismissive force to suggest disappointment that a human network, rather than superlative Auric abilities, had been the source of Gauvain's knowledge.

There was little illumination in the small cabin, one medium-sized light ball, but Neve would swear the mage blushed.

The cabin grew quiet. In the other room, Leo let escape a soft snore. Santon and Gauvain continued their discussion, their voices hushed. With nothing to contribute, she slipped into the other room and unrolled Santon's pallet. After all they had endured, she was more than happy to join Leo in slumber.

Neve woke as two women from the village entered the main room, placing trays bearing bowls on the table. In the dim light of early morning, she could just see a look of contempt twist the lips of the older one. Fair enough, the place had certainly looked – and smelled – better, before the congestion of four occupants. At least the most recent intruders didn't slam the door as they left. Neve sat up. Beside her, Leo slept on. In the main room, Gauvain shifted but didn't wake. Santon was rising to his feet, looking straight at her and gesturing for quiet. She nodded. The two older men needed the extra sleep, even if it meant cold, congealed porridge later. She rose and approached the table, studying the bowls. "Safe?" she asked in a whisper.

"Probably. They aren't out to kill us, just keep us from John." Santon stood across the table from her, sharing her frown at the mess in the bowls. With a grimace, he added, "We'll need the energy today, I suspect."

They quietly pulled the chairs out from the table and sat, each choosing a bowl and making a start. After a swallow, Neve shook her head and rose to fetch her pack. Silently she held up a water flask. Santon flashed her a grim smile. They washed the breakfast down as needed, before the other two men woke.

"The fog?" she asked, keeping her voice low.

"I don't feel it. I think I'm free."

"Should I check in on John?"

"I believe it's safe. I was thinking about this last night. We agree they aren't mages?"

Neve nodded.

"My guess is they have a limited repertoire of skills," Santon continued. "Most of their actions have been logical, anticipating what we'll do, so I seriously doubt they have some spooky way of predicting us. And we need to know what his situation is."

Gauvain stretched and sat up. "Blasted pallet," he muttered. "Hard as bare ground."

Santon and Neve both turned to look at him. "Have some breakfast, if you can stomach it," Neve said.

Gauvain's mouth twitched. Rising, he joined them, sighing at the sight of the bowls. "Anything new?"

"Not so far," Neve said. She retreated to the other room and sank into trance with her back against the wall. Although all evidence suggested John was well taken care of, she wasn't going to be comfortable or focused until she was sure of her brother's safety.

A short time later she returned to the main room, puzzled. "I can't reach him."

Santon looked up from where he had been tracing wet patterns on the table. "At all?"

"No. Usually, that means he's out of range."

"But we know he's at the other end of the village," Gauvain said. "Within your capabilities, surely."

Neve was too troubled to be offended by the mage's officious tone. "It doesn't feel like a block. So, he's not there."

"Let me try." Gauvain turned his back on her and went into the small room, where Leo was just beginning to stir. He took her place on the pallet, sitting cross-legged, and entered a trance.

He emerged soon after. "I can sense him, but not close by. Likely he's left the village. I tried to get him to respond, but—"

"He wouldn't know to be listening for you," Neve said.

By now Leo was up. Judging from the twinkle in his eyes, he was greatly refreshed by his long sleep. "Stop squabbling and listen," he said.

Silence pervaded the cabin as they gradually became aware of unusual sounds from the village square. Only Leo calmly ignored the hubbub and helped himself to the remaining bowl of gelatinous porridge, taking the chair vacated by Gauvain. "They're upset. Could be John made his own way to safety."

Santon locked eyes with Gauvain. "Do we risk it?"

The mage nodded. "Only if we have no choice."

Before she could ask what they were talking about, running feet pounded the ground outside, and someone – their guard, Neve figured – shouted, "Wassit? What's going on?"

"Bastards been using magic," another voice said, followed by a crash as the door was shoved open and rebounded against the wall. Two men of middle age entered, both lean, well muscled, and very angry.

"Where's the kid?" one of them demanded.

"We don't know," Gauvain said. Leo calmly dug through his porridge.

"Liar," the man said, getting right in Gauvain's face. He backed away, a look of offended fastidiousness crossing his visage.

Neve's tentative chuckle turned to alarm as the second one said, "Bring the woman. She's kin. She'll know."

As both men advanced on her, her eyes locked on Santon's.

"Now," Gauvain said.

Santon bullied his way in front of the men coming to take her. He snatched her hand and muttered, "Hold on." She vaguely registered that Gauvain had done the same with Leo. Then the two mages converged in the middle of the room, hooked their free arms together, and... and...

... the room was gone. In fact, everything was gone, lost in a mad, swirling ether that barely let Neve breathe. She couldn't see her companions, but used her free hand to grip the stone in her pocket. Her body soared, out of her control. Her eyes were open, but there was nothing to see, just... void. She bit back a scream.

An eternity later, she felt rough, solid ground beneath feet that refused to support her. Limp, she fell, sensing Santon collapsing next to her. The arm that had linked them to Gauvain now lay across her middle, holding her against him.

She squirmed into his embrace. Whatever had just happened, she couldn't deal with it now.

"We seem to have been successful," Gauvain said from somewhere close by.

"A little warning next time," Leo said. His voice was shaky; he had no doubt been taken as much by surprise as she.

Her eyes finally registered the low, ruined walls of the tower. She lay on the baked dirt floor near the center. "Bergen?" she asked.

"Bergen," Gauvain confirmed. He was closer to the wall and had already pulled himself up to a sitting position, supporting Leo.

Santon gave her a squeeze, then rolled over to flop on his back, arms and legs outstretched. "Never, ever, did this place look so good," he said, sounding slightly breathless.

The unexpected comfort of his arm gone, Neve also sat, growling. "What the hell?"

Santon grinned. "You've picked up my swear word."

"Couldn't help it, the amount of time we've been in each other's pockets." She felt unexpectedly light, despite having no brother nearby.

Anticipating her, Gauvain said, "I'd say our visitors confirmed that John escaped the village." He gave a curt nod, as if his words were all the ratification needed.

Santon stood and reached out a hand to her. She pulled herself up with his help, wondering how many more unexpected traumas lay in her immediate future. "We planned it last night," he said. "There was a good chance we'd have to leave in a hurry, and that we weren't going to make it through the gap. They'd have no trouble keeping it well guarded."

"This is related to the way you and John made such good time getting to Bergen, isn't it?" Leo said. Neve noted that he still clutched the spoon he had been wielding when they were... taken?

"A variant." Gauvain's tone was mildly dismissive, as if what they had just done weren't one tick short of a miracle.

"Be happy for a hot bath and food that doesn't involve lentils," Leo muttered. He, alone of the four of them, seemed almost nonchalant by their sudden transport. But then, he was accustomed to Gauvain's powers.

Gauvain, naturally, acted as if translocation were an everyday event, but there was a new element of relief behind his eyes; he hadn't been as confident as he'd let on.

Neve walked over to the remains of the western wall and stood on tiptoe to stare at the place where the path disappeared in the thick hedge. There was no sign of John. But then, she hadn't really thought there would be. "We might have stayed," she said. "He might have come back. He might need help."

Santon joined her, a loose arm draped around her shoulders. "No. They were going to separate us, and we had no idea what kind of future they had in mind, beyond that they couldn't let word of their doings escape the village. Come on."

Reluctantly, she turned from the wall and let Santon lead her along the rough trail back to Bergen. He shifted his arm from her shoulders but held her hand all the way to the bridge. She was glad, but she wasn't ready to think about what it meant. Not yet.

Chapter 39: The New Normal

The wonders of heat. Santon stretched his back, the most the short tub allowed – his knees were still dry – and let the water work its miracle. Besides being exhausted, every muscle in his body felt tense to shattering. It all came down to the translocation spell; never had he thrown so much of himself into a working, but even so he seriously doubted he'd have been able to pull it off on his own. His respect for the Black Mage had gone up several degrees in the last day.

Clean and refreshed, if disgustingly weak, he dug a clean tunic and trousers from the clothes he'd left behind in Bergen, then made his way to the common room. Leo was already there, tucking into a bowl of meat stew. "Ready to build a road tomorrow?" he asked. "We're behind schedule."

Santon used an unacceptable word to convey what he thought of the schedule. "If we don't take a day or two to put ourselves back together, we'll make mistakes or fall ill. Which, I think," he added ominously, "is a distinct possibility."

"True enough." Leo wiped a dribble from his grizzled chin. "Besides, I feel the time has come to activate that stone of yours. And where better than in the tower?"

The implications didn't bear thinking about, but Santon nodded. "Agreed."

"I had thought today, but you're right. You and Neve both need to be in top form. So, tomorrow," Leo continued.

"As a safeguard, we'll place it on something, so neither of you is holding it."

Gauvain had appeared behind Santon as Leo spoke. His burned hand bore fresh bandaging; from the smell, a new herbal poultice had been applied. "This isn't healing in a hurry."

"Not a surprise," Leo said with impressive indifference. "Wounds from magic have a way of healing in their own time. Given that the stone clearly took umbrage..."

"My burn healed surprisingly quickly," Santon countered.

"You're much younger," Leo said flatly. Over Gauvain's glower, he added, "Will you be leaving for home soon?"

The serving girl brought out two more bowls of the stew. Gauvain sat, and he and Santon both tucked in.

Outside, the sun hung almost directly overhead. Some careful questioning had confirmed they had neither gained nor lost time in the hills. The work crews had made themselves useful over the two and a half nine-days they had been away. Santon hadn't really absorbed it, but he did note, as they had dragged themselves to the inn from the tower, that the roads in the village were graded and freshly cobbled, and a couple of derelict buildings now were shored up. He made a mental note to speak to Leo about compensation.

"I find I'm in no rush to return to Orlan," Gauvain said to Leo. "The cuisine suffers in your absence. As I'm this far south, it makes sense to continue." He spoke around a mouthful of meat and vegetables. They were all too starved for decent food to bother with conventional manners.

Neve entered the common room, already holding a bowl of stew. Her hair was still wet, and her tunic hung on her. She had lost weight, despite the physical work and available, if unpalatable, food that had occupied their days in Upper Wem.

Santon was glad to see her. Very glad. Something to explore, and no more telling himself *later*. Soon.

"John?" she asked as she sat.

Gauvain shook his head. "I can only assume he's heading for the Midland. I expect he'll meet us when we reach the south."

Frowning, she scooped up a mouthful of stew; unlike the men, she swallowed before she spoke. "You told me we can't cross to the Midland."

"It doesn't follow we can't return to Borgonne," Gauvain said. "I know John well. He's resourceful. You're not to worry." He spoke as if his words were a commandment and she should put John out of her head, but Santon knew it wouldn't be that easy. Over their time together, he had learned a lot about her family, her closeness to her brother.

The meal finished, he and Neve set out of one accord to walk along the road, ostensibly to survey the work ahead. The road became a mere track just after the bridge, which would be their next engineering challenge. Santon was looking forward to it.

So, it appeared, was Neve. "I was thinking about the embankment," she said, and began to explain her idea, her hands illustrating her points.

He followed, but found himself far more interested in the way the reddish highlights in her hair, now dry, caught the light than he was in the best methods for shoring up the bridge.

Interested enough that he failed to notice she had stopped talking until she nudged him gently on his arm, scrupulously avoiding his sore ribs. "What do you think?" she asked.

He debated, very briefly, pretending he had heard a word of her outline, then shrugged. "Sorry. Mind somewhere else."

"Oh?" Her brows went up. He had the feeling she saw altogether too much.

But that wasn't the worst thing that could happen. "Think we need to talk?" he asked, faking nonchalance.

"Do you suppose Gauvain's right? Is John going to be okay?"

Ah. No surprise their minds had struck out on diverging directions. "Yes. The man's obnoxious, but in this I believe he knows what he's talking about. John was familiar with the village and the first part of the trail west. He'd have known he couldn't get to us, and that he had to escape. He's young and healthy and strong. He'll make it, you'll see. But unlike our beloved mage, I don't dare tell you not to worry."

"No, but you can keep me distracted. Let's go on down the track a ways. Too many people around here."

Distracted... almost without thinking he took her hand as they crossed the bridge and struck out to the south. Neither of them made a move to turn off toward the tower. Nor did she withdraw her hand.

She promptly took the proposed conversation in another direction he hadn't planned. "I was thinking about that place you lived, before your mage got killed."

"It's nice. Clean, spacious. Herb gardens, all that."

"Who runs it now?"

Santon kicked a stone down the dusty path. "No one, as far as I know. Most of the locals are afraid of it."

"Can't say I blame them, from what you've said about Duncan. But... would it work for our academy?"

"Our—?"

"We talked, before the hills. About a school for all the hedge mages and village healers." She whirled around in front of him, grasping his other hand as they drew to a halt, face to face. "Let's do it, Santon."

He was caught flat-footed. He hadn't considered their conversation about a school since they found the stone and made for the hills. The idea was seductive because, after all, what else was he going to do? Being forced to abandon his training had left him heartsick. Surveying was an honorable profession, and he could earn a decent living. But did he really want to be a surveyor for the rest of his life, putting aside all his hard-won skills? Was he now any different from all the other unqualified people out there with some access to the Aura but no training?

He rejected that outright. He hadn't been able to complete his work with Duncan, but he was a mage to the tips of his toes. A mage without a credential... Neve's idea of a school might open a different door, a way to practice without subservience to the dictates of the College of Mages.

But still...

"That wasn't exactly what I wanted to talk about."

She blushed. She knew.

But he moved slowly. "Traveling with you... it worked out okay. Back when we met, I thought we might kill each other. But... yeah. I like you, Neve."

She tried to free her hands, but he held on. She stared at their feet. "Yes," she said. He leaned in to hear. "It's been... good."

He hadn't expected shyness or... nerves? He'd assumed she would reply with her customary incisiveness.

The way it usually went, he'd sense interest in a woman, a serving girl or someone in a bar. They'd make eye contact, and the rest would follow, pleasure with no commitment. Clearly, that wasn't going to happen here. Neve would require courting. Worth it? Likely. Definitely. "I'd like us to explore this. Get to know each other better."

"Yes," she said again, faintly. Her eyes were glued to the ground. "As long as we don't blow anything else up."

I think we're going to be explosive.

But all he said was, "Let's start here, shall we?" He freed a hand to put a finger under her chin and lift her face, then he leaned forward and kissed her, very gently. "Okay?" he murmured.

A shiver ran through her, communicated to him by their still joined hands. He almost asked, then decided not to and kissed her again. Slowly, an exploration. This time, she responded and placed her free hand on his arm. He let the kiss go on, drawing her closer, moving his lips against hers, changing the angle, touching her lower lip with his tongue. Her hand snaked around his back, fingers digging in. He'd never taken it so slowly before. He liked it – or maybe he only liked it because it was Neve. But however tantalizing it might be, the rest of his body was growing uncomfortable in a hurry.

Neve stepped back. She was breathless, but the old confidence had returned. She met his eyes. "Really?" she said, without the expected challenging inflection.

"Really." He reeled her in for a hug; she responded as if he were the last solid point in a shifting sea. Neither of them considered the lingering ache in his ribs. He could have stood there on the trail and held her, felt her clutching him, all day, if the stimulation wasn't on the verge of becoming painful. This close, she would be aware of his arousal. But today wasn't the day to do anything about it. "I think we should walk some more," he murmured into her ear.

"Or try to." She pushed back and grinned, glancing down at his groin and back up again. Then she broke free and headed out, catching him by surprise. When he caught up, she said, "I've... I guess I've got a lot to think about. More than I expected."

"Me, too, except... I've been wondering about us, ever since that near disaster with Tess. Maybe before then." His turn to shiver; that had been one close call. He'd never know, now, what the girl actually was like, even what she looked like. Whatever the future, if any, with Neve, he had been in no doubt whatsoever how he felt about Tess and Upper Wem. The instant he and Gauvain cut the fog had felt like freedom.

Now, as his body gradually calmed down, it felt right to walk with Neve along the track they would soon convert to a road, taking them to the south.

Chapter 40: The Stone

Three days later, acknowledging they all needed recovery time despite Leo's itch to move on, they convened at the ruins of the tower. Neve faced Santon across an improvised stand made by placing a stump on end between them. It reached just above knee height and stood at the exact location where they had excavated the stone. Santon had his back to the hills; Leo and Gauvain completed the square.

Clutching the stone, she met Santon's eyes across the makeshift platform. In Neve's mind, the last two days had been magical as she and Santon explored... the local environs, and each other. The shades had been raised on the man, his reality, as they hiked along the river or took the road south, or followed the high hedge that hid any view of the meadow and the route into the hills.

At night, their explorations had been much more personal, and much more thrilling.

Today, there was an almost painful honesty in Santon's eyes, meeting hers calmly but making no secret they were in this together, whatever happened next.

And next could be anything at all.

Neve gave the stone a final rub with her thumb and placed it on the log, oriented so its long axis pointed to the two of them and to the hills. Leo and Gauvain were spectators only, there if needed to pick up the pieces.

"It's going to be okay," Santon said.

"I know, or at least I hope. It's sad and scary."

"You must attempt not to give the stone human properties," Gauvain grumped. "It's annoying for the rest of us and makes no logical sense."

As if there were anything logical about the stone, or the hills, or Upper Wem and its inhabitants. Amazing how easy it had become to ignore Gauvain's pompous assertions. "Are you ready?" she asked Santon.

"As ready as I'll ever be."

Santon reached out; she matched his movements, lowering her hand slowly. Their fingertips touched as they made their final descent to the stone.

At first, it seemed as if nothing had changed. Then everything happened at once.

The log went up in a blaze that seemed to expand to fill the ruin. Neve screamed as a violent wind caught her and hurled her into Gauvain, driving them both to the ground.

The flame disappeared into a void of darkness, while the land heaved and cratered; the sound of the wrenching earth threatened to split her eardrums. Helpless to move, she lay in terror, her eyes pinched shut, reaching blindly for anything human and normal. Her hand found another's and grasped it. Something about the eerie darkness and grinding noise terrified her, worse than the flame she had been sure would consume them.

Abruptly, it all stopped, settling with a sound like a sigh, as if the earth itself had exhaled.

Leo was the first to recover, if you could call it that. At least he was mobile, arriving at her side on hands and knees. She felt his hand on her shoulder. "Neve?"

From somewhere that seemed far away, Santon groaned and shifted. "Hell," he muttered; she heard a shuffling sound, and a moment later felt a touch on her shoulder, quickly withdrawn.

Her eyes had been pinched closed in terror, but logical thought and feeling were returning. Now that the land lay quiet, she allowed herself to crack a lid. "Why's it so dark?" she asked. They certainly weren't in daylight anymore; the obscurity felt like the inside of a building at sunset, after the light had fled but before full night.

She opened her eyes fully and glanced around. Santon sat with his head in his hands; he was chanting, very quietly. Gauvain lay on his front beneath her. He had yet to move, but his hand clutched hers with a death grip. Leo squeezed her shoulder gently. "I think you should get off him, my dear, if you can. He may be injured."

As her mind began to recognize something like normal consciousness, she heaved free of Gauvain and pulled herself upright, a host of minor pains suggesting multiple scrapes and bruises.

They were on the flagstone floor of the tower – the no-longer-a-ruin tower – which now loomed a good three stories above her. A narrow stair wound its way around the wall, vanishing into obscurity at the top. The walls and enclosing roof effectively shut out the day; only a few small windows part way up its walls allowed light to enter.

Leo knelt beside Gauvain, frowning. "I can't find a pulse."

Neve stared at Leo, stunned. To lose one of their number now, when they had survived the hills? And Gauvain, who gave every indication of being indestructible? Impossible. She twisted toward him despite the near enervation flooding her limbs.

"I'll help." Santon was shaking, but his hands closed on her shoulders, supporting her.

Shock, head trauma... use your training. Neve took a few moments to collect herself and turn inward, accessing the energies arising from the earth. Then she went to work, the rhythm of healing gradually overtaking her, allowing her to forget the cataclysmic action of the stone. She worked one-handed, reluctant to free her other hand from Gauvain's grip. The flagstones seemed to be a magnifier; she could feel the extra healing power flowing through her to be absorbed into Gauvain's body.

Santon's hands stayed warm on her shoulders. She sensed he was sending air energy to match Gauvain's, through her.

Leo watched her as closely as he watched Gauvain, or so it seemed to Neve. In the gloom inside the tower, nothing was sharply visible. She was grateful; it helped her maintain her focus.

After an interminable time, Gauvain sighed, muttered something that sounded irritated, and relaxed against the paving stones, as if he had been in thrall to a great tension. It wasn't over yet, though. Neve continued throughout the morning, pulling energy up from the earth and feeding it into the Black Mage, until her strength gave out and she sagged forward. Gauvain never released her hand.

Santon pulled her back to lean against his chest. Leo had grasped Gauvain's other hand and was chafing it, restoring circulation, while speaking quietly, recounting what had happened.

What had happened?

Reading her mind, as he had come to do over the last two days, Santon said, "Our stone packed quite a punch. It looks like it's rebuilt a derelict tower, although I can't imagine why or how. And frankly, I'm reluctant to see what happened outside."

Neve glanced around. The gap in the ruin's wall had become a door. She could see faint daylight around its edges. "Even a spell can't build a tower at the snap of fingers. Can it?"

"Something did." Santon wrapped his arms around her. She welcomed his support; she had nothing left of her own.

"We need to get him back to the inn," Leo said. "See where he's injured, clean up his wounds."

"And I guess it's up to us to open that door." Neve gently freed her hand from Gauvain's, and between them she and Santon stumbled to their feet.

"What if...?"

His fingers touched her mouth. "It has to be okay. The stone likes you, remember?" When she couldn't bring herself to give him an answering smile, he merely took a step and tugged, compelling her to follow. Like two survivors of a plague, they staggered across the floor. Santon dropped a quick kiss on her cheek, then opened the door.

Outside, facing east toward the village, all seemed to be as it always had been. The dusty trail, the stony landscape. Even the hewn stones, which they had believed to be from the original destruction of the tower, were still in place. Santon made a little 'Hmm' noise in his throat.

Feeling more confident, they circled the tower. On the side facing the hills, nothing was the same. The hedge was gone, as was the meadow. Before them lay a bleak expanse much like the one surrounding the tower, extending almost as far as she could see before the first of the hills rose to meet it.

"Did we walk that far in the meadow?" she asked, awed.

"Didn't seem like it." Santon stared at the changed landscape. "We should have expected this, I guess. We already knew the others didn't experience the meadow the way we did. It was all spell work."

"The hills," Neve said as if that explained everything, which, in a way, it did.

"The hills. Let's figure out how to get Gauvain back to Bergen, shall we?"

Leaving Leo with Gauvain, they hiked toward the bridge until they came to a good-sized tree and relieved it of several sturdy branches. Even with the Aura's assistance, it was a difficult and time-consuming task using only their trail knives. At the tower, which now could be seen to be as black as the one in Orlan, they scavenged the men's tunics and Neve's loose trousers to create the bed of a rough litter to transport Gauvain. Just before they left, Neve darted back into the tower. The stump, she noted, had vanished. She found the stone against the south wall, unbroken. "I'm afraid to touch it again," she said to Santon, who had silently followed her.

"I'll keep my distance, but I suspect even if we both touched it again it wouldn't do anything."

She nodded and reached a finger, then her hand, and cradled the stone in her palm. "San," she whispered, "it's still fizzing."

"Not good news. Probably means it has more to tell us, don't you think?"

"Should we take it from here?"

"Ask it."

Neve half smiled. She had developed a habit of talking to the stone, if only in her mind. She thought the question, listened, and nodded. "I think it wants to get out of here as much as we do."

She dropped the stone into its familiar pocket as she and Santon left the tower. Carrying the litter, they made their stumbling way back to the village.

Chapter 41: On the Road Again

"Just to warn you, it won't be comfortable," Santon said. "This is the last town of any size until we get to the south."

Gauvain shot Santon an irritated look. "When we're this close? You could hardly imagine I would forego the opportunity."

"It's not that close. Another four or five nine-days, at a minimum. Before, we were just improving existing roads. Now, we'll be building them."

He and Gauvain were sharing a table in the inn's common room. Chops and roast vegetables were on the menu, and both men were hungry. The room was half full, but neither Neve nor Leo had appeared yet. They had been out with Santon and the team all day, restructuring the bridge, so he had a very personal idea of how tired they all were.

Gauvain had spent the three days after the cataclysm following Neve's prescriptions to restore his health. Santon was impressed by the mage's willingness to accept and obey her instructions. Gauvain's injuries were healing, his perennial headache was almost gone, and his color was better than it had been when Santon first met him.

Yeah, a lot less cadaverous.

"I guess you can ride in one of the donkey carts."

Gauvain tossed a bored hand in the air. "I assure you, that woman has instituted a complete protocol. You have no other objections, I assume."

"No." Santon shifted in his chair. "In fact, as long as you know what you're getting into, I'm glad you're coming with us. I'd like to talk to you about the journey south."

Here goes nothing. Deep breath.

"When Duncan was killed," he said, "I was left hanging. I hadn't quite finished my training. So, I'd like... that is, I want to ask whether you'd be willing to accept me as an apprentice."

"Yes, yes. Duncan was full of your praises." Gauvain's voice was dismissive, but his gaze was sharp. Santon had the feeling he had anticipated this conversation and was ready for him. "My personal opinion," Gauvain continued, "is that Duncan was much too fond of you. I doubt he would have let you complete your studies on schedule. He would have found a way to delay."

Santon's mouth quirked. "Likely you're right. He wasn't a nice man."

"However, you're much too old and experienced for me to take you on as an apprentice."

Santon's heart sank. "What, then? I don't have anywhere else to go. It's not right, given how close I am to completion. In fact, it could be dangerous, as you know."

Gauvain stated terms. "As we travel, I will set a series of tests. You will undertake them without demur. If you continue to display the abilities I have already seen, there should be ample time to complete my assessment. Assuming you are successful, I will then confirm you as a mage in my lineage."

"Will I be able to learn or clarify techniques I may not know?"

"I expect it."

And probably look forward to it, if it will prove you the superior mage to Duncan.

"I accept. Thank you." He kept his voice formally cool, but the relief Santon felt was massive. He'd been gearing up for this conversation for days, ever since he had come to know Gauvain as they worked to rend the fog, then to transport their party away from Upper Wem.

"Don't get too comfortable. Your first assignment is to attempt to contact John. With my diminished health, I find the process draining. Come to me after work tomorrow and I will instruct you in the technique."

"With pleasure."

"Don't expect enjoyment."

As they spoke, the serving girl placed their plates in front of them. Santon picked up his fork and knife, gave Gauvain a confirmatory nod, and tucked in.

Santon saw Neve later that evening, when they both adjourned upstairs. She had been sitting with a group of their construction team for the meal, a move they both considered strategic because the workmen kept a closer finger on the pulse of the village than they were able to. Their presence, once so welcome in Bergen, had become problematic with the drastic, impossible-to-explain changes west of town. The residents were edgy, distrustful.

"Leaving the day before Solstice isn't going to be popular with the crew," he said as he lounged back on her bed. Technically, he shared a room with Leo. Neve supposedly shared, also, but Elin had acquired a definite preference to sleep elsewhere – neither Neve nor Santon cared to know more than that – so she had the space to herself.

"True enough." Neve sat against the wall, well out of touching distance, as aware as he that their chances of rational conversation diminished in proportion to physical proximity. "But maybe not as bad as we feared. They're picking up hostility, same as we are, despite having nothing to do with the so-called 'magical events'. Solstice in town is liable to be a bust if we're here – or cause a riot, when everyone's into the beer."

"I've confirmed things with Gauvain."

"I guessed as much." Neve knew about Santon's plan to petition Gauvain for a spot in his apprenticeship program.

"Not as a student. He'll test me while we make our way south. I agreed, but we have work to do, and that uses my powers, too. I hope I won't be so exhausted at the end of the day I can't handle his assignments. And it may affect my time with you."

"That was expected. To get the credential, San – it matters."

"I suppose you have to stay across the room from me?" When she looked up at him, he recognized the sad half-smile. "You're thinking about John."

She nodded and looked down again.

"My first assignment is to try to contact him. I'll do my best."

She gave him no acknowledgment. She was delving deeper into sadness, and that couldn't be allowed. It affected her work, the team... and him, with a heart-clenching echo of her own misery. He straightened and left the bed, settling on the floor next to her. No words needed; she turned into his arms like a lost kitten returning to its mother.

Mother. He scoffed. But he knew a wounded animal when he saw one. As her tears ended, he drew her to her feet and toward the bed. They were perfectly capable of generating heat enough to burn down the inn, but tonight wasn't about passion. It was about kindness, and tenderness – the depth of his caring still bowled him over sometimes – and comfort.

Santon reveled in this novel approach to lovemaking, thoughtful and controlled, and just as satisfying in a different way. Neve fell asleep, her head on his shoulder and an arm across his chest. He shifted just enough to drape a light linen cover over them before dropping a kiss on her head and settling in for the night.

Chapter 42: The End of the Road

Neve pushed filthy hair away from her face, which she then swiped with the hem of her tunic. The last four and a half nine-days had been hot, physically grueling, and scary, due to an acute shortage of water. Only once had they been able to bathe and replenish their supply. Otherwise, it had been carefully rationed, and Neve remembered few days when she hadn't been thirsty.

Then, two days ago, the trail had ended, crossing a trickle of a creek to reach a wide, golden plain.

She looked south. A herd of horses – she had never seen one before but had been assured they were indeed horses – grazed in the distance. To the west, the hills were lower; instead of towering above them, they rolled to the horizon. That didn't change their magic, though. Santon had already tried to cross over into the Midland, and failed. One moment he had been moving forward, the next he found himself back where he'd started. She had heard tales of similar adventures back home in Orlan, when those with no Auric connection attempted to cross the hills.

At least with the dry weather her tunic didn't stick to her skin. Although the creek had solved the drinking water issue, given the heat she literally had no moisture to sweat out. They were halfway to autumn equinox and the hope for cooler temperatures. She could do with something more temperate.

And a bath. She'd love a bath.

Gauvain stood next to her. The stone's violent reaction had caused him ongoing pain throughout his body as well as occasional, ferocious headaches, but his health, after a decidedly shaky start, had improved steadily over the trek. His color was better and the aches had diminished; her chore was to heal him, just as Santon's had been to please him by executing the tests the mage assigned with near faultless precision. Her opinion of Duncan had gone up; Santon's training had been solid.

He had whispered to her his suspicion the Black Mage actually preferred that he fail occasionally, to enforce his own dominance. That was fine with Santon; the occasional stumble was always a good learning opportunity.

"The administration building and stables in the area over there," Gauvain said, gesturing to a flat space close to the end of the trail – where, in fact, they had already set up their camp.

"Residences first, or you won't have anyone to staff the admin or maintain the horses," she countered.

"I'm troubled about the shortage of building materials." He frowned, as if he took the grassy plain as a personal affront.

"We'll utilize timber from the forest on the flank of the foothills, and the exploration party reports a decent supply of stone in that area." She gestured to the northeast. "We'll need to build an aqueduct of some sort to channel the water." Whether the creek could provide enough in the long term was a concern.

Santon joined them. He, too, looked better. A few days ago, Gauvain had – grudgingly, Neve thought – approved his appointment to the College of Mages. In a way, Santon had enjoyed the challenge of Gauvain's testing, so she hadn't fully realized the stress he had been under until it was lifted. Had any previous candidate ever been put through such a rigorous screening? No doubt it had its roots in the old rivalry between Gauvain and Duncan. "Are you ready?" he asked her.

"As I'll ever be." To Gauvain she said, "See you later." It was amazingly simple to walk away from him once you put his deliberate air of superiority aside.

She and Santon left the plain behind, making their way north along the path. They had already agreed on a spot, an open space downhill from the trail, at a distance from the spindly riparian forest that followed the creek.

They had also weighed the potential consequences. But they both had a strong intuition that whatever spells coated the hills, the fewer of them the better. The camp was well distant, and the crew were all out on the plain, either assessing building materials or plotting the best way to round up the horses. It was as safe as it ever would be.

The sere landscape seemed... poised and waiting, Neve thought, as if it knows what we're about to do. She extracted the stone from her pocket and placed it on the ground. "Ready?"

As before, Santon positioned himself across from her, although this time she took the location closest to the hills. Without giving themselves time to overthink it, they touched fingers and slowly squatted, lowering their hands to the stone.

The first thing Neve noticed was warmth, a soothing heat that spread from her fingers throughout her body, quite different from the atmospheric heat she had endured for days. Then the world around her wavered. The land gave a gentle throb. A bird trilled from the crown of a stunted tree upslope from her.

When did she last hear a bird?

She met Santon's eyes, and of one accord they removed their hands from the stone. Around her, the world had changed, not dramatically, but as if spring had come after winter.

The greening of the land. "The spell made things worse," she observed.

"Keeping people away, I bet. Listen to the creek."

She focused, then hurried toward the riparian forest, which already appeared healthier. Even before she approached the creek, she knew the flow had strengthened a hundredfold, the water bouncing over the boulders in its way as if it were celebrating its freedom.

"Relieved?" she asked.

"Oh, yes. But the ford will be flooded. I think we have one last bridge to build."

They hugged. The rush of clear water held them both in thrall.

She turned away, returning to the place of their shared magic, and retrieved the stone. It lay inert in her hand, the familiar tingling gone.

"Thank you," she whispered.

Santon joined her. "It gave us everything it had," he said. "The least we can do is take care of it."

Neve fixed him with a look. He shrugged. "I know. It's just a stone now. Still..."

"That's what I like about you," she stated. "A mix of magic and reality and whimsy."

"I could say the same." He turned her toward him, his voice dropping to a husky promise of things to come. "And for a few other attributes, too. Tonight, I intend to prove it."

She grinned. "And I intend to wash my hair." A shiver crept through her as she led them back toward the camp, half excited by the improved water source, half anticipating the night to come.

❖

That night, Santon lay next to his woman in their tent, lazily touching as they sketched out plans for their school. How to determine affinities, how to instruct, what successful completion would mean. And the place itself, of course.

"Gardens," Neve said, more lost in a dream than paying attention. "Fountains, courtyards. Serenity."

"We can do it. Now that I've been admitted to the College of Mages, we can even be official."

"We have to allow for the very real possibility our students will blow stuff up."

His fingertips traced idly over her breast, creating a visible frisson. He loved that she couldn't control it. Her hand, as he very well knew, was positioned to transmit a more acute sensation.

Good. Very good.

"We'll need to hire people," she said. "Fire and water specialists. We can't do everything."

"We're meant to be talking about how we'll publicize the school. It's not much good having the employees and courtyards if nobody comes."

"Town criers. Word of mouth." Her hand wasn't resting anymore. He had a feeling that nothing was going to be decided this night. He stretched and shifted to give her better access. "I think we know enough about fire magic. One aspect of it, anyway."

Neve giggled. He shifted his hand from her breast to her fine, firm posterior, pulling her against him.

"Inflammatory?" she asked. "Burn down the tent?"

He grinned. "Sizzling." He could add, he already was – but she had eyes, she'd know.

Oh, yes. "I think we'll need a separate residence. A long way from student housing."

"For sure." He wasn't going to be capable of words much longer if she kept up her ministrations.

Who needs words?

The temperature in the tent was rising. "Anything else?" Santon rumbled, his tone clearly suggesting there had better not be.

Neve's lovely smile blossomed. "Not a thing."

"Wench," he said, keeping his voice low. "You please me."

She wrapped her arms – those strong arms, toned from years of physical labor – around him. "See to my needs, man," she growled in his ear, her voice husky.

So, he did, until they both collapsed, sweaty and sated.

She hummed against his skin. Holding her tight, he rolled them onto their sides. "Sleep," he commanded, his voice soft.

"I will."

He grinned; she was already half gone.

For Santon, slumber didn't come so readily. Talking to her, it all sounded easy. And maybe it would be. But Duncan's bastion, so far north, was a different reality. They had a lot to finish here before they could act on their dreams.

Nothing more to do for the moment.

Nothing except hold his woman, keep her safe, love...

Love?

Might as well admit it. Santon shifted to cradle her more comfortably, feeling no need to do more than be grateful for the upheaval this one woman had caused in his life.

Chapter 43: John

Three nine-days later, the station was beginning to take shape. Santon and Neve had worked nonstop, seeking out and blasting rock to build the first structures. Gauvain was given the dual jobs of site development and floor plans, while Leo masterminded the entire project. A roof would be going on the barracks soon – a work crew was in the forest, harvesting the logs they would need for rafters. A low wall marked the beginning of a stable.

Unfortunately, the explosions needed to create building stone had spooked the herd; a scouting team reported they were a day away, far down the valley.

The whole crew had been waiting ever since they arrived for someone from the Midland to cross the hills. So far, it hadn't happened.

Santon was more than ready for a day off. Even while exerting his considerable mage-based powers to provide building materials, he also had been monitoring the airwaves, hoping to find some hint of Neve's beloved baby brother. But there had been no clear signal from him since they left Upper Wem. The lack of news was weighing on Neve, although she tried to keep it hidden.

He dusted his hands on his filthy tunic – no one was taking time to wash work clothes these days – and walked across the low grass plain toward their camp, which had a feel of permanency now. Gauvain ruled from the largest of their tents, surrounded by the smaller ones that formed a temporary barracks. Cooking was outdoors; Santon worried about a possible change in the weather with the approaching equinox, only about three nine-days away. There had been rain recently, laying the dust, but he couldn't judge how frequently it would occur. The grass had greened after the rain but was already browning again.

Santon sniffed; definitely meat in the stew. A supply wagon had arrived from Vienne a nine-day ago, the first to test the new road. The staples it brought, combined with hunting, meant they ate well. In the distance, he could see Neve and Leo talking to one of the work crews, several people heading from the plain into the forested hills. And emerging from the path leading to the Midland...

He squinted. No, the heat wasn't addling his brain. Two children.

Children?

"Hey! Kids! Wait a minute!" He changed direction, jogging for the trailhead. The kids saw him coming and vanished back along the trail. Santon drew up, frustrated by the impossibility of following them. Several times either he or Neve had tried to cross and ended up back at the giant boulder marking the entrance to the trail.

Could the boulder function like their green stone? If they blew it up, might the spell go away?

Gauvain arrived at his side. "They know we're here," he said. "Now, maybe they'll take the trouble to make contact."

"And bring John with them."

Gauvain shook his head. "If he were this close, I have to believe we'd have been able to contact him by now."

"Or not." Santon had little faith in anything being as it should be with the hills interfering.

Gauvain made a discontented grumble in his throat and turned away. Santon followed more slowly. He was confident Neve had seen the boys – he thought they were boys. She'd be hovering on a knife edge between hope and despair.

Around mid-morning the next day, the situation changed again. The kids reappeared, but this time accompanied by a man and a woman. Wasting no time, the woman took the lead, striding across the grass.

Santon was standing with Leo, reviewing plans for the stable. Neve spotted the group from the Midland and was hastening over, her eyes scanning... hopeful, Santon thought. But there was no sign of John.

They didn't even know if residents of Borgonne could cross the hills from the Midland at this point. He'd really like to find a way to lift that particular spell, because being blocked from crossing the hills skewed the trade alliance in the Midland's favor. Perhaps he and Neve could scan the area, now that they knew, in general terms, what to look for. Somewhere close, something controlled this spell.

Gauvain emerged from the tent just as the woman spoke, her voice welcoming. "I am Constance Devereaux. I head the trade mission for the Midland. My colleague, Dal, represents the Motherhouse." She gestured to the austere looking man accompanying her.

Leo made the introductions, including Neve and Gauvain, who by then had joined the group. Constance gave Gauvain an appraising look as they were introduced. Dal and Gauvain clearly knew each other, but a stiffness in their acknowledgment suggested they were not friends. But after all, with whom had Gauvain ever been friends?

"You've accomplished a lot already," Constance said. "But I don't see the horses."

"They were spooked by the blasting," Neve said with a smile. "We'll soon be done with that. We could use some advice, actually, about what kind of weather to expect this winter, so we'll be better able to prioritize our construction."

"Happy to help. But first... Timmie?"

One of the boys held a large bag gingerly, as if it might explode. He crept closer and thrust the bag at Constance, then both boys darted back toward the trailhead. Constance in turn held the parcel out to Leo. "You probably haven't had fresh eggs in a while. I hope you'll enjoy these. Next trip, we'll try to get some ground hens over for you."

Leo's eyes widened and Neve leaned over to peer in. "Dozens," she whispered.

The bag got passed to Santon with the clear intention that he deliver it to the cooking team. No point arguing, and he had no wish to stand on precedent. The others could play politics; he'd just get the eggs safely to the cookfire and contemplate the feast in store that night.

As he turned away, Gauvain joined him. "I hadn't been aware that the Motherhouse would play an active role in this," he growled.

"Makes sense, though." Santon was pleased overall with their new acquaintances. The potential for a smooth relationship seemed strong.

Gauvain's grin wasn't pleasant. "It's a training facility, not administrative. I wonder if they're looking to expand their power base."

Santon shrugged. "Perhaps they'll be no more involved than, say, you are. Setting up the system, then letting it run."

Gauvin was silent for a pace or two before making a dismissive gesture with his hand. "I suppose they couldn't do more, given their watered-down understanding of the Aura. It's all about everyday skills like music and healing, rather than building a foundation of its more esoteric aspects."

"That doesn't sound so bad to me," Santon replied. "It's more or less what Neve does. Maybe they have more earth-based mages?"

"Or that their powers are limited. The Aura is weaker on the other side of the hills. At least that man is competent."

"I gathered you know Dal. Have you spent much time there?"

Gauvain answered with a grunt as they reached the cookfire, where the eggs were received with the expected jubilation. Duty done, Santon hastened back to the group gathered around Constance.

Gauvain, he noticed, returned rather more slowly – the man just couldn't resist showing his contempt for the world in general. Well, that was Gauvain. They were colleagues now, equals in a sense. He had learned to tolerate the senior mage and respect his powers.

Now it begins.

Neve officially headed their trade mission, although Gauvain's presence complicated the order of precedence. But the two had, over the nine-days, managed to establish a working relationship. Gauvain let Neve take the lead; Neve deferred to Gauvain as needed.

Pleasantries were exchanged first – the trip south, the landscape and climate, staffing their depot, the town on the other side of the hills that would host the Midland's depot. None of their team mentioned Upper Wem. Finally, and naturally, they moved to planning, the first nuts and bolts of their incipient business relationship. After a while they all adjourned to one of the tables set up around the cookfire.

Santon looked on with approval as Neve and Constance forged a relaxed, respectful relationship, both firm in their requirements but neither demanding or hostile.

Immediately after a late lunch – mixed beans and grains, fresh raw greens from the water pastures around the stream – Constance rose to leave.

"So soon?" Neve asked. "You're welcome here."

"Thank you," Constance said, "but it's not a short trip. The hills are a lot less intimidating this far south, but the days are growing shorter, and I'd rather be home before dark." She and her party began to gather their possessions and prepare for the return walk.

Dal, who had been a quiet, enigmatic presence throughout the visit, saying little but missing nothing, dug in the pack he carried and extracted a piece of paper. He addressed Neve as he held it out. "One last thing. A few days ago, we received this."

Neve forced herself not to grab the note out of Dal's hand. Accepting it with outward calm, she gave in to her excitement and turned her back to rip it open. "John," she blurted. She could barely get the words out. Having scanned the note, she looked up, frowning. "He's okay. But he's... I don't understand."

Gauvain snatched the sheet from her. He read, then read again, his hand clenching the small scrap as if he might demolish it.

"We've been waiting for Neve's brother," Santon said. "He was supposed to meet us here."

"He says he didn't think he could cross to this side, if he came south," Neve reported. "So, he went north instead. He's—"

Gauvain's roar interrupted her. "The total, absolute *fool! Traitor!* Why would he want to go there?" Gauvain flung the page to the dusty ground – the effect was neutralized by the paper's floating, rather than crashing down – then tore away from them, letting out a single, enraged bellow as he went.

Neve watched, dumbfounded, then turned to Santon, her eyes wide, and blurted out the news. "He's gone to the Motherhouse."

Epilogue

Leo and Gauvain had left by donkey cart three days ago. Now it was Neve's turn. It was the spring equinox, almost exactly a year since she left home. Soon, her adventure to the south would be over. Santon was in the stable, overseeing the final packing and preparing the horses for their departure.

In the late morning sunlight, Neve chatted with Constance and Benjaman, a stocky man of middle years who would be taking over administration of the depot. She enjoyed the other woman's company. They had grown to trust and like each over the course of the winter. Benjaman... well, despite superficial politeness it was obvious he'd be happy to see the back of her.

Neve and Santon had found no way to cross the hills to the Midland. Even in Constance's company, the two of them inevitably found themselves turned around and delivered back where they started. So, her meetings with Constance were conducted here, on the southern Borgonnian plain. Dal accompanied Constance occasionally, his presence valuable as he lent his considerable healing powers to ease inevitable injuries associated with construction and horse wrangling. They were still a very new outpost.

In two seasons, the depot had come into being. A barracks and dining hall, a small office, and a spacious stable with training grounds had risen from the short grass plain. The structures were sturdy, had already withstood a couple of mild quakes, and gave every indication of permanence. They had sources of food and water. The trade route was open and functioning, with agricultural products arriving regularly, to be sorted and dispatched north by donkey cart. The horses promised to the Midland in trade had to be gentled and trained before they could cross the hills, but the first two had been delivered and five more were in the stable. A new era had dawned; soon, the mysterious Midland wouldn't be so unfamiliar, although they couldn't get there in person.

She would miss it.

"Let me know how it goes," Constance said with a smile.

"I will."

"You ladies seem to be forgetting there's work to do," Benjaman fulminated. "Let's get that contract finalized."

Neve suppressed her irritation. Benjaman would never accept that a woman could be as capable as a man, but he wasn't her problem.

They walked across to an outdoor table, where three copies of the final trade agreement, along with pen and ink, awaited. "I've read this a dozen times," Constance said after scanning one copy. "I'm ready to sign."

As she inked her signature, Benjaman, who was less familiar with the document, studied another copy, then held out his hand for the quill.

Constance pointedly ignored him. "You negotiated this," she said to Neve. "I'd like you to sign it."

Neve grinned. "Both of us, I think, since Benjaman will be the one to execute it."

Glowering at the women, Benjaman scribbled his name on all three copies of the document before handing the pen to Neve – grudgingly, she thought. Too bad. When she met the other woman's eyes as she accepted the pen, she saw amusement. Constance was indomitable; she'd cope with Benjaman just fine.

Neve accepted the quill and added her signature below Benjaman's, who snatched up the depot's copy as if afraid she would purloin it. "I'll file this in the office."

Unable to resist, she said, "Be careful you don't smudge it." It would take a while for the berry-based ink to dry.

Benjamin snorted. "Safe trip," he said. "I have work to do." He left them, holding the page by a corner as he crossed the yard toward the office.

With more care and less haste, Neve and Constance took their copies, rolling them carefully. Neve's would go to Orlan, the economic center and de facto capital of Borgonne.

"It's time." Santon had arrived with their horses as she and Constance chatted about inconsequentials. "As I'm sure you know," he said, addressing Constance. "it's been a pleasure."

"Indeed, it has." Constance squeezed his hands. "We've inaugurated a new era. The best of luck with the school."

Constance wrapped Santon in a hug, then Neve in a longer one. "Be safe," she whispered.

"Is that a protection spell I sense?" Neve joked. But it wasn't really a joke. Constance's Auric powers were such that she was more than capable of draping their small group with a new energy.

Constance just smiled.

"Take care." Neve couldn't risk saying more; her throat suddenly closed – even though this was a happy time, not a sad one.

Constance gathered up her small entourage and set off along the trail to the Midland. Santon draped his arm around

Neve, pulling her close. They stood and watched until the party disappeared from sight, then turned to their own trail.

Santon waved toward the office, where Benjaman had just emerged. "We'll be in touch," he called.

He was answered by a brusque nod. The new depot chief turned away, heading out onto the plain.

She and Santon mounted their horses – a new thrill. These weren't the youngest or swiftest beasts, but suitable for her skill level on the trek north. She expected they would overtake Leo's donkey cart within a day or two.

The work crew had thrown a party last night; farewells had already been said. One last look, and they turned their horses' heads toward...

Home, she thought. The farm, Orlan, a familiar world. And then Duncan's complex, housing the new school, a new adventure. With Santon.

He must have caught the sheen of tears in her eyes, because he reached over to touch her hand before drawing his horse into the lead.

The path entered the forest bordering the stream, hiding the plain from sight. Settling into the horse's rhythm, Neve cast one last look at the plain before turning resolutely to the future.

About LizAnn Carson

It's interesting, trying to condense who you are into a paragraph or two. I live on Canada's west coast, in a city that's large enough to have all modern conveniences, but not so large as to have hours-long traffic jams or heavy-duty pollution. I can follow a trail to my local supermarket, or I can be downtown in twenty minutes.

Yes, I spend much of my time writing (and editing, formatting, critiquing for other writers, battling computer problems, and occasionally tearing my hair out). But beyond that, I enjoy a variety of crafts. I play early music on a baritone ukulele and struggle to produce attractive paintings in oil pastel. I walk a lot and enjoy weight training and yoga. My career was in Information Technology, but once, a long time ago, I owned a yarn shop, and for a while I taught English as a Second Language.

Sometimes, I just watch my cats sleep.

See more about my books in the worlds of both fantasy and romance on my website, www.lizanncarson.com.

www.ingramcontent.com/pod-product-compliance
Lightning Source LLC
Chambersburg PA
CBHW020305200626
46814CB00006BA/2085